Light My Fire

By
Christie Ridgway

D1531228

Light My Fire
© Copyright 2014 Christie Ridgway
ALL RIGHTS RESERVED

Chapter 1

The children of America's premier rock band learned early to sleep through anything. Late night jam sessions, liquor (and worse) -fueled arguments, raucous parties raging from dark to dawn that were peppered with wild laughter, breaking glass, and the squishy thud of fists against skin. At twenty-four, Cilla Maddox had not lost that skill, though she'd recently come to view it as something less than a gift.

Still, she didn't stir from her curled position on the edge of the king-sized bed when a tall, broad figure entered the room in the middle of the night. No streetlights disturbed the darkness this deep in Laurel Canyon and the newcomer found the bed only by deduction. When, at his sixth cautious step, his shin met an immoveable object, he dropped the motorcycle boots and duffel bag he carried to the plush carpet and took a leap of faith by tipping his long body forward. Finding firm mattress and feathery pillow, he instantly fell into sleep.

Hours later, Cilla came awake to the sound of birds tweeting and chirping their odes to another Southern

California morning as they flitted through the shrubbery and tall eucalyptus trees that grew inside and outside the canyon compound where she'd grown up. Eyes closed, she breathed in the country-scented air, such a surprise when the famous Hollywood Boulevard and its twin in notoriety, the Sunset Strip, were less than a mile away. Flopping to her back, she stretched to her full five-feet, five inches. Then she pushed her arms overhead and swept them back down until her fingertips met—

Something solid. Warm. Alive.

On a gasp, her eyes flew open and her head whipped right. She yanked her hand from a man's heavy shoulder to press it against her thrashing heart.

As it continued to beat wildly against her ribs, she stared at her bedmate. Though his body was plastered to the mattress belly-down, his face was turned toward hers and it only took another instant to realize he was no stranger. But recognition didn't calm the overactive organ in her chest that continued sending blood sprinting through her body.

She blinked, just to make sure her eyes weren't deceiving her. They apparently had told the truth, she decided. After years of adolescent fantasies, she was actually sharing a bed with *him*. With Renford Colson.

No mistake, it was her teenage fantasy man. His glossy black hair that tangled nearly to his shoulders. His days'-old stubble of beard that made his mouth look softer, fuller, more kissable if that was even possible. Those were his spiky lashes resting against his sharp-angled face.

Yet...was he really here? To make herself believe it, she mouthed his name. *Ren.*

As if he heard the silent syllable, his eyes flipped open.

She started, their distinctive color—a silvered green,

just like eucalyptus leaves—jolting her to the marrow.

Dark brows met over his straight nose and she watched the drowsiness seep from him as his gaze sharpened. "Priss?"

She frowned. He was the only one to call her that nickname and it had annoyed her since she was old enough to understand it telegraphed something about the way he viewed her. "Excessively proper," she remembered reading in the dictionary. "Prim."

"Cilla." Her voice sounded morning-husky as she made the correction.

One corner of his mouth kicked up. "Priscilla."

Ugh. That was worse. To her mind, Priscilla was the name of some old-fashioned china doll that was deemed too nice to play with and so grew dusty on a high, forgotten closet shelf. As the youngest "princess" of rock royalty (an article in *Rolling Stone* had described the nine collective children of the Velvet Lemons in just such terms), she'd often been overlooked. Likely Ren hadn't given her a single thought in the nine years since she'd last seen him.

"Why are you here?" she asked, sitting up.

His gaze dropped from her face to the size XL T-shirt she wore, an authentic Byrds concert souvenir, one of the several such clothing items she'd collected (read: purloined from her careless father) during her lifetime. "Priss," Ren remarked with a note of mild surprise, "you've grown up."

Grown-ups didn't react to the red flush they could feel crawling over their skin. Grown-ups didn't check out their chest to determine if it was a modest B-cup that led him to such a conclusion. So ignoring both compulsions, she repeated her question. "Why are you here?"

"Couple reasons." Ren flipped over then jackknifed on the mattress to face her. Both palms rubbed over his eyes and down his cheeks, his beard making a scratchy sound. He'd fallen asleep in his worn jeans and wrinkled dress shirt. On the floor near him were a pair of battered boots and a leather bag, both as black as his hair. His hands went to the buttons marching down his chest.

She swallowed. "What are you doing?"

"I've been wearing this damn thing for—Christ, who knows?—it's got to be a couple of days. However long it took me to get here from Russia with a fucking long layover in Paris."

Her gaze didn't leave his nimble fingers as they continued unbuttoning to reveal a stark white undershirt beneath. "You didn't stop off in London?" That was where he was based. Ren had started as a roadie for the band, then moved into concert tour planning and security. When he'd left the employ of the Velvet Lemons, he'd set up shop across the pond and continued doing the same thing—but for other bands.

Cilla couldn't blame him for giving up working with their fathers. The three Lemons might as well have been named the Odd Ducks. They'd achieved superstardom in the 1970s and when they were nearing forty, somehow decided they wanted more than sex, riches, and scandalous reputations. Each had produced three kids before declaring their paternal urges satisfied. No mothers came attached to the children they'd fathered. They'd been bought off or wandered off and as long as Cilla could remember the nine rock progeny had spent their childhoods in the expansive Laurel Canyon compound that consisted of three separate houses and then this smaller cottage where she and Ren had chosen to sleep.

Inspecting the hand-tied quilt covering the bed, Cilla ran her fingers over the psychedelic-inspired design. "You know about Gwen?" she asked, referring to Guinevere

Moon, an original Velvet Lemons groupie who'd been the closest to a mother figure the band's offspring ever had. This had been her house.

"Of course," Ren replied. "I couldn't get here for the memorial service, but I came as soon as I was able to make arrangements for my replacement."

As head fixer for some other band's tour, Cilla supposed. "Her real name was Donna Carp," she said, her heart squeezing to think that the spiral-curled, caftan-wearing gentle soul was now gone. "Gwen's, that is."

There was a short silence, then Ren laughed. "Baby, you didn't think she really had Guinevere Moon on her birth certificate?"

Mortification spread heat over Cilla's face once more. Okay, so she had. "Thanks for thinking I'm a fool," she said, glancing up to glare at him.

The spit in her mouth dried.

Ren had tossed his shirt over the side of the bed and then stripped free of the undershirt he'd worn too. Beneath that...

He was cut. Ripped. His abs were perfectly defined above the waistband of his jeans. His pecs were slabs of thick muscle that drew the eye to broad shoulders that led to arms that were sinew, bone, and more muscle. Over his left pectoral began a primitive-yet-elegant tribal tattoo that swirled in black ink over the cap of his shoulder to reach as far as his elbow. Though most of his forearm was unmarked, on his wrist was a lone, stylized half-curve. She stared at it and then his long fingers, unwilling to let her gaze wander back to that beautiful chest.

She'd been fifteen when she'd last seen him. He'd been twenty-two. Then, she'd only dreamed of his kisses, chaste kisses at that, and hadn't wondered about his body or his hands or what he could do to a woman with them.

It was what consumed her thoughts now.

That, and how they were sharing a bed.

Galvanized by that fact, she leaped from beneath the covers, her bare feet landing on the carpet. The overlarge shirt swung around her body, the hem tickling the top of her thighs. With Ren's gaze on her, her attempt at escape seemed a foolhardy choice. Suddenly her legs felt too naked, and she was acutely aware of what was under her tee—just a scrap of lacey panties. In another not-so-suave move, she swiftly re-inserted herself under the quilt and between the warm sheets, pulling them high to conceal more of herself. "It's, uh, cold out there," she said, by way of explanation. Her breathless state made her voice sound reedy.

Ren's expression had gone blank and his thoughts were impossible to interpret. Staring at her, he ran a palm along his stubbled jaw. "You cut your hair, Priss."

Her fingers flew to the bobbed ends. She still wasn't accustomed to how the dark blond stuff curled and waved now that eighteen inches of weight had been taken from its length.

"I thought you'd vowed never to take scissors to it," he continued.

He remembered that? She shrugged. "Like you said, I've grown up." The haircut hadn't been her idea, though, and a wave of humiliation at the memory of it washed over her.

Ren's gaze narrowed. "Priss..."

"*Cilla.*"

"Cilla, then. Something wrong? Something bothering you?"

A lot was bothering her. Up to and including the fact that her old longing for Renford Colson was not dead, but just hibernating until the day his hot body arrived on the doorstep. Now her hormones were stirring and she felt oddly out-of-sorts and unfamiliarly ravenous. Not unlike the California black bears, she figured, that would emerge from their hollow trees and mountain caves in a few short weeks.

"It's been a lousy month or so," she said. He couldn't doubt that. "Gwen's passing, the wild circus the Lemons made of her memorial service before they rushed back out on tour, and then there's the Beck situation."

"Beck?" Ren frowned. "What about Beck?"

The Velvet Lemons' drummer had named his three kids, Beck, Walsh, and Reed—all boys—after musicians he admired: Jeff Beck, Joe Walsh, and Lou Reed. Ren's father had given all three of his progeny, two boys and a girl—Renford, Payne, and Campbell— the surnames of their long-gone mothers. Cilla never got a straight answer from her own dad. She figured he didn't remember why he'd picked out Priscilla, or why he'd chosen Brody and Bing for her twin older brothers.

She took in a breath, stalling. Beck was the oldest of the nine and Ren was the next closest in age. How would he take the news? "He's missing. Nobody told you that?"

Ren went still. "I don't have regular communication with anyone."

The princes and princesses of rock royalty had scattered as each came of age, but she hadn't realized how out of touch Ren had been. "You don't talk to Payne or Campbell?"

Ren was shaking his head. "Not very often."

"Beck hasn't been in steady contact with Walsh or Reed either. That's why we don't really know exactly how long he's been missing."

"Missing," Ren repeated.

"He took a freelance assignment to do a long piece on

the Nile for one of the nature magazines. About nine months ago. No one has heard from him since."

"Hell."

"His dad and the magazine put feelers out, though it's not clear whether Beck is actually lost or merely following the story. It just seems weird that he's been silent for so long."

Ren relaxed, and ran his hand through his hair, giving Cilla another glimpse of that interesting, incomplete-looking tattoo on his wrist. "I'm sure Beck's fine."

Cilla wished she had his certainty. "I hope you're right."

"I am." He half-turned to punch the pillows behind him then settled back, crossing his arms over that magnificent chest. His biceps bulged.

Gathering the covers closer, Cilla pretended she didn't notice them. "So...you're just, uh, passing through on your way back to London?"

"Moscow to London via Paris and L.A.? I know we had shitty upbringings, Pri—*Cilla*, but our schooling wasn't so bad. Pretty sure you'd see there's no logic in that."

There wasn't logic in anything at the moment. Particularly how she was absolutely electrified by the presence of Ren who was gazing on her like she was a ditzy puzzle and not a desirable woman.

Though she'd been doubting the desirable part for months already. Her fingers wandered again to the shorn ends of her hair.

She forced her hand to her lap. "So what exactly does bring you home?"

He drew up his knees and rested his wrists on the top of them, his big hands dangling. "I got a package from Gwen's lawyer, telling me about some box she left me, as well as a key to this place. Then Bean tracked me down. That was a first."

"String Bean" Colson, the band's lead guitarist and Ren's father. "What did he have to say?"

Ren shrugged. "The gist of it was he wanted me to come to the canyon, look things over at the compound since the band's been gone for months. That, coupled with Gwen's death..." Looking down, he ran a finger over the tattoo on his wrist. "I decided to check in."

His gaze lifted to her face. "What are you doing here, Cilla?"

Hiding. Licking my wounds. Trying to resurrect my sense of self in the one place where I always found comfort. "I received my own package from Gwen— including a key as well. So I decided to leave my place at the beach and move to the canyon for a while. She left me her costume collection and I thought I might sort through it from here."

A brief smile gave her a glimpse of Ren's straight white teeth. "You always liked to play dress-up."

Didn't that make her feel five years old? "It's my business now," she said, bristling a little. Cilla's career had been seeded by Gwen. The older woman had left home at sixteen and become an infamous band groupie. Over the years she'd amassed a vast number of costumes from the most renowned rockers in the world and Cilla had always been fascinated by them. "I make custom clothes for professional dancers, skaters, and yes, even music stars."

"We really have been out of touch," Ren said. "I had no clue."

Cilla lifted a shoulder. "Every Lemon kid left the compound as soon as he or she could and never looked back."

He studied her. "Which means you, as the youngest,

was alone at the end."

At the beginning and in the middle too. But they'd all had to raise themselves with only Gwen as a stabilizing figure. "I'm okay." She had been, anyway, until Tad Kersley.

"Sure you are," Ren murmured, his gaze not leaving her face.

His steady regard lifted chill bumps on the surface of her skin. She suppressed a shiver and tried to think of something to drop into the awkward silence developing between them. Her tongue darted out to wet her lips.

Ren exploded into motion. "I've gotta get into a shower."

Cilla drew back. "Oh, sure. And I can make you some breakfast before you leave."

"Leave?" Ren paused in the process of scooping up his discarded clothes.

"You know." She made a vague gesture. "I'm here. I'll keep an eye on the compound."

"All alone? It's pretty isolated."

It was better than sharing that isolation with him. Cilla wasn't up for dealing with the way he made her tingle all over. Even if she was only just looking, her sexuality was already messed up enough without having to brush up against Ren-tosterone on a daily basis too. "Really, I'm good."

He was looking at her again, in that intense fashion of his. One hand absently traced over the bare skin covering his ribs, re-drawing her attention to all his masculine bone and muscle. God, he was gorgeous, she thought, her own flesh turning hot and her breath catching once again in her throat.

"Yeah," he agreed softly. "I can tell you're good."

Not if he could read her mind. Not if he could know

how his sexy body and his beautiful green eyes made her hyper-aware of every erogenous zone between her head and her heels. "So then..."

"We'll talk about it after I shower."

Her palms went damp in desperation. "Really, Ren—"

"I'll think about it."

"Look." She grasped at straws. "It's not seemly."

"What?" he asked, clearly puzzled.

Did rock royalty even comprehend such a word? Cilla waved her hand. "Even if you stay at Bean's house, your old house—"

"If I stay, I'm staying here."

"Well, *I'm* staying here." She had to spell it out for him? "So, you know...*you* can't. Two single people, one a man, one a woman, sharing close quarters..."

A smile split his face. "So that's not 'seemly'," he said, shaking his head. "Priss—"

"*Cilla.*"

His smile didn't dim. "C'mon. 'Two single people'? Surely we're more like...like..."

Oh, don't go there, she thought on an inner groan. *I've enough doubts about myself and my attractiveness to the male sex without you saying what I think you're about to say.* But then, of course, he did.

"...brother and sister."

Ren exited Gwen's small, canary-colored cottage that dripped with gingerbread trim and strolled into morning sunshine, its warmth immediately starting to dry his shower-damp hair. Narrowing his eyes against the California-brightness, he sucked in a breath and tried shaking off the strangeness of the morning.

Jet lag was seriously screwing with him, he decided. Usually a few hours of sleep would clear his mind. But today, he'd opened his eyes and things had gone from weird—an unexpected woman in his bed—to weirder.

Priscilla Maddox's mouth had turned his normal morning wood to a rod of aching steel.

Shit.

Shoving that thought from his head, he turned in a circle, taking in the pool and tennis court in the distance as well as the three homes where he and the other rock royalty had grown up. At seventy-five yards away, Bean's place was closest. Western-styled, with a shake-shingle exterior and a front door sporting a steer skull, it looked the same as when Ren had lived there. Beyond it was where Mad Dog Maddox had built a rock-faced castle-type abode, with a Rapunzel tower which Ren remembered had been a particular refuge for little Priscilla. The third member of the band, Hop Hopkins, had a severe glass-and-chrome two-story home where Beck, Walsh, and Reed had grown up.

His mind snagging on the missing member of that family, Ren pulled his phone from his jeans pocket and pressed a speed dial number.

"Yo," a male voice answered. "Isn't it like the middle of the night wherever you are?"

"I thought when you went home everything was supposed to seem smaller," Ren said to his half-brother Payne, by way of answering. "It's all so...*so*." So sun-drenched. So lush. So bright with flowers and birds and colors.

The arresting blue of Cilla's eyes.

There was a small silence. "Are you telling me you're at the compound?"

"Yeah. I needed a break." When he said it, Ren realized it was true. He'd been on a grueling schedule for months, years, maybe, and if he told the complete truth, learning of Gwen's death had thrown him a little. "And Bean put the pressure on me to personally ensure the place was doing okay in the Lemons' absence."

"That's bullshit. A gardener comes by. The pool guy. Seven of the nine of us live within an hour's drive if traffic isn't jammed. We'd look in if asked."

"Well, I'm in California now." And not resenting the arm-twisting so much. He *did* need a breather. Then his brother's words sank in, *seven of the nine,* and he remembered his purpose for calling. "Why the hell didn't you call and tell me that Beck is missing?"

"I didn't know you'd care."

That rankled. Ren paused as he started up the path that led toward the fruit orchard planted on the hillside behind the pool. "Way to make me feel like an asshole."

"I didn't mean to," Payne responded mildly. "We all live pretty independently."

"Shit," Ren muttered under his breath. "Give me a Cami report," he ordered, referring to their younger half-sister, Campbell. "And I don't want to hear that— surprise!—she's married with a passel of children."

"As if any of the Lemon progeny are eager for that state," Payne said, "given that not one of us knows what a normal, healthy relationship looks like."

Ren grunted. His brother had that right. "So, she's what...?" Not much would surprise him, not after he'd realized that little Priss—Cilla—had actually grown up and now had a *career*.

"She runs one of my wrecking yards by day," Payne said. "Getting gigs to sing by night."

"Hmm." Ren ran his fingertips over the yellow skin of a lemon as he breathed in the scent of their blossoms. That's what Cilla had smelled like this morning, he realized. Citrus blossoms. He remembered that Gwen used to rinse the little girls' hair with water infused with the tiny flowers and he wondered if Cilla continued the practice. "The wrecking yards doing okay?"

"I'm in my element."

Ren knew that was true. His brother had been crazy for cars—and totaled a few—before he'd even had a driver's license. They'd all learned to drive a golf cart around the seven-acre compound as soon as they could reach the pedals. Payne had convinced a handyman to strap blocks on them so he could crash and burn earlier than the rest.

"So how long are you staying?" Payne asked now.

"I don't know that I am," Ren said, grimacing. As much as a vacation sounded like an appealing idea, there was the issue of Cilla to consider. Finding her sharing the pillows had been a surprise, and a bigger shock came when he realized she'd gone from the coltish adolescent he remembered to a lovely, blue-eyed blonde with a tight body and an adorable tendency to blush.

It scared the hell out of him.

No, scratch that. His reaction to the succulent small package that was Cilla Maddox was what alarmed him. And the intensity of that alarm was only further alarming.

Shit.

She was too sweet for a man like him. Too good for what he'd wanted to do to her, with her, the minute he'd put his eyes on her. But her bare legs and the touch of her pink tongue to her lush upper lip had made him ache like a raw nerve. As much as he found her worry about seemliness amusing, she had a point.

Two single people, one a man, one a woman, sharing close quarters...

Too bad it sounded so damn tempting.

A crackling noise came over the line from Payne's

end. Likely the sound of him breaking into a package of his favorite breakfast of strawberry Pop-Tarts with sprinkles. "You came all this way just to take off again?" his brother asked around a mouthful of unhealthiness.

"Cilla's here."

"Yeah?" Payne munched again. "Cami ran into her at a club where she was playing a couple months back. She's into costume design or something."

"Mmm." Ren swung around to glance at the cottage and his gaze instantly found the woman in question. She'd wandered out of the cottage too, and stood in a shaft of sunshine. It caught all the gold in her cap of wavy, bouncy hair. A pair of cropped jeans hugged her curvy hips. The outside seam on each side of light denim was embroidered in a dark blue pattern that was repeated on the straps of the sleeveless, peasant-y top she wore. The hippie-chic style suited her. A dozen narrow bracelets circled one wrist and he remembered that each of her fingernails had been painted a different color.

The Byrds T-shirt had looked damn good on her too, the logo of five swirly letters in red and yellow on black cotton draping her high breasts.

"She had a boyfriend with her," Payne added.

Ren went instantly alert. "What?" Maybe that was why Cilla wanted to get rid of him. She was at the canyon for nookie-time with the man in her life.

"They broke up, though. Cami and Cilla made a date for coffee and when that day came, Cilla said the guy was history. Cami figured she'd really decided to move on because she'd also lost her long mane of hair."

Something about that story sent a cold finger down Ren's spine. He shrugged the uneasiness away and ran his palm over his clean-shaven cheek. "She's not a big fan of being at the compound with me."

"What's the big deal? You're practically a brother to her."

Except Ren wasn't, he thought, closing his eyes. He was seven years older and back in the day, he'd had little contact with her. And no man who was practically a brother to a woman would be experiencing this unsettling and powerful surge of raw horniness every time he looked at her.

Maybe he should have gotten laid more often in Moscow.

What warned him next, he couldn't say. But he opened his eyes in time to see a couple of scruffy young men summiting the ten-foot wall that separated Gwen's cottage from the narrow, one-lane road that led to the compound. Cilla still remained in her ray of sun, unaware of the strangers invading her bucolic moment right behind her back.

A wave of protectiveness welled in Ren's chest and he started toward her at a run. "Gotta go, Payne," he told his brother. "But just so you know, Cilla's no sister to me."

Chapter 2

Cilla passed a long fence board into Ren's waiting hand. He took hold of it without looking at her, fitted the piece against the rail, then pounded nails into it with angry vigor, as if he was using the hammer on the heads of the two strangers he'd thrown off the property an hour before.

"I think they were harmless," she said.

He paused to send her a disbelieving glance over his shoulder. "They reeked of weed. God knows what else they had in their systems."

After he'd dealt with them, he'd gone on a mission to inspect the perimeter of the compound. At the discovery of a damaged section of fencing in the northeast corner, he'd appointed himself chief mender. She'd tagged along to provide assistance.

His hand stretched back for another board in silent request. She slipped him a piece of the wood stacked in the wheelbarrow they'd brought along. Both had been found in the storage shed at another corner of the compound. "You may have scared them straight," she said. "As a matter of fact, you might have scared me a little."

He grunted, then continued hammering.

"That's a pretty menacing mask you're able to pull out of your back pocket," she mused. When he'd confronted the strangers, his face had gone furious and his body predatory. Truth to tell, she'd experienced an embarrassing, almost sexual thrill in the pit of her belly as he'd bumped chests with the first man who'd made a brief show of blustering bravado.

Ren turned to her. "Cilla, it's not a mask. I'm not a gentle guy."

"Oh." She waved her hand like she was batting the idea away.

A short sigh blew out of him. "No joke. I knew how to deal with those guys today because I've been just like them. Drugs, too much booze, that was my scene too. I pulled myself free of it, then went to work as a bouncer in a bar where I handled people hopped up like that all the time."

"Oh," she said again. He'd been into drugs and booze?

"And concert security? I've had to use my fists more times than I can count." He spread the fingers of his free hand. "See the scars on my knuckles? Those aren't from beating on a computer keyboard, though I've been tempted to do that a time or three too."

Looking down as instructed, her stomach tightened on another illicit trill. But it wasn't thinking about how he could use the appendage to hurt anyone that caused the low vibration. Instead, she was contemplating how the backs of his fingers, crisscrossed with marks of violence, would feel tracing the curve of her cheek. The slope of her breast. The span of flesh between her hipbones. Shivering, she realized that now, *now*, she really was a little scared.

Of how easily he affected her.

Turning toward the fence, Ren reached behind him

and yanked off his T-shirt. "Getting damn hot," he muttered.

Me, too, Cilla thought, staring at his naked back. There were a thousand muscles moving beneath his smooth, golden skin. As he shifted, so did they, the sun catching a ripple here, a smooth bunch of power there. The valley of his spine called out for her fingertip. She wanted to press her palms against the heavy wings of his scapulas. Her mouth practically itched to touch the bulge of a tricep.

As if sensing her turmoil, Ren glanced back. His green eyes narrowed and she took a quick step away. One dark brow rose. "You're really afraid of me, Cilla?"

Yes, yes, *yes*. She shook her head. "I'm, uh, just thinking again it would be best if you leave the compound. You know, because we really don't know each other well..."

And I want to get to know you, oh-so-bad, up close and very personal. That was scary. She wasn't good with men, particularly in that arena. Tad Kersley had made that clear. It had been clear to her before then too, when in the privacy of her own head she'd had to acknowledge that kisses, tongues, and touches never took her anywhere close to the paradise promised by books and porn movies.

Yes, she'd watched a few, trying to find out where and how it always went wrong for her.

"What the hell is going through that brain of yours?" Ren asked.

Not answering *that* truthfully. "I'm just saying I'll be fine here alone."

Turning to face her fully again, he crossed his arms over his chest. Oh my, more smooth skin and fascinating masculine contours. "Baby," Ren said, "after what happened today you think I'd let you stay here by yourself?"

"They were looking for the Lemons," she protested. "Their favorite band."

His brows rose. "And what do you suppose might happen when the next set of impromptu visitors are disappointed to find them away from home?"

"They would go on their way."

"Like those dudes were so happy to do today? I had to get in their faces, Cilla. I don't think the outcome would be the same if a beautiful woman insisted they take their leave."

Ren thought she was beautiful? Or was that just an automatic turn of phrase?

Before she could decide, his back was presented to her again and he returned to pounding nails. "I've got a couple weeks for you," he said over the hammering.

Two weeks alone with Ren. Two weeks of torture in his presence. Not just because she'd be tormented by being near someone she suddenly, viscerally wanted so bad, but also because she'd surely give away her stupid fascination with him. She'd trip, she'd stammer, she'd blush, surely she would (she already had!), and he'd guess her secret.

Then pity her.

Backing away from him, she tried thinking of other arguments. Other options. Maybe she'd pack up Gwen's costumes and return with them to her own small place near the beach. Her fingers slid into her pants pocket to grip the key to the storage room built behind the older woman's cottage. Though she'd examined the pieces displayed in the main part of the house, Cilla had yet to take a look at the full collection.

If she was going to escape forced seclusion with Ren, she had to figure out her next move.

Leaving him to finish the fence repair, she set off for the storeroom alone. Inside the windowless, 15 x 30-foot space, the air was cool and smelled like lavender and lemon, scents Cilla immediately identified with Gwen. She stood in the dimness and breathed it in, thinking of the woman who had brushed her hair when she was small, who had explained the mysteries of pimples and periods as she grew, who had encouraged Cilla to explore her interest in fashion design.

Leaving the door propped open, she flipped on the light and approached the rolling racks of clothes that were stacked against three of the walls. On the fourth, the one with the entry opening, floor-to-ceiling shelves displayed footwear: white patent leather go-go boots and outrageous sequined platform shoes. Knee-length, lace-up moccasins and spike-heeled stretches of black suede that would reach a woman's crotch. Most of Gwen's collection was women's clothing, but adjacent to the shelving was a short rack of striped bellbottoms, billowing poet shirts, and velvet jackets with epaulets, gold stitching, and brass buttons that had belonged to male performers.

There was a fawn-colored suede vest from which swung beaded and feathered fringe that she remembered her dad, Mad Dog Maddox, had worn during a Grammy performance.

Cilla ran her fingers through the long strings of leather, a smile on her face. She loved these vintage pieces. *Thank you, Gwen*, she said, ignoring the little sting at the corners of her eyes. *Thank you for these costumes and everything else you gave me.*

She drifted toward a selection of dresses. There were three white pleather minis likely worn by the back-up singers of some Sixties band. They would have been hell to wear (and sweat beneath) under stage lights. Nearby hung a halter maxi dress made of Stevie Nicks-styled lace and filmy layers. As her hand brushed over it, a long, matching scarf fell to the carpeted floor. Cilla snatched it up and on a whim, flung it around her shoulders and over her head, for a moment channeling her inner music diva.

Closing her eyes, she whirled and dipped, again Stevie-style, humming a song in an old game of pretend that she'd entertained herself with as a lonely little rock princess (influenced by Gwen who'd been a huge Fleetwood Mac fan, naturally). With her arms overhead, wrists crossed, Cilla swayed her hips and twirled to a rhythm playing in her head as she lost herself in dance. A throat cleared (not her own), freezing her mid-swoop-and-turn. *Oh, damn.*

Dropping her arms, she yanked off the scarf and let it trail to the ground. Her gaze flicked to Ren's face. "If you tell a soul..." she said in a low, menacing voice.

He was grinning. "I think there's a lot about you I don't know, Cilla."

"Well, you're not going to get a chance to find out exactly what that all is," she grumbled, walking to the rack of dresses to drape the fabric over a hanger, her jerky movements causing the whole wheeled contraption to slide sideways.

"What do you mea—" he started, then broke off as his gaze widened.

Cilla glanced behind her, and saw what had caught his eye. There was something behind the clothes, something large and colorful, and then Ren was shifting some of the metal contraptions to the middle of the room so they had an unencumbered view.

It was a photo, blown to life-size proportions and hung on the plaster surface. In the middle of the shot, wearing one of her long calico dresses, Gwen sat cross-legged. Her elbow-length graying curls framed her happy grin and sparkling eyes. Gathered around her were the nine

Lemon kids, ranging in age from ten (Cilla) to eighteen (Beck). Silent, she and Ren stared at the image.

The day was sunny. They were gathered on the grass beside the tennis court. She couldn't remember how or why Gwen had managed to corral all of them together. Despite being raised at the same compound with fathers in the same band, they'd never been like one big family. Cilla wasn't even that close to her own siblings, maybe because twins Brody and Bing were six years older and always perfectly partnered with each other.

The photographer had caught the two of them mid-wrestle, their long bangs flopping over their sixteen-year-old foreheads. Dark-haired Beck looked off into the distance, likely already thinking of the wide world he was eager to explore. His brothers Walsh and Reed mugged for the camera, bookending the group on either side. Cami and Cilla sat next to Gwen in poses that mimicked hers. Both of them had a hand on one of the woman's knees. Behind Cami, Payne stared coolly at the lens, a smudge of motor grease on his cheek. Ren slouched in his place behind Cilla, striking an insolent pose in a leather jacket over a white T-shirt. His hair was messy, a silver cross dangled from one pierced ear, and he had a cigarette clamped in the corner of his sulky mouth. A quick tremor snaked down Cilla's spine.

No wonder she'd developed a crush on him. It was so clear now.

He'd been the ultimate bad boy.

Now Ren made some sound she couldn't interpret. She glanced over at him. His gaze was still trained on the photo. Though he'd grown into a man, she could still see some of the brooding half-grown adolescent behind the silver-green of his eyes. Maybe it was the Stevie Nicks moment she'd just indulged in, but she thought suddenly of

Stevie's solo song, "Edge of Seventeen." Ren would have been just that age—on the brink of so much. He could have fallen into real danger, she knew, recalling his confession about drugs and booze.

They all could have, given their unstructured, ungrounded lives.

It was odd, she thought, but nonetheless true that despite their similar backgrounds (or maybe precisely *because* of their similar, dysfunctional backgrounds), they'd not all bonded into one cohesive, happy unit.

Looking at Gwen, she figured that's what the loving woman had hoped for. She'd started out a groupie, hadn't she? She'd always wanted to be part of something bigger. And then she'd come to the compound and stayed, doing her best to be a maternal influence on nine motherless kids whose fathers', at best, treated them with benign neglect.

"I'm lucky I'm alive," Ren suddenly muttered, letting her know his mind was traveling along some of the same lines as hers.

"Yeah," she agreed.

So stay here with him, a voice said. It was Gwen's voice. *Stay with Ren at the canyon. Give the both of you a little time to be glad about that together.*

Why glad together? Cilla wondered. But the voice didn't speak again.

Still, as woo-woo as it might sound, she knew in that instant it was the woman's wish. Gwen wanted her to take these weeks with Ren.

Cilla couldn't refuse, because she owed the older woman just that much. Not to mention Ren's own desire for a respite at the compound. Whether it was to appease his guilt over missing the memorial or because he'd promised Bean or because he needed the vacation (likely some combination of all three) he was committed to staying. Surely Cilla could be woman enough to ignore her overactive hormones for a short period so the sex god of her fantasies could have what he wanted as well.

Turning away from the photo, she started for the storeroom exit.

"Cilla?" Ren said. "What's next?"

"A morning meal," she said. "Didn't I promise you one?"

Ren got an evening meal out of Cilla that day, too. He was ostensibly teaming with her to make the chicken-and-vegetable kabobs, rice pilaf, and fruit salad, but so far he'd nursed a beer while watching her move around Gwen's kitchen, a plain white butcher apron protecting her clothes.

Covering up most of her hot little figure.

He still got the rear view if he chose to look—and the jaunty bow tied at the small of her back only did more to draw the eye to her fine ass—but he was resisting with every scrap of goodness he could find in his black heart. If they were going to co-habit for a couple of weeks—she appeared to have accepted that now—then the she-was-like-a-sister-to-him angle was the best way to go. He was going to cement that attitude by bedtime tonight, he promised himself.

As she chopped a zucchini into chunky coins, she shot him a glance through her thick lashes. "What?"

Tipping the bottle back, he finished his beer. "I didn't say anything."

"I can hear you thinking from over here."

Shit. Honesty was not the best policy in this case, so he scoured his mind for what he'd ask a sister-type he'd been out of touch with for a long while. His mind went back to his conversation with Payne about their sibling, Cami. "Uh...you ever been married?"

"Not once."

"Shacked up with a guy?"

"Nope."

He nodded. "I would have guessed that."

Cilla sent him another look, this one, he thought, holding a trace of hurt in it. "Gee, thanks."

Double shit. "Hey, I didn't mean it like that. You're, uh..." *Ren, don't go there.* "I'm sure some men find you...cute, or whatever." Did that sound brotherly? He thought so, though her reaction was difficult to judge as her focus was back on the green vegetable. Was she wielding the knife more viciously?

He resisted the urge to cover his crotch and tried a different tack. "What are you going to do with the costume collection?"

Cilla drew a colander of washed mushrooms toward her and began trimming the ends. "Various things. Gwen and I discussed it."

A stab of guilt had him crossing to the refrigerator for another beer. Though the time from the older woman's diagnosis of pancreatic cancer to her death had been swift, he should have found a way to come back, if only for an in-person goodbye. "And...?"

"If I can establish the provenance—who wore them and when—of the better pieces, I'll store them safely or display them in my studio. The others I might try incorporating into my designs. A blend of vintage and contemporary, if that suits my client's taste."

"I'd like to see some of your work," Ren said, realizing he really did.

She looked over, as if gauging the truth of that. "Yeah?"

"Yeah."

With another assessing look at him, she wiped her

hands on the apron front then crossed to a laptop sitting closed on the kitchen's granite-topped island. In moments she had it open and had navigated to a webpage, "Cilla Design." Drawing closer to her, he watched the screen as she clicked through a gallery of images. Some of the clothing hung on padded hangers, other times they were modeled—he presumed—by her clients. The pieces were colorful, beautiful, and clearly well-designed. As she'd told him before, there were brief and glittery ice-skating costumes, sweeping dresses and matching suits for ballroom dancers, and a selection of lacey-though-simple dresses and Western-styled jackets worn in the publicity photo of an up-and-coming country band. "I know those guys," Ren said, pointing his beer at the screen. "They're good."

Then he tapped his bottle on the back of her head in a gesture of brother-like affection. "You too, Cilla. You're really good."

She turned to face him. They were so close he could smell that citrus scent of her hair. She had a shallow dent in her chin, like someone had pressed their pinky fingertip there. How had he never noticed that before? Her mouth was soft, two pink pillows that drew his gaze until he jerked it up to land on the brightness of her blue eyes.

There was a smile in them. "Thanks for the compliment."

He didn't remember a word he'd said. Not when every damn cell in his body was screaming for him to yank her even nearer, to taste that mouth, to have those eyes close in surrender. But his big hands would leave marks on her tender skin, he wanted to clutch her close that bad. He'd bruise her flesh.

Mar her life when he disconnected, like he always did. Like he was so damn good at.

So he drew back to take another pull of beer and reined in his lust. "You're welcome," he said. "It's pretty amazing to think Mad Dog Maddox could pass along that kind of talent."

She sidestepped away from him—thank God—and moved back to the cutting board. "Mad Dog is color blind. I'm thinking I may have gotten it from my mother. Gwen said she had a distinct sense of style."

"You've never met?" Ren searched his mental files for what he knew about her. Nothing, he concluded.

Cilla shook her head. "She had the twins and me, but her relationship with our father was on-again, off-again. After I was born, she roamed away with another band and was killed in a crash of their tour bus."

"Oh, Cilla."

She shrugged. "Never knew her. I was a couple of weeks old when she left. I have to think hard to recall her name." There was a glass of white wine on the countertop and she took her first sip. "You?"

"I always knew the name of my mother, of course. Her last one, anyway." Ren smiled wryly. "I think that's why Bean named Payne, Cami, and me the way he did...so he'd remember the surnames of the women who bore us."

"You've never met her?"

"Actually, I have." The legs of a bar stool screeched against the tile floor as he pulled it away from the island. He hitched a hip on the woven rush seat and set down his beer so he could scroll through the images on Cilla's website again. Pretty. Original. Sexy. Like their designer.

"Well?" Cilla demanded. "What did you think of her?"

"My mother?" He shrugged. "She didn't throw open her arms when this twenty-year-old tough with long hair and piercings showed up on her doorstep in Pasadena."

"Pasadena," Cilla said knowingly.

"Yeah. Wears pearls. Married a doctor. Has a couple of kids with him. He knows about me, they don't."

"So you don't spend Thanksgiving and Christmas with that side of the family either?"

He shook his head. "It was clear right away I was an unpleasant reminder of a now-embarrassing period in her life."

Cilla winced. "That had to hurt."

"I didn't think it affected me much." Gaze dropping, Ren studied the tattoo that swept from a sharp point near his inner wrist to make a curve four inches higher on his forearm. "Until the girl-of-the-moment refused to go through with our couples' tattoo after my meeting with not-so-friendly Mom."

"Couples' tattoo?" Stepping closer, Cilla scrutinized the black ink.

"This is like your dancing, okay?" he warned her. "What's said or done in the compound stays in the compound. Right?"

A little smile twitched the corners of that sweet mouth. "I can agree to that."

"It was an incredibly stupid idea, but remember I was twenty and this girl, she gave the most amazing blo—" He broke off, just in time. "Let's say she was, uh, skilled in the sack and she extracted a promise from me in a vulnerable moment."

Cilla's brows were high over her big blues. "'Couples' tattoo'?" she repeated.

"Yeah, see, she was supposed to get the same design as me, but on her left wrist. So, when we held hands—now don't laugh—they'd make a heart."

Silent, she was staring at his arm.

"All right," he said, shaking his head. "Go ahead and laugh."

"I don't want to." Cilla looked up and her gaze caught his. "She didn't follow through with it, you said."

He had no clue what was going on in Cilla's head and his powers of deduction were distracted by her lemon-sweet scent. "Not after I found my mother. I was never one for warm-and-fuzzy, but I went both a little wild and a lot remote following that meeting. The girl didn't stick around much longer."

Though of course Ren had never emotionally attached to her anyway.

"You could have the half-heart removed," Cilla pointed out. "Don't they do laser or something?"

"Have never opted for that. First, that procedure hurts like a mother." He winced. "No pun intended. Second, it's a good reminder."

"A reminder of what?"

"I suck at anything other than solitary."

After that moment of sharing, she went back to dinner prep. He topped off her wine and got the grill started. They ate out on the patio just off Gwen's kitchen, under a propane heater that radiated warmth on their head and shoulders. A single votive candle illuminated the small table and the darkness closed around them like a loosely held fist.

The food tasted good and when his plate was clean, he kicked back in his chair and breathed in the clean canyon air. They could have been the only two people in the world. Though L.A. with all its neon excitement and larger-than-life dreams was a car ride down Laurel Canyon Boulevard, this was Eden. Ren decided he felt a little buzzed. Not on beer, but maybe on all the oxygen exhaled by the thriving flora at the compound. Or maybe it was Cilla, who seemed as content as he to enjoy the...contentment.

He couldn't remember the last time he'd slowed down enough to absorb quiet. Christ, and he'd never told a soul about the visit to his mother and the story behind the tattoo on his wrist. Maybe he really *was* buzzed. Picking up his third beer, he squinted at the label, then grunted. Nothing he hadn't imbibed before.

He transferred his gaze to Cilla. She was cradling her wine glass and staring off into the distance. The candlelight flickered across her face, giving her silky skin a golden glow and shadowing her eyes and that small depression in her chin.

She could break some man's heart, he thought. That vulnerable expression belied an upbringing as messed-up as his own. For whatever reason—did there need to be one besides their oddball childhoods?—the nine Lemon kids were a prickly, wary lot, not much good at reaching out to one another, let alone to anyone else. Yet that didn't show on Cilla's fine features and in her fathomless blue eyes. Someday a man was going to come along and be drawn to all that delicate outer beauty but then find, to his dismay and unending frustration, that she was too well-armored to let him in all the way. He'd only be able to dip his toe into Cilla's essence, because she wouldn't let down her guard and allow him any more of her than that.

What had Payne said? *Not one of us knows what a normal, healthy relationship looks like.*

It was bad, sad, sadder than he'd ever considered, when he thought about Cilla Maddox, forever the lonely little rock princess, as inaccessible to love as if she was truly locked up in her Rapunzel tower for the rest of her life.

The notion shook him, and he stood so abruptly, his chair rocked violently against the flagstone patio surface. Cilla looked over in surprise. "Don't get up," he told her.

"I'm on dish duty."

Still, she trailed him into the kitchen, and they managed to do the clean-up without any fuss or much conversation. Glancing at the clock, he noted it was barely nine o'clock, but he was ready to retreat. Like he'd said, he was best when he was solitary and he could use the time to put her soundly into the no-touch column in his head. He moved around the small house, locking doors and windows. Then he strolled back into the kitchen to address Cilla, who was sipping at a cup of hot tea while she surfed the internet on her laptop.

"Jet lag still has its claws in me," he told her. "I'm going to bed." He'd stashed his duffel in the cottage's second bedroom. It was free of Cilla's scent, unlike the one he'd woken up in this morning. That way, he hoped, her nearness wouldn't disturb his sleep.

Why would it? a little voice in his head mocked. *Remember, she's like a sister to you.*

Ignoring the taunt, he started for the hall, glancing at Cilla as she followed on his heels. "I'm tired too," she said.

When he paused with his hand on the doorknob to his bedroom, she hesitated as well. He looked down at her. "Well...goodnight."

She smiled. Then, placing one hand over the tattoo on his wrist, she lifted to her toes and placed a kiss on his cheek.

Both touches burned.

As she fell back to her heels, they stared at each other. At the flutter of her pulse in her neck, he knew her heart was pounding as fast as his. At the flags of color on her cheeks, he knew that fire was pouring into her veins, just as it was into his. At her wide eyes and their expression of very real alarm, there was no doubt in his mind that this white-hot physical attraction was going both ways.

Her hand was still on his skin and his muscles went hard as he clamped down on the need to take her into his arms, to jerk her up to meet his mouth, to drag her to his bed and slake this inconvenient, throbbing, *aching* lust.

If he was anyone else, he would. If she was anyone else, he would.

If they were anyone but the messed-up, mistrustful progeny of the careless, hedonistic kings of rock 'n' roll, there might be a chance for something here. Temporary, of course, but that didn't mean it couldn't be satisfying.

But nothing was going to happen, because they *were* the messed-up, mistrustful progeny of the careless, hedonistic kings of rock 'n' roll.

"Fucking Lemons," he muttered, jerking away from her and from temptation.

Her eyes went even bigger, but then a little smile curved her pretty mouth. God, she was going to kill him. Her voice was soft as a whisper when she spoke. "Do you remember what Gwen always told us?" she asked. "When life gives you the Lemons..."

He shook his head, remembering all too well and not believing for a second anything sweet or good could come out of this unwelcome connection between him and Cilla. "Make lemonade."

Chapter 3

The morning air was beginning to warm as Cilla approached the pool, considering a swim. If she was at her place near the beach, she'd be preparing for a run on the sand, but the canyon roads were narrow and wound around each other in intricate coils. If she went out for her usual forty-five minutes of exercise she was afraid she'd either get lost or hit by a car. Bending over, she dipped her fingertips into the aquamarine water, yelping when her flesh met the much-too-cold wet.

Nope, no swimming for her. Resigned, she turned toward the pool house, half of which was filled with top-of-the-line exercise equipment including a varied set of dumbbells, a weight machine, an elliptical, a stair-stepper and a pair of treadmills. It was a good thing she'd worn her running clothes just in case.

When life gives you the Lemons, make lemonade.

The echo of that line halted her footsteps as her mind replayed last night, the moments right before she and Ren exchanged their halves of the line.

What impulse had led her to do it? She didn't know,

but she'd hadn't thought twice about giving Ren the most casual of goodnight kisses. It had been just a little peck on the cheek, really.

But then something had happened that made the walls of the hallway close in like a blood-pressure cuff. Ren had looked at her, merely looked at her, and the smolder in his eyes had sent her pulse pounding and her body temperature soaring. She'd felt turned on and terrified. Aroused and afraid.

It was one thing when she was the host of a solo passion-party, but entirely another when an unexpected guest arrived, ready for party games.

He'd looked that way, felt that way, his arm turning to steel beneath her hand.

But if he actually wanted her, despite how attracted she was right back, Cilla knew there was no possible way she could do anything about it. She was terrible in bed. Awkward, cold, essentially embarrassed by the entire procedure that was intrusive, intimate, and, ultimately, messy.

Just the thought of going through that with Ren—with the guaranteed result of experiencing his disappointment in her performance—made her want to dive into the freezing pool and never come up again.

Her only hope was she'd imagined the moment.

Somewhere in the night she'd started wondering about that. Besides "Fucking Lemons"—and there could be an untold number of reasons for him expressing that sentiment, as she well knew—he'd not given away what was going through his mind. Perhaps that smolder and that tension had all been on her side and she'd been, well, projecting.

With her hand on that unfinished heart, the defiant symbol of his solitary nature, perhaps she'd romanticized the moment. Gone girly, fantasizing she was the one who could be his other half.

Except it actually hadn't felt like *romance*, per se. Instead, it had felt the opposite of anything dreamy and idealized. To her, that moment had throbbed with raw power. Raw sex. Making clear to her that going to bed with Ren would mean she'd be stripped bare of more than just clothes.

Oh, it had to be all in her head!

The phone in the pocket of her hoodie buzzed. She stilled. Ren? But she'd left him—presumably—still sleeping back at Gwen's, and anyway, she hadn't told him how to reach her.

How could she be thinking he wanted to swap bodily fluids when he didn't care about swapping cell numbers?

The screen read "Jewel" and Cilla quickly took the call. She'd run into the other woman at the Canyon Country Store a few days before. Under the photos of The Doors and The Lemons, beside the shelves of expensive liquor and the section of English foodstuffs stocked for the famous expat Brits who lived in the canyon, the two women had re-connected.

Or maybe connected for the first time ever. Jewel had been a couple of years ahead of Cilla in school and they'd never been more than nodding acquaintances even though they lived on the same street—Cilla in the compound and Jewel at her grandmother's funky rambler down the road where chickens roosted in the trees and a couple of goats lived and were loaned out to help with weed abatement.

But their chat had been friendly and Jewel had promised to stop by one day soon and introduce Cilla to her newborn baby daughter. That day, apparently, had arrived.

Hurrying to the narrow side gate where Jewel said she

was waiting, Cilla was grateful for the distraction. Jewel was a willowy brunette, already slim at the waist though her baby was just a few weeks old. She slipped through the now-unlocked opening, an infant wrapped in a soft pink blanket in her arms.

Cilla peeked at the small face revealed between the folds of the blanket and a bow-topped pink band circling a nearly bald head. "Oh, she's precious."

"This is Soul," Jewel said, then made a wry face. "I know, I know, it's horribly Laurel Canyon of me to choose such a hippie-dippy name, but there's an old song...'Heart Full of Soul,' that means a lot to me."

"I love the name Soul," Cilla assured her. "What's her daddy think of it?"

A flush crawled over Jewel's face. "Soul's father is...not around at the moment."

"Oh, I'm sorry." In the store, the subject hadn't come up. "I hope I didn't make you uncomfortable..."

"No, of course not—" She broke off, her gaze shifting over Cilla's shoulder. Her body went still. "Has Beck come back?"

Cilla craned her neck, and saw the tall, dark-haired figure in the distance. "No. That's Ren. Ren Colson," she said as he seemed to spot them and began heading in their direction. Crossing her arms over her chest, she tried appearing calm and collected, as if a simple kiss had not caused her an inner riot. "Do you know him?"

"Just by reputation," Jewel said, and then she was smiling in response to the dazzler that Ren directed her way as he strode up.

A glance was flicked at Cilla. "Company?" he asked, and Cilla swore she saw him checking out the other woman's bare left finger. Telling herself that was good news, she pasted a smile on her face and made the necessary introductions.

Ren shook hands, gave the baby a quick look, then smiled at their neighbor again. "So, Jewel and Soul?"

The brunette shifted her daughter to her shoulder and laughed. "And I actually make jewelry for a living. What can I say? Native of the canyon."

"Me, too," Ren said. "We've got that in common."

Was that an interested gleam in his eye? Cilla stared at his face, trying to determine if he was truly flirting with a woman he'd met just this minute—who was also a brand new mother to boot.

"What are you frowning at me for?" Ren asked, glancing her way.

"I'm not frowning."

"Yes, you are." He pointed at a spot between her eyebrows. "It's giving you a furrow right there."

Cilla resisted the urge to iron the spot with her fingertip. "I don't furrow."

"Well, you glare pretty good," he muttered.

Turning away from him, she addressed Jewel, who appeared to be biting back an amused smile. "You said on the phone you had something to ask me."

"That's right." The baby began making snuffling noises and her mother started swaying while rubbing the tiny back. "My grandmother is after me to get out and I wondered if you want to visit one of the music clubs on Sunset with me tonight. I know it's short notice, but I've been wanting to hear," she glanced over at Ren, "someone you both know. Cami Colson."

"Cami!" Cilla snatched at the chance. Not only did she like Jewel and also Cami's music, but going out for the evening would free her from Ren's unsettling presence. "I'd love to."

"Count me in," the man on her right added.

Cilla let loose her glare once again. "Did I hear her invite you?"

"It's my sister," he pointed out. "I'm curious. And by the way, you're furrowing again."

Jewel laughed over Cilla's *humph* of outrage. "Of course you're invited, Ren," she said. "Meet you there at eight o'clock?"

"Eight o'clock it is," he answered.

How could Cilla protest? Under what pretext could she say she didn't want another evening in Ren Colson's company? So she stood there, stewing over her helplessness while a few minutes of wind-up conversation transpired. Then Ren held the gate open for mother and child to exit through. "Cute little thing," he said, watching the two walk away.

"Jewel's nearly six feet tall," Cilla objected.

He sent her a weird look. "I was talking about the baby."

"Oh. Well." Still, wasn't that just as strange? Did Ren actually have an opinion on infants?

"Were you headed into the gym?" he asked, nodding toward the pool house. "I was thinking of taking a spin on one of the treadmills."

He was dressed for it, in running shoes and a pair of long shorts and V-neck shirt in a quick-dry fabric. "Um..."

"At dinner last night you mentioned there was a pair of them." He gave her a grin. "We could race."

It was that white smile that undid her. It was relaxed, confident, and...not the least bit sexual. It *had* all been in her mind!

And so, she and her pride decided there was no good reason for not following through with the work-out she'd intended all along. With luck, it would help alleviate the sudden bad mood that had dropped on her out of nowhere.

Already unzipping her hoodie, she strode off.

Of course there was no racing on a treadmill. And she didn't even try matching Ren's pace, because with her shorter legs she didn't have a prayer of keeping up. Now, maybe if she had Jewel's height...

"You seemed surprisingly interested in baby Soul," Cilla heard herself say, her feet thumping a regular rhythm.

He glanced over at her, a question in his eyes.

"Is that a sign you want kids of your own?" Maybe the exercise was loosening her tongue as well as her muscles.

"What would I know about raising a kid?" he asked, his response as easy as his gait.

"That doesn't mean you don't want any," Cilla pointed out, then heard her mouth keep running on. "Do you have a significant other in your life at the moment?"

He adjusted the treadmill's speed, upping it a little. "Told you I do better solitary."

"Pretty sure that isn't the same as celibate," she said drily.

His lips twitched. "No."

She hesitated, then thought, *in for a penny, in for a pound.* "So, is there a regular casual visitor to your London bedroom?"

He glanced over, his lips twitching again, as if he was enjoying this little game. "I haven't seen the inside of my flat there, Cilla, for over three months."

Her face must have given away her frustration, because he laughed.

At the low sound, she went a little breathless, but she'd been jogging for approximately five minutes, so it was likely anaerobia kicking in. "Never mind," she said, lifting her nose. "It's none of my business."

Another of his chuckles rolled down her spine. "Don't

get in a huff. No, baby, there's nobody 'regular casual' at the moment."

She glanced over to see him grinning at her again. When their gazes met, he wiggled his brows. "But maybe I'll meet some lucky lady tonight."

Her eyes rolled. "Lucky to meet you, I suppose you mean."

And he just laughed harder.

Yep, he wasn't looking at her sexually. He was *laughing* at her. So that moment of mutual lust must have all been in her head. What a relief.

It was!

And...it wasn't.

Ren held the door open for Cilla so she could proceed him into the music club located on Sunset Boulevard, wondering how hard he should try keeping his gaze off her ass. Sure, he'd gawked when she'd traipsed out of her bedroom in the outfit-of-the-evening, but he'd had time to get used to it by now.

His eyes drifted and he quickly jerked them up again. No, not used to it.

Couldn't forget about it either. The image was burned on his retinas. She'd made a mini-skirt out of a black Lemons' tour T-shirt, of all things. She'd explained the process while he'd been rolling his tongue back into his head. Something about cutting off the sleeves and neckline and using a sewing machine to create new, hip-skimming seams. An elastic waistband. A hem that hit right where she wanted.

Mid-thigh, damn it.

And the design was engineered so that the silk-screened image of an open, full-lipped red mouth dripping multi-colored flowers was on the front. The list of the band's 1978 tour dates stamped over with "SOLD OUT" lovingly cupped the curve of her butt.

She wore it with a black tank top and a pair of strappy spike heels. Her blond hair was a mass of waves and half-curls and her lips were painted a ripe raspberry.

His libido had taken one look at the whole package and declared, *Yeah, desperate to tap that.*

He'd sicced his good intentions on the impulse and the two had wrestled during the short drive from the compound to the club. But no matter which ended up on top, Ren was determined to keep his hands off the titillating blend of innocence and sex appeal that was Cilla Maddox. To that end, he was planning to do just as he'd told her.

Find some other woman on whom to focus his attention.

He had some early luck. Once he'd paid their cover and they'd made their way inside, it was to find Jewel sitting with Ren's half-sister, Campbell "Cami" Colson at a four-top near the small stage.

She jumped up to hug Cilla, then stood back, her gaze sliding over him. He sized her up too, shaking his head as he took in her slight figure wearing a loose white blouse dripping delicate lace tucked into torn jeans with motorcycle boots. Even though the lights were somewhat low, he could see her eyes were still the same grayish-green as his own. Her hair, though, was a combination of auburn and gold and brown. She self-consciously fussed with the long, side-sweeping bangs and the blouse's cuff slid to reveal a tooled leather cuff on her wrist and the beginning of a trailing vine tattoo on her inner arm.

"Looking good, Cam," he said.

"It's been five years." There wasn't a shred of condemnation in her words.

He nodded. "You and Payne met me in Paris for your twenty-first birthday."

She grinned. "Bean sent us a case of champagne and that dance troupe as entertainment."

"'Dance troupe'." Ren winced. "It was a handful of male and female strippers who weren't averse to offering extras after the music ended."

Her eyes bugged. "I didn't know that! You and Payne hustled them out before a single zipper came down." She looked a little miffed.

"One of the few times we were good brothers to you, Cam."

A smile lifted a corner of her mouth and he recalled that sweet lopsided grin from her babyhood. Something moved in his chest and he reached out to pat her awkwardly on the shoulder. "It's music for you now, huh?"

She glanced toward the stage. "Yeah, and I gotta get to it. Maybe we can talk between sets?"

"Sure. Look for me by the bar..." But she was already gone.

He was about to do the same, his gaze roaming over the single women milling about, when a cocktail waitress came by with a loaded tray of drinks that she set on the table. "From the talent," she said, nodding toward where Cami was setting up.

So what could Ren do but sit between lovely Jewel and his sexual nemesis Cilla?

He sipped at the whisky with beer chaser his sister had bought and kicked out his feet as he surveyed the club. A good crowd for a weeknight, he decided. Lots of men dressed in jeans and tails-out button downs like he was. The women were in everything from do-me heels to sheepskin boots. His gaze wandered to a table of females in short silky dresses who were also looking his way. With a smile, he toasted them with his glass. Two returned friendly waves.

On the verge of shoving back his chair to test his chances with them, Cilla leaned close, her citrus sweetness tickling his nose. "They look nice," she said, her whisper blowing warm air against his ear. "Perhaps even lucky."

Brat. To put distance between him and her, he twined his fingers in the back of her hair in order to draw her off. Mistake. The fine strands clung to his skin like cobwebs, trapping his touch. Instead of moving her away, it made him want to bury both hands in the stuff and bring her closer.

Without thinking, he tilted back her head and turned his, aligning their mouths—

And the room went dark.

The surprise made him release his grip. He huffed out a breath and dropped his hand to his lap. When a spotlight shown on the stage, highlighting his half-sister, Ren spun his chair around, careful to create more space between him and Cilla.

Cami sat on a simple stool, a guitar cradled in her lap, her focus on her fingers as they began to pluck a rhythm on the strings. The crowd went quiet. Ren had worked with musicians for over a decade and he recognized when one was comfortable in their skin while at the same time supremely aware of their audience. His half-sister snuck a short look in the direction of the table where he sat with Cilla and he wondered if their presence made her nervous.

Then she started to sing and he no longer thought at all.

Her voice, throaty yet pure, was perfect for the folk/bluegrass vibe of the first song about a wandering lover. As the last chord was strummed and the crowd broke into applause, he shared a glance with Cilla. She smiled at him. "I've heard her before. Great, huh?"

"Great," he confirmed, wondering if Bean had ever seen his daughter perform or even knew she played. Ren regretted this was his own first exposure to her talent.

Then Cami swung into the next song, a cover of Colby Caillat's "Brighter than the Sun." His half-sister smiled as the audience started clapping, taking up the rhythm. At the chorus, she stopped picking and strumming to drum on the body of the guitar while she sang the lines a cappella.

After that, the crowd was hers and the set ranged from country covers, a pop standard she made new with her own little twist, and then a sweet rendition of "Baby, Now that I've Found You," reminiscent of Alison Krauss. As the applause from that died down, Cami stroked her thumb over the guitar strings. "This will be the last number of the first set, but I'll be back for a second."

Ren glanced at the table of single ladies he'd spotted before. The minute his half-sister left the stage, he'd head for them. When he returned his attention to Cami, it was to see her peering through the glare of the spotlight directly at him and Cilla. "This one's an old spiritual that's been covered by a number of artists. I hope you'll enjoy my version."

She started to pick out the notes on the guitar, then leaned into the mic and sang:

> *Motherless children have a hard time*
> *When their mother is gone*
> *Motherless children have a hard time*
> *When their mother is gone*
> *Motherless children have a very hard time*
> *All the weepin', all that cryin'*
> *Motherless children have a hard time*

When their mother is gone

The verses continued and she delivered them in a voice filled with heartbreak and loneliness. As the song's last word faded away, Cami didn't wait for applause, but just slipped through the curtain behind her.

It wasn't until the house lights came up that the audience reacted, clapping wildly. Ren joined in, noting that Jewel was looking over at Cilla in concern. He whipped his head around and caught her wiping away tears. Surprised by the show of emotion, he scooted close and rubbed his thumb over her cheek. "Are you okay?"

"Sure." She pushed at his hand and grabbed a cocktail napkin to blot her cheeks. "I'm an idiot."

"No," he said, pushing back his chair. "Hold on. I'll be right back."

Without a second glance at the table of pretty women, Ren stalked past them to knife into the crowd gathered at the bar. He was back to Cilla in moments, glasses of wine for her and Jewel in hand as well as another shot glass—this one filled with tequila.

"Drink," he said, pushing the hard stuff toward Cilla. "You look like you need it." The tip of her nose was pink and she hadn't let go of the balled-up napkin. In his mind, he could still feel the dampness of her tears against his skin.

"I'm fine," she demurred.

"A sip," he insisted.

With a roll of her eyes, she took the glass, touched it to her lips, then sputtered as a few drops of tequila landed on her tongue. "Gah!" she said, frowning at him. "I only drink tequila when I've been bitten by a rattlesnake."

"Funny." He removed the glass from her hand and downed the rest himself. "And you call yourself a rocker's daughter." Then he rubbed his thumb along her cheek again. It warmed under his touch and Cilla's wary gaze cut to his, her big blues looking at him as if she considered *he* might be a dangerous reptile. Instead of backing off, he caressed her again and leaned closer. "I'll ask again," he said, his voice low. "You okay, baby?"

"No," she whispered back. "Not okay when you touch me, Ren."

And before he knew how or what to respond to that, the lights were extinguished. Cami returned to the stage and Ren was grateful for the excuse to turn from Cilla and give his attention elsewhere. Except he mostly didn't. Throughout the next set he was hyper-conscious of her every move. From the corner of his eye he watched her lift her wine glass to her lips. He saw her fiddle with the neckline of her tank top. When she crossed her legs, he tracked the heights to which her hemline rose.

And wished like hell he'd ordered himself a big glass of crushed ice.

The instant the second set was over, he was heading straight for the single ladies' table, he told himself. Goal: at least one phone number.

Not okay when you touch me, Ren.

Booting the echo of her whisper out of his head, he forced himself to ignore Cilla's next leg-crossing and the inches of bare, sleek thigh the action revealed. To Ren, the forty minutes crawled by, though Cami performed another spectacular set, concluding it with a cover of Dawes' "Time Spent in Los Angeles." He clapped like hell, then rose from his chair when the lights came up. Not looking back, he strolled over to the land of Short Silky Dresses.

Ren discovered the natives of that particular country were very friendly.

It relaxed him enough that he chanced a look in the

direction of where he'd been sitting, no longer quite so concerned about a Lemons miniskirt or the track of tears on a beautiful woman's face. Jewel was nowhere to be seen, but Cilla stood, half-turned from him, conversing with a man in slacks and a starched shirt. His arm was curled around a woman whose long blonde hair nearly reached her hips.

As Ren watched, Cilla gave a jerky nod and then the half of her mouth he could see in profile moved up in faux good humor. He tensed, his eyes narrowing. Why was Cilla faking a smile? The answer to the question seemed glaringly obvious to Ren. Had to be some guy from her past.

One of the short silky dresses put her hand on his arm to reclaim his attention. He turned back, trying, really, to focus on the words coming from her pretty mouth. They were numbers. Her cell number.

Instead of feeling gratified, Ren's mind couldn't get past Cilla and the fake, strained smile.

"Excuse me," he said to Short Silky. "I'm sorry, I've got to check on something."

In ten strides he was touching Cilla's tense shoulder. She jolted, then he felt a little of the steel go out of her. "You," she said, and he saw the emotional storm brewing in her eyes.

Cutting his gaze to the couple, he turned to them with an easy smile. "Ren," he said, reaching out to shake their hands one at time.

"Tad," the man said. "And this is Tracy."

"Tad and Tracy," Ren repeated. It sounded like a tween series on Nickelodeon TV. He tucked his arm around Cilla's waist and drew her against his body. "You ready to go?"

The other man's gaze narrowed on Ren, clearly trying

to figure out what he was to Cilla. *Yeah, keep on guessing, buddy.*

As if he didn't notice a thing, Ren slid his hand up Cilla's spine to bury it in her soft cloud of hair, his palm molding to her scalp. "Baby?"

"Um. Uh, sure." Her eyes flicked to Tad and Ren felt a tremor roll through her.

Shit. What was that about? Did this guy *scare* her? He took hold of her hand with his free one, squeezed. "You all right?" he said against her ear.

Her lashes swept up and looking directly into his face, she gave a small nod.

Despite the assurance, those big eyes did him in. And her soft hair that was twined around his fingers. Not to mention the memory of her desolate expression following Cami's song. *Motherless children have a hard time.* The combination compelled him to do something more.

As distraction? Comfort? To nullify the apparent unease she felt upon encountering this preppy stiff named Tad?

Ren couldn't decide.

So, without a further thought or search of soul, he followed his sudden compulsion and bent his head and pressed his mouth to hers.

Cilla's warm lips opened on a gasp of surprise.

Lust punched into his bloodstream with the instant power of a hypodermic. *Jerk away*, he thought, *disconnect from her*, but Cilla had already melted into him and separating their bodies would clearly cause serious harm.

Mental anguish.

He sucked on her bottom lip, then took his time with the upper. She clutched at him, one small hand wrapped around his, the fingers of the other digging into his side. It wasn't a lascivious kiss as kisses could go—he kept his tongue to himself—but it was soft and intimate and sweeter than he could have ever predicted.

"Ren?"

Cami's voice yanked him back to sanity—and yanked his mouth from Cilla's.

Hauling in a breath, he stepped back and so did she. Her face was flushed, her lips were swollen and her hand reached up to smooth the tangle he'd made of her hair. *Well, hell*, he thought, remembering how he'd wanted this to go—and how easily he'd lost this round of the fight.

Current score: Impulse, 1; Good Intentions, 0.

Chapter 4

Cilla sat in the front passenger seat of Ren's BMW rental, grateful they were bringing Cami back to the compound with them. She'd tried to insist the other woman ride shotgun, but Cami had climbed into the backseat with her guitar as if Cilla hadn't said a word. Still, she made an effective buffer between her and the Mighty Kisser.

Cilla was calling Ren that in her mind.

He'd slayed her with a single press of mouth-to-mouth.

Melted her with the soft suction of her lower lip.

Dizzied her by sipping at the top one.

Who but a man with *beso* superpowers could do such a thing? And *why* had he?

Swiveling her eyes, she checked out his profile. In the glow from the dashboard, he looked relaxed. Calm.

While her heart had yet to settle back into place in her chest, fifteen minutes later. It still beat against her throat, making her feel breathless and helpless and not just a little bit gauche.

If Ren knew what he'd wrought with a ten-second kiss

(maybe not even that long!) he'd laugh. Tad Kersley could take some of the blame, though. He'd been introduced to Cami's music through Cilla, so it shouldn't have come as quite so much a surprise to encounter him at the club (he'd enjoyed it that much). But to see him squiring her long-haired replacement...

She hadn't known whether to slap his smug face or steal the other woman away for a private word of warning.

Instead of doing either, she'd worked on maintaining her dignity. That's what she intended to do in the aftermath of the Mighty Kiss too. She was rock royalty, wasn't she?

Cami made a little sound as they drove through the compound gates. The fairy lights that wound through the trees and iced the fence surrounding the tennis court twinkled in the darkness. "Sometimes I forget," she murmured.

Ren glanced at the rear view mirror. "I know you said you're good with sleeping at Gwen's, but I can get us into Bean's place if you'd rather. Bet it's been a long time since you rode the mechanical bull in the basement."

She laughed. "Maybe another time. Right now I just want a bed. Thanks for saving me from the long drive back home with my sound check guy. His truck is a bucket of nuts and bolts." Leaning forward, she brushed Cilla's shoulder. "And thanks for letting me crash here."

"Don't mention it. Gwen would love the idea of you being at her place."

"You and Ren, too," Cami said. "I think she always wondered if—"

"There'd be as many as even three of the nine of us in the same place at the same time again," Cilla hastily put in. Not that she thought for a second Gwen entertained the possibility of any...kissing or whatever between Ren and herself, but it sounded like that's what Cami had been about to say.

Their arrival at the cottage prevented any more dangerous talk. Cilla breathed a sigh of relief as she walked through the small house, turning up the lights. She asked Cami if she wanted tea or something stronger, but the other woman refused and practically zombie-walked down the hall to the room where Ren had slept the night before.

Though Cilla had insisted she'd fit much better, he'd volunteered to get his shut-eye on the couch in the living room. So she dug out a pillow and some bedding, set them on the cushions, and then escaped to her bedroom while he was still in the hallway bathroom. After going through her own nighttime routine in the en suite, she stretched out on the bed and directed sleep to take her away.

Sleep stubbornly refused to cooperate.

After nearly an hour of ceiling-inspection, Cilla decided to venture out for a cup of herbal tea. She could be quiet and quick if she used the microwave to heat up a mug of water.

The cottage was dark and quiet as she made her way in slippered feet to the kitchen. She swung shut the door between it and the living area without taking a peek at Ren. The light over the stove gave her enough illumination to prepare her mug. Just as the microwave beeped off, she happened to glance outside the French door to the adjacent courtyard.

Ren was out there, sitting in one chair, his booted feet propped on another.

Asleep?

She hesitated, then decided she couldn't leave the man dozing out there in the cooling air. Turning the knob, she called softly into the darkness. "Ren?"

He glanced around. "What are you doing up?"

She raised her mug. "Tea. Would you like some?"

Shaking his head, he got to his feet and came toward her. She pushed the door open wider, telling her heart to stop pounding like the Lemons' Hop Hopkin's heavy foot on the pedal of the kick drum. Ren came into the kitchen, bringing with him the perfume of fresh breezes, night-blooming jasmine, and a faint but delicious man-scent that she'd been so up-close-and-personal with as they'd kissed. Some sort of rare European aftershave, she supposed.

The kitchen shrank to the size of her tea cup when he swung shut the door behind him. Cilla instantly made for the one she'd closed that led to the rest of the house. She needed more air and another escape to her bedroom.

"Cilla." Ren's low voice sent a skitter of chills down her spine.

Her toes curled in her slippers. "Um, yes?" Thank goodness she'd donned her calf-tickling robe over another vintage T-shirt. Still, she was embarrassingly aware of her breasts, bare beneath the layers of cotton. The lace of her panties tickled in places she'd never noticed before.

"We should talk," he said.

Throwing a glance over her shoulder, she tacked on a sophisticated half-smile. "No need. No need at all."

"Cilla—"

"Really," she tried smothering the rise of panic. "No need."

"When you can't look me in the eye," he said, his voice implacable, "there's a need."

Damn. He wasn't going to let her off the hook.

So just get it over with, she decided, spinning on her heel. The tea sloshed dangerously close to the lip of her mug and Ren reached over, plucking it from her hand to place it on the counter. "We don't want you to get burned," he said.

Yes. That exactly. But the back of her neck was already on fire. Inhaling a long breath, she forced herself to meet his gaze. Sophisticated, remember?

Those pale green eyes studied her until she had to fight off a squirm. "What?" she finally said, pushing at her hair then rubbing her hand over her mouth. "Do I have toothpaste drool on my chin?"

A sudden grin split his face. "'Toothpaste drool'?"

"You know what I mean."

His laugh was that low and quiet one which flipped her belly. "I find you highly entertaining, Cilla."

She huffed and crossed her arms over her chest. "Yay."

He shoved his hands in his pockets and lowered his head, shaking it so the glossy darkness caught the low light in the room. Did he have to be so damn beautiful? And the way he kissed...

His head came up as if he'd heard her thought. "We have to talk about the kiss."

"Oh, no," she said, lifting her hand and moving it in the air as if erasing the memory. "There's nothing to talk about there."

He stepped back to lounge against the countertop. His large hand slid from his pocket to lift her mug. He took a swallow of tea, his eyes on her the whole time. "I don't want you to think—"

"I don't think anything," she hastened to say, as mortification spread the heat at her neck across her face. "Not thinking at all. Not about anything." She tapped the side of her head with the heel of her palm. "Hear that echo? That's the sound of emptiness."

He was grinning at her again. "Cilla, did you just insist you're an air-head?"

Whatever it takes. "I'm making clear we don't need to

have this conversation."

"Well, you're wrong," he said, returning the mug to the counter with a little *clack*. His expression turned serious. "I've got to make sure you know not to worry... Look, I'm not going to push anything, I promise. Believe me, I don't want to take things any further."

She stared at him, her mind scrambling for some mature, dignified rejoinder. Instead, a question popped out. "Well, why'd you kiss me in the first place?"

He returned his free hand to his pocket and the look he gave her teemed with frustration. "I can't say exactly. You seemed...a little lost, I guess."

"Oh, great." Cilla groaned. "I get it now. Thanks for the pity kiss."

"It wasn't pity," he ground out. "It was..."

The long pause only made her more humiliated.

"It was..." He frowned. "Cilla, it was—"

"Don't bother," she snapped, and kept right on talking. "I don't need an explanation. I also don't need you assuring me you're not going to take anything further either. I know my kissing skills are lacking, like all my skills when it comes to sex. I'm bad at it, and I'm aware of that. Foreplay, afterplay, and all the mortifying middle stuff too. Terrible at every single step in the process."

Now he was staring. "What, exactly, is 'afterplay'?"

"You see!" she said, flinging out a hand. "I don't even know. But it stands to reason that if there's a fore, there must be an after. Newton's Law, right? Anyway, I'm bad at all of it."

"What exactly do you mean by bad, Cilla?" he asked, tilting his head.

She shrugged a shoulder, feeling defensive and moody and wishing her mouth would stop moving. "I don't ever really feel anything, okay?"

His eyebrows shot up. "You didn't feel anything when I kissed you?"

Her good sense finally came alive and started shouting at her. *Shut* up, *girl! Put the brakes on this convo, right now!* "Well, we don't have to get into that, do we? Because you've just said it was a one-time thing."

"Do you really never feel anything?"

"Can't we just leave this alone?"

When he merely stared at her in silence, Cilla finally broke. "Look, Tad told me I was a lousy lay."

Ren's expression turned rock-hard. "*What*?"

"Lousy lay." The words didn't get easier with repetition.

"He *said* that?"

"On the day we broke up." Cilla looked down at her nails, inspecting the polish for chips. "Before that he said I needed to loosen up a little or maybe watch some porn before our dates."

Ren made a noise. "That guy's a dick." There was disgust in his voice.

It teased a small smile out of her. "I was beginning to think so myself. But he wasn't wrong about me finding it hard to relax."

"You melted against me, Cilla," Ren said. "In my arms you were sweet and soft and willing as hell."

She glanced at him. "Gee, thanks. Rub it in."

"Mercy, please," he said his eyes rolling heavenward. "One minute you're complaining about your lack of response, now you're annoyed when I point out you were plenty responsive to me."

"Fine." She returned to inspecting her fingernails. "It's possible I'm not quite reasonable on this topic, okay? I'm a little raw about it, actually."

"Cilla—"

"Let's drop it. Drop it forever."

"I don't think I can. My conscience won't allow me to let you wander around with the misunderstanding that you're what...cold, frigid?"

"Well, I am. And not just with Tad, either."

Ren was shaking his head. The kind—pitying—expression in his eyes made her want to cringe. "Let it go, please," she begged him.

"Cilla, you've got some kind of negative feedback loop going on in your head."

Spare her bedroom advice from the Mighty Kisser, she thought, temper beginning to kindle. "Hey—"

"Honey," he continued, "it's not that hard—"

"If you think it's so easy, or if you think I'm so responsive, then why don't you want to do something more about it?" The words exploded from her mouth. "But that's right, you don't want to take things 'further.'" She put air quotes around the word.

He grimaced. "Because—"

"Let it go, Ren. Let it go and leave me be, unless, that is..."

His eyes narrowed. "Unless what?"

In the back of her mind, her good sense was shouting again, but Cilla wasn't thinking clearly. She hadn't been thinking clearly since Ren came back into her life and now after the evening she'd had, seeing Tad with Cilla's replacement, and then that unexpected kiss...

"Unless you want to teach me," she said, feeling reckless and rash. "You're going to be here for another couple weeks. You could do something useful with your time."

Ren took his hands from his pockets and straightened away from the counter. "Like what, exactly?"

Cilla slammed her arms over her chest. "Mentor me."

Shocked as she was at her own words, they continued to flow from her mouth. "You could be my sexual mentor."

When she saw him start in surprise, she told herself again to shut it down. But some impetuous part of herself couldn't leave well enough alone. "What do you say, Ren? I dare you."

Early morning, and Ren was navigating the L.A. traffic, getting his sister to the auto salvage yard where she worked. He glanced over at her, noting the way she was sucking down the coffee they'd stopped for at the Laurel Canyon market. The place had been busy, some business types and entertainment moguls heading into skyscrapers or studios for the day, others looking like they were winding down after an all-night jam session or a frenzy of painting or sculpting. Canyon country contained all kinds.

Cami must have felt his glance. She looked over. "What?"

"I'm wondering how you're keeping up with this double life of yours. Salvage gal by day, Lady Music by night."

She held up her paper cup. "Caffeine, and lots of it."

"Payne treating you okay? Is he paying you a decent salary?"

"I like the job," she said. "My particular yard's more of a holding facility. Not too many buyers come by. I sit in a trailer most of the day and when I'm not keeping up the inventory on the computer or dealing with the occasional customer, I can play my guitar, do some writing."

"Payne's not in your face, then?"

She shook her head. "He's good to me."

For some reason the warm affection in her voice felt like a blow to Ren's chest. He cleared his throat. "Are there any other men in your life?"

"Just my mystery man."

"Who?" Curious, he slid her another look.

A small smile played around her mouth. "An occasional client. Makes an appointment. Comes late at night. I indulge him because he doesn't complain about the prices I jack up just for him."

"Is that safe?"

"Don't worry." She waved a hand. "He's harmless."

Ren refocused his gaze on the ass end of the Lexus in front of him. "What about you and Cilla?" he asked in a casual voice. "You see her often?"

"No."

"But you girls were the last two left at the compound. Didn't you...bond a little?"

"Some, I suppose. But I'm older. We were in different grades. Lived in different houses."

Ren knew all that, but it was the first time he'd considered what that meant. "So not really like sisters."

She shrugged. "We drifted apart after growing up."

The knowledge gnawed at him a little. Cami had Payne in her corner. But Cilla... Maybe she'd managed to build a life for herself, but she was still alone, it seemed.

In her bed, as well.

You could be my sexual mentor.

Those words ran through his head for the millionth time.

Damn woman. All sweet on the outside, innocent-looking, but she knew a way to skewer a man. *I dare you.* He might not have been particularly close with the other Lemon kids, but all were surely conscious of one of Ren's particular foibles.

Despite a broken arm as the result of an attempt to climb the outside of the Maddox Castle, the loss of high school graduation ceremony privileges due to a prank pulled on the principal, and that Halloween when he'd been arrested three times in the same night—all incidences that had occurred before his eighteenth birthday—Ren had never been one-hundred-percent successful at turning down a dare.

To make that matter worse, there were additional personal weaknesses he'd never completely conquered even though he was now thirty-one: 1) like every other guy on the planet he'd been known to let his cock make decisions for him, and 2) if he wanted something, really wanted it, he went for it. Even if having it might be bad for him.

Even if it might be bad for her.

He contemplated this on a sigh as they hit some infamous L.A. traffic. Cars were at a halt in every lane and it gave his mind ample time to recall that light in her eyes and that sassy tilt to her dimpled chin when she said, *You could be my sexual mentor.*

And he'd replied, *I'll think about it.*

I'll think about it!

What was wrong with mentioning that wasn't a great idea or even laughing it off and pretending she wasn't absolutely serious—even when he knew she was. This dilemma could be over now, already behind him, instead of something he was going to wrestle with through forty more minutes of a crawling conga line of cars to drop Cami off then another forty to get back to the compound.

But he hadn't laughed it off then because it would definitely have hurt Cilla. She'd been serious as a heart attack...like the one he'd nearly had when she'd made the request.

You could be my sexual mentor.

By the time Ren dropped his sister at work, turned around, and made his return to Laurel Canyon Boulevard, there was a snake of autos slinking their way from the San Fernando Valley toward Hollywood. He was going against the flow, thank God, and edged through the compound gates still struggling with his decision. His brain said one thing. His cock another. And between the two was a place he was trying to ignore as much as possible.

Who would have thought Ren Colson had a heart?

But he'd discovered he did and it wasn't a big fan of that lost look he'd seen on Cilla's face the night before. He was even less of a fan of her thinking she was frigid. Jesus! She'd been a flame in his embrace.

Still uncertain of how to handle the situation, Ren let himself into Gwen's house. Though it was early and Cilla might conceivably be asleep, he could feel the place was empty. In the kitchen, he saw a half-full carafe of coffee on the burner and a flowered mug on the counter. He wandered down the hallway in the direction of the bedrooms. The door to the one where she slept was open. He glanced in, noting a pile of clothing on the quilt, the rhinestones and flamboyant colors suggesting the items were part of the collection left by Gwen to Cilla.

It made him think of that little girl she'd once been. He hadn't noticed her all that often, but he had a memory of her draped in scarves, a man's heavy-buckled leather belt wrapped twice around her waist and a crown of daisies in her hair. What game had her imagination conjured? One, he supposed, to entertain the lonely child she'd been.

Though Cilla was all grown up now, she still retained a decided innocence factor. And he was in the kind of business that jaded a man early...meaning they were not a good match—even a temporary one.

Except, exactly how innocent could Cilla really be? Just like him, she'd grown up around the Lemons and that meant she'd been exposed to a lot more than most women of any age...

Which might also go a long way to explaining her inability to relax when it came to sex.

Certain she was nowhere in the house, he took a stroll through the grounds. He should probably spend his time searching for the box that Gwen had willed to him, but his mind was on his housemate instead. As he approached the pool, he heard the wet *splish* of someone moving through the water. His hand on the gate leading to the deck, he stopped, arrested by the sight of Cilla swimming. She wore a one-piece suit that clung to the curves and hollows of her body. As she was moving away from him, arm-over-arm in a front crawl stroke, he could appreciate the flare of her hips and the cute roundness of her rump. But when she flipped and headed in his direction, he started forward, spurred by the suit's blue hue.

How her lips nearly matched its color.

As she reached the shallow end, he bent to catch one wrist. Sputtering, she looked up and he caught the other, hauling her from the pool and onto the deck in one move.

She blinked at him, her lashes spiked, her eyes wide. "Hey—"

"Hey nothing." He dragged her toward a lounge where he spied a long terry robe. With efficient movements, he bundled her into it, then took up a towel and started blotting at her hair. "What do you think you're doing?" he demanded.

"Um, swimming?" Her teeth began to chatter and a shiver ran through her body that he could detect even beneath the thick robe.

Shaking his head, he rubbed her hair more briskly. "The pool temp is fifty-seven degrees. I checked it yesterday."

"So?" She tried grabbing the towel, but he caught her

wrists in one hand and held them down while he continued getting the moisture from her hair with the other. "Ren!"

He ignored her protest. "You are a silly woman."

With a wild movement of her arms, she broke free of him. Then she caught the towel and ripped it from his hands to hang around her neck. The rest of her might have been cold, but her glare was molten. "Do you mind?"

He glared right back. "I mind you freezing on my watch."

"Have you thought that's maybe what I wanted?" she yelled. "That maybe I was trying to freeze my brain?"

"Why the hell would you do that?"

"So I could stop thinking about what happened last night, okay? So I wouldn't remember what an idiot I made of myself with my overshare." She turned on one bare foot and stomped off in the direction of Gwen's.

Ren watched her for a moment, and though she was covered in yards of thick fabric, something about the way her cute ass twitched as she hurried off made his blood rush south. Like he was led by a chain, he followed in her wake, bemused by his own reaction and the sense of inevitability swamping him.

She glanced over her shoulder, and that swift look of apprehension only caused him to quicken his footsteps. He'd always known he was a very bad man.

As she reached the door to Gwen's, so did he, and he pulled it open before she could. With a shrug she swept over the threshold and he had to swallow his laugh. Clearly she was nervous now, and it only served to make the predator in him more keen for her.

Yeah. Bad Ren.

With him at her heels, she headed for the hallway. Before they reached it, she swung around to confront him. Her hands went to her hips.

He was gratified to see her lips were back to their normal rosy color and her cheeks were pink too. Ren smiled at her. "Warm now?" he asked.

Cilla ignored the question. "Last night, why didn't you just tell me I was giving too much information? Three letters, a T, an M, and an I, and I would have set aside my tea and taken myself off to bed."

"I accept," he said, cutting to the chase.

She blinked. Her body went still. "Accept?" she whispered.

"The dare. The role. I'll be your sexual mentor."

Her nostrils flared. More color rose from her neck to infuse her face. "Um..."

"Unless you want to back out," he offered.

She stared at him. "Um..."

"Yes? No?"

"Yes."

"You want to back out?"

"No!" Her fingers fisted around each end of the towel hanging over her neck and she continued to stare at him, round-eyed. "I...I... Really?"

God, she was so fucking adorable that he was going to do this right or kick his own ass. Cilla deserved to experience all of life's pleasures. "Really, baby. I'm going to prove you're not the least bit cold. Starting now, we'll discover every one of your buttons and I'll show you how much fun it is to push them."

She only goggled more.

Fuck. Adorable.

"Now?" she whispered.

"Right now."

With a hand on her shoulder, he turned her, then pushed her in the direction of her bedroom. "Put on some clothes. We're going hiking."

Her head came around. "Hiking?"

He smiled. "Hiking," he said, then let his grin go wolfish. "As the sexual mentor, baby, I make the rules and that's where we start."

As she set off down the hall, he told himself the heat coursing through him was a decided sense of satisfaction. Bad Ren was actually going to do good here. If he helped her get comfortable in her own skin, if he was able to give her confidence and a strong sexual identity, then she'd be able to climb down from her Rapunzel tower and find a man with whom she could make a strong connection.

Not him, of course. But he'd take her on a two-week tour of sorts, during which he'd smash her hang-ups and banish her inhibitions, in order to free her to find true love.

Yeah. Jeez. He really fucking had some semblance of a heart.

Who knew?

Chapter 5

Ren accelerated north through Laurel Canyon, green trees and shrubs passing by, the sky as blue as summer. It was winter in Southern California, which meant if the sun was out the temperature could easily edge toward a high of eighty degrees. The BMW's sunroof was pulled back, allowing in a breeze that teased the tendrils of wavy blonde hair caressing Cilla's cheeks.

He wanted to reach over and tuck them behind her ears.

But part of the game plan precluded putting his skin to hers just yet. From the instant he'd made clear he'd take on the mentor role, it was obvious her nerves had leaped to high alert, as if she expected him to toss her to the nearest bed and jump in right after. That wasn't going to happen. He was an old hand at sex and had learned the pleasures of a slow seduction.

Pleasures he was determined to pass along now.

So instead of getting naked, they were going on a hike.

He glanced in the rear view mirror, checking on the

insulated backpack perched on the rear cushions. Lunch had required another trip to the Canyon Country Store. They'd hit the deli for sandwiches, the refrigerated cases for cold drinks, and a rack by the register for the pack to carry them in.

The car neared Mulholland Drive and Ren flipped on the radio. As if the universe knew mere minutes ago they'd been parked at the intersection of Kirkwood and Laurel Canyon Boulevard, mere yards away from the "Love Street" home of the late Jim Morrison, the rocking beat of "L.A. Woman" by The Doors poured out of the speakers. Ren shot a grin at Cilla who was smiling too, as if tickled by that song hitting the airwaves at this particular moment.

Taking a right turn onto Mulholland, that infamous section of roadway that edged the ridgeline of the Santa Monica Mountains, they got their first view of the San Fernando Valley stretching northward. Ren slowed the car, giving them both a moment to enjoy the sight as The Doors lead singer growled about the City of Night. But it was daytime, and the dark ghosts and the deep shadows of Los Angeles were in retreat—at least until the burning circle of the sun met the silvered Pacific at sunset.

Until then, it was all bright optimism.

They followed the curve of the road. It was a thoroughfare made for motorcycles. He glanced over at Cilla. "You ever travel this on a bike?"

"If you mean like a Harley or a Honda, then no," she said, shaking her head. "Only you boys had motorized two-wheeled vehicles. Anyway, I barely learned to ride a bicycle."

His eyebrows rose and he shot another look at her.

"What, you think Mad Dog Maddox would think to teach me?" she asked.

Ren tried to remember how he'd learned. "I stole

Beck's," he said, the memory returning. "Fell a few times and lost some skin before he discovered what I'd done. Then I got my balance right quick so I could pedal the hell away from him. He's mean when he's mad," Ren said on a chuckle.

"Later, you showed Payne and Cami how to do it."

"Yeah, I did." One of his few brotherly acts. His gaze flicked to Cilla again. "Bing or Brody...?"

"Bing and Brody were always too caught up working on a tree house or a fort. They had them squirreled away all over the canyon."

In his mind's eye, he could see two near-identical figures hanging from the trees like monkeys. "They used to pitch pine cones at my head."

"They now use all that excess energy in running their home-building empire. Still busy, busy, busy."

At the wistfulness in her voice, his hand left the steering wheel, compelled to stroke her cheek in comfort. But then he recalled his strategy—no skin-to-skin—and he snatched it back. *Take this slow, Ren*, he reminded himself.

A few miles more, and he pulled onto a side street. "We're here," he said, parking in a small lot beside a trailhead. "If it hasn't changed over the years, I can promise a good path and a great view."

Swinging the straps of the backpack over one shoulder, he waited while Cilla bent to adjust her canvas slip-on shoes. In a heroic feat of self-restraint, he studied the peeling trunks of the surrounding eucalyptus trees instead of her round ass covered by a pair of well-worn jeans. Peeling strips of bark in red and gold and silver shifted in the slight breeze that also stirred the medicinal scent of the leaves into the air.

"Ready?" Cilla's voice drew his attention. A UCLA ball cap was pulled low on her forehead, the pale blue color only serving to make the more jewel-tone of her eyes stand out. Her tentative smile told him she was still on edge.

Trying his best to look harmless, he gestured with his hand for her to precede him. Second thoughts instantly popped up. Three miles of staring at her sweet behind wasn't going to work for him. With her one step ahead he was already focused on her two back pockets and his mind was busily conjuring images of him sliding his hand beneath the denim there and then into her panties to fill his palm with one silky-skinned cheek. The heat of her skin would send a prickling response up his arm and down to his cock.

Which was already starting to harden.

In two strides he was past her, taking the lead. "I better go first," he said, his voice gruff.

She didn't reply, though he sensed her falling in behind him.

His fingers curled around the strap of the backpack, holding fast as he plowed ahead, following the red-dirt trail that wound among heavy boulders and dense patches of chaparral and coyote brush. The twisty branches of the manzanita were blooming, their tiny bell-like flowers the color of a young girl's blush.

The sun heated the top of his head but the going was easy. A mile-and-a-half in, he came around a corner and drew to an abrupt halt. Cilla made a small sound of wonder as she came to a stop too, her shoulder brushing his upper arm.

"Still a great view," he said, unnecessarily.

There it was, laid out before them.

Los Angeles.

To their left, the Hollywood sign stood braced against the hills it was named for. Then there was downtown Los

Angeles, from this distance the skyscrapers almost like the towers of some magical kingdom's massive castle. Hollywood was in the foreground, huddled close to the mouths of the canyons, and to the west was the blue smudge of the ocean, with Catalina Island seeming to float on its surface like exotic flotsam.

"Ren," Cilla said. "You never see it like this."

"This," he supposed, being the epitome of the golden promise it had offered to so many for so many years. Dreams had been dashed against those thrusting metal spires and drowned in those seemingly serene waters, but every day others took their place because the sun and sky, the mountains and beaches, produced fantasies with the ease and speed that other landscapes grew dandelions and crabgrass.

The Lemons had arrived from Missouri and West Texas and Ohio, riding a cultural wave and spurred on by their undeniable talent. Between them, they'd built an unrivaled musical platform and along the way fathered native Californians—even more rare, native Los Angelenos—children steeped in unlimited sunshine and limitless possibility, decadent desires and unspoken needs.

Ren swept his gaze across the vista before him, feeling the visceral tug of home. People thought Southern California was too shallow to take root, but it ran deep inside him, he realized now. No wonder so many of the rock royalty had stayed put.

"I'd forgotten what it's like here," he murmured.

"How did you find this spot?" Cilla asked.

He glanced down at her. "Good location for getting drunk or high. Or drunk *and* high."

Cilla's eyes widened.

"Baby," he said, laughing. "Come on. I was that kid everyone's parents warned them about."

"*I* never thought you were bad."

"You were too young to imagine how bad I could be."

She rolled her eyes. "I wasn't so naive."

"No, you were just a goody-goody," he said. Her expression went disgruntled, and he wanted to kiss her pouting lower lip so bad he had to dig his fingers into the backpack straps instead of sinking them into her hair to bring her mouth to his.

"Priss is a nickname—it's not me," she said. "And by the way, don't think Ren Colson was the only wild one in the canyon."

"You weren't, though," he said, certain of that. But something inside him lurched, thinking of what other untamed sorts she might have encountered growing up. With no one looking out for her—Mad Dog and her brothers were apparently useless in that regard—she could have fallen in with a bad crowd.

Like his old crowd.

He narrowed his gaze. "There's a rough clique in every school. Did you keep clear—?"

This roll of her eyes was even more dramatic. "I didn't need to be at school to encounter rough, wild, or bad, Ren. The Lemons? Hello?"

Shit. That was true, of course. Before he'd been old enough to completely understand, he'd glimpsed drugs, drunks, and the opening acts of full-blown orgies. Later, he'd been called upon to referee naked water polo games in the pool and to judge nude relay races on the tennis court. Once Cami started walking and talking, though, he'd pulled their father aside and pointed out it wasn't safe or sane to subject his young daughter to the same kinds of sights.

Bean hadn't cleaned up his act, but he had kept it behind locked doors.

Who had looked out for Cilla? Another uncomfortable pitching in his chest. "Baby." He reached for her, only at the last minute checking the movement so his fingers merely clutched the half-sleeve of her T-shirt. "Jesus, Cilla," he said, still fighting a protective urge that wanted to snatch her close.

"Don't look like that," she said. "Gwen kept an eagle eye out...and made absolutely sure I understood not to get myself into any precarious situations. I was always on guard, Ren."

He stared at her. Fuck. Fuck that. Pretty little Cilla, walking around *on guard*. He'd figured as much, but hearing her say it out loud set his hackles high. No wonder she'd preferred to play in her Rapunzel tower. No wonder she thought she was frigid.

No wonder he wanted to carry her off somewhere and show her how it could be if she let down her walls.

"Ren..." Her expression went cautious and she backed out of his hold. "Are you all right?"

No, he wasn't all right. He was tense and angry and wanted to use his fists. It was years too late, but he wanted to take down any danger that had put itself in her way thanks to their fathers and their crazy rock 'n' roll lifestyle. "Fucking Lemons," he spit out.

For some reason that made her smile a little. "We've been over that, Ren. Lemonade, remember? Let's make lemonade."

Maybe there was some to be had, he decided as he led the way back toward the car after they'd eaten lunch on a low rock by the spectacular view. In this pissed-off mood, he didn't dare touch her. His temper wasn't conducive to the slow and easy seduction he had in mind.

Instead, he found it put wings on his feet. His strides ate up the dusty trail and as he hiked up the incline to the parking lot, Ren realized he'd left Cilla behind. He glanced back, then turned to watch her gamely making her way toward him, even though the silty, uphill slope was difficult to navigate wearing the smooth-soled shoes she had on her feet.

She was panting a little as she neared, her face flushed.

God, she'd grown up beautiful.

As if she heard him—or maybe she could read the thought on his face—she jolted, and the movement caused her to lose her balance. The wobble started her sliding backward and Ren could see she was a second away from landing on her cute ass. Leaping forward, he circled her bicep with his hand, then hauled her close. Her body landed against his, their gazes colliding as well.

Fire poured into his bloodstream. His cock twitched, going hard as her quick breaths pushed her breasts against his ribs. He could smell her citrus scent and he hauled more of it into his lungs, wanting to bathe himself in Cilla. Wanting to taste her skin, her mouth, her sex. His fingers tightened on her arm and he watched her eyes widen. Did it look as if he wanted to take a big juicy bite out of her? Because he did. Oh, yeah, he did.

"Ren..." she whispered, then she swallowed and his gaze dropped to watch her throat muscles ripple. It stayed on the thrumming pulse that drummed against her fragile skin. "Ren."

He glanced back at her eyes, their blue outshining the sky. "Yeah, baby?"

"I want this," she said, her voice still low.

Yes, she did. He could feel her trembling against him but her flesh was heated and she was pliant in his hold, yielding to the powerful attraction that ran between them. It was sexy as hell.

Ren bent his head to communicate that with a kiss, but Cilla had another thing to say.

"Just be careful with me, okay?"

The quiet words made him instantly drop his hold on her. He stepped back, his open hands raised to shoulder level. *Not armed, honey. Not a danger to you.*

He shouldn't have put a finger on her yet! Hadn't he promised himself he wouldn't go skin-to-skin?

But Christ, even without touching her, she was touching *him*. With her sweet looks and her sweet scent. With her talk about bike-riding and being on guard... Damn. Cilla was finding her way beneath his flesh, rattling his bones...unsettling something that lay even deeper than that.

Cilla stood at the kitchen counter, mashing avocados in a bowl with the back of a fork while silently cursing herself. Through the open door leading to the adjacent courtyard came the murmur of Ren and Jewel's voices. At Cilla's request, the other woman was joining them for dinner.

Which only served to stretch her nerves to the breaking point.

She hadn't considered this when she'd extended the invitation. That had happened following their Mulholland hike, when she'd still been reeling from the sensation of Ren's hard body pressed to her softer one. Once inside the car (which had shrunk to the size of a tuna can) she'd gone on full babble about dinner and decided to make her Mexican casserole. That had necessitated another swing by the market where she'd encountered Jewel and latched onto the idea that dinner with the other woman would stall the commencement of Ren's mentoring.

Dumb idea.

One, because Ren's mentoring was what she'd told him she wanted (and she really did, in a breathless, I-can't-believe-myself kind of way), and two, because postponing the start of his lessons was making her walk a knife's edge. One wrong move and she'd fall into full-blown panic.

Lesson singular, she reminded herself. The start of his one lesson. She shouldn't actively consider it would be more than a lone event, especially if she went into it so tense she'd shatter at the first touch.

Warm hands slid onto her hips.

Cilla managed to swallow a shriek, but the fork fell from her hand to clatter against the metal bowl. Glancing over her shoulder, she met Ren's gaze. "Uh, hi."

His fingers squeezed, a gesture she thought he meant to be reassuring. "Is there something I can do to help?"

She shook her head. "Casserole is in the oven. I'm just whipping up guacamole. I'll bring it and chips out shortly. How spicy do you like your avocado dip?"

The corners of his lips tipped up and his hold tightened on her again. "Hot."

Oh, God. She felt a rush of prickling chills speed over her flesh. Lifting her wrist to her forehead, she blotted suddenly damp skin. "I'll chop a jalapeno."

He grinned. "Make that two." Then he moved off to the refrigerator, leaving the kitchen with a beer in one hand and a glass of white wine in another.

Pursing her lips, she blew out a long breath. *Be calm*, she told herself. Before the command had time to sink in, Ren was back. He returned to the refrigerator and in moments he held another glass of wine, this one he slid in front of her. The heat of his body soaked through the cotton of her shirt and she stared at that stylized half heart on his lower forearm.

The fork slipped through her fingers again and

smushed avocado bits spattered onto the countertop. With a frustrated sound, she moved for the sponge, but Ren was there first, wiping away the mess with a paper towel. She snatched it from him and shot a glare over her shoulder. "Go away, will you? You're a distraction."

He tousled her hair as if she were two. "You're welcome for the wine."

Cilla resisted gnashing her teeth and replied as sweet as could be. "Thank you for the wine."

His grin flashed and then he was out the door.

Closing her eyes, Cilla tried to get hold of her galloping pulse. If she couldn't find normal, he was going to run far away from her and her skittishness. And she wanted this. She'd asked for it!

With new determination, she finished her preparations and then put together a tray that she walked out to the patio. Upon seeing her, Ren immediately rose, taking it from her hands and guiding it to the table.

"Such good manners," she said.

"As you'll find out," he murmured in a soft, sly voice. "Ladies first and all that."

Cilla froze, struck by the seductive rasp. Ladies first, she thought, now succumbing to the panic. Oh, God. A man had never managed to make her orgasm. What if, despite his mentoring, she couldn't with Ren, either? If he intended to hold out for his own until after she climaxed, he might be waiting forever.

Unless she faked it really well.

She had a terrible feeling that Ren was good at spotting fakers.

On slow feet she made her way to the chair he politely held for her. She dropped into it then scooped up her wine glass that sat beside the chips and dip. A long swallow went down cold and bracing.

It was then she noticed Jewel across the table and remembered her hostess duties. "I'm sorry to be so long," she told the other woman, who was holding a sleeping baby Soul in her arms. "I hope Ren's been entertaining you."

"He was just about to describe his business for me. I know nothing about tour management."

Ren grimaced. "If I'd thought more about it ahead of time myself, I might have gone into something easy, like grizzly wrestling."

Jewel smiled. Cilla noticed the tender brush of her thumb over her baby's cheek. "So, I'm guessing herding a bunch of temperamental artist-types from one venue to another isn't loads of fun?"

"It's a job that's part travel agenting, part accounting, and more than a little babysitting. We've got a dozen bands we're currently working with and I have forty-five people on staff to keep things running smoothly."

Cilla stared. "Forty-five employees?" He was the head of an actual company? She'd thought...well, she'd just never considered him doing more than squiring pop and rock stars about Europe.

"Yeah. There's the people in the London office who do the administrative work and then the big, mean-tempered commando-types that go out on the road with the bands."

"Rule by intimidation?" Jewel suggested.

"Nothing gets a lead singer out of bed in the morning quicker than a six-and-a-half foot former college fullback with a three-day-old beard and a no-nonsense attitude."

"I didn't realize you have an actual staff," Cilla said, still marveling that dark and dangerous Ren Colson was also a businessman.

He glanced over. "I can't be everywhere at once. My

assistant, Raina, says I could stay in London and avoid the road altogether. We have an able group of cruel-looking characters besides myself to motivate the bands."

"But you'd miss the travel," Cilla guessed. And the action and the music. The women, she supposed, too. Though they wouldn't be hard to find for a man who looked like Ren, wherever he was.

"I've had my fill of travel," Ren said. "But not sure I want to spend all my time at the offices in Pimlico, either."

That led to a discussion of London's neighborhoods. Jewel had spent a semester abroad there during college and she and Ren traded anecdotes about their favorite haunts. Cilla sat back in her chair, the warmth from the patio heater and the alcohol in the wine finally dispensing some of her anxiety.

I'll be your sexual mentor.

It was a crazy idea, wasn't it? Under her lashes, she sneaked a peek at Ren. He sat at ease in the chair, one elbow braced on the table, his other hand resting on the solid column of his thigh. Her gaze lingered there, at the quad muscle she could see beneath the denim. If she really went through with this, that muscle was going to be naked against hers, she thought, redirecting her gaze to the stem of her wine glass. Those legs would slide between her thighs to make space for his hips and for his—

A fingertip touched the top of her own denim-covered leg. Despite her quick jerk, it began to draw a lazy pattern just above her knee. Her eyes went wide. Under cover of the table top, Ren was teasing her skin.

Her temperature spiked like a fever and her inner muscles clenched, then went soft. Oh, God. Oh, my God. The sensation was light and lazy and it conversely put her whole body into a state of painful hyper-awareness. Her lungs shut down on her last breath as Ren continued the languid stroking. His conversation with Jewel didn't let up either, and they chatted with seeming ease while Cilla sat at the table, her hearing gone, her eyes unseeing, her whole being focused only on the sensation of that wandering finger igniting sparks of reaction along her flesh.

The ping of the oven timer going off took a long moment to register. By the time it did, both Jewel and Ren were staring at her. The other woman grinned. "You were miles away."

"Mmm. Yeah." She scooted back her chair, sending a quick glance to Ren as he started to get up. "No, no. You stay and keep Jewel and Soul company. I'll be back with plates in just a minute."

Thank goodness he listened. She snatched up the appetizer tray so quickly the bowl wobbled on its surface, but she didn't let that halt her hurry into the kitchen. Once there, she deposited the tray on the counter, flicked off the timer and slid the casserole out of the oven.

Then she merely stood, fanning her face with lobster-shaped oven mitts. *Gwen*, she thought, *I bet you didn't suspect your little out-of-this-world encouragement to stay in the cottage with Ren would lead to this.*

He'd agreed to be her sexual mentor.

Of course, Cilla could back out of the arrangement. No iron-clad promises were in place.

Reaching into a cupboard, she considered the wisdom of going that route. Just beg off, cry uncle, run away from the whole intimidating idea like a little girl scared of her shadow.

Never get to know what it was like to caress Ren, kiss Ren, find out if she could be something besides a failure as a woman with Ren in her bed.

Her inner vixen wailed in disappointment.

Cilla blinked, astonished. She had an inner vixen?

While trying to come to terms with that piece of new information, she plated up the food. Then she carried it outside, her gaze sliding over Ren to see that Jewel had put the baby in the stroller at her side. Cilla delivered the three plates and they dug into the meal.

It was one of her favorites, but it might as well have been beach sand and oak leaves. Jewel didn't seem to notice her preoccupation, but she could feel Ren checking her out from time to time. It only made her duck her head closer to her plate and fork more food into her mouth. Her dinner companions had declared it tasted delicious and she chose to believe them.

When the last bites were eaten, Jewel excused herself to use the bathroom. Cilla slid into the other woman's chair so she could watch over (and admire) the snoozing Soul. The baby's lids were so translucent she could see the trace of veins beneath them and every few moments the infant would pucker up and make an endearing suckle-face, nursing in her sleep.

"You all right?" Ren's voice rumbled from across the table.

She flicked a glance at him, then returned her attention to the baby, minutely adjusting the blanket tucked around her. "Sure."

It was a word she re-thought immediately. Why didn't she tell him the truth? Be upfront about her nerves, her lack of orgasm achievement, the fact that she was ridiculously anxious. Wasn't honesty always the best policy?

"I—" she began, but Jewel was back before she could get any of that out.

The other woman took Cilla's seat then sent Ren an impish look. "I think that glass of wine has made me just tipsy enough to pry into your love life," she said.

"Ren doesn't have a *love* life," Cilla said, trying to make clear she didn't imagine that would change once he took up his mentoring duties.

Jewel laughed. "All right, though I don't know what else to call it." There was more mischief in her smile. "It's just that when April and Alana Speckleman have their annual summer party, they always get really drunk and brag about this night when you and the two of them—"

Ren groaned. "Do not talk to me of the Speckleman twins."

"The Speckleman twins?" Cilla stared at Ren. "You and *both* the Specklemans? At the same time?"

He didn't even have the grace to look embarrassed. "It was a long time ago, Cilla. I told you I was wild back then." His shrug was more rueful than repentant.

"The Speckleman twins." Cilla tried to wrap her mind around it. She'd been seconds away from confessing her anxiety over being mentored to a man who had apparently banged the notorious sisters at the same time. The notorious sisters who were said to have had an unnatural relationship with their pony, back in the day, not that she'd ever believed it for a second. The Ren story...now *that* she believed.

Jewel stifled a laugh behind her hand. "If it makes you feel better, they're always very complimentary."

The legs of Ren's chair scraped across the patio. "Didn't you say you needed to go soon, Jewel? I can walk you and Soul home now."

With another smothered laugh, Jewel got to her feet. Then mother and baby were on their way with minimal fuss, Ren pushing the stroller. Cilla did the kitchen clean-up, though he'd told her to leave it for him. Next, she settled onto the cushions of the patio's jumbo, double-wide lounger, a throw wrapped around her, her gaze on the stars in the sky.

When he returned, she was going to renege, she decided. There were a million good reasons why that was a good idea—honestly, the Speckleman twins!—but a new one had just occurred to her.

While she had that ability to sleep through anything, she'd never been able to *fall* asleep with a man in her bed. Whether it was a privacy issue or a trust issue, either way, she always had to sneak away from the sheets and take a pillow to the nearest couch (if at her place) or drive home (if at his). She just couldn't see herself explaining that embarrassing situation to Ren.

As if thinking of his name conjured him up, there he was. "Move over," he said, and slid onto the cushions without waiting for her to comply. Putting several inches between them, she glanced over. "Ren..."

He groaned. "Can we have a few minutes of silence, please? That baby started squalling when we were a quarter mile from Jewel's front door and my ears are still ringing."

"Hmph." Cilla crossed her arms over her chest. "Ren—"

"Five minutes, Cilla."

Wiggling, she put another two inches of space between them. Okay. Fine. She'd give him the requested quiet and then she'd tell him in no uncertain terms that she was letting him off the hook. So what that he'd think her...well, whatever he'd think of her. It didn't matter.

Closing her eyes, she relaxed into the cushions. The quiet *was* soothing, she discovered. It was the right decision to back out of the whole mentoring deal.

She yawned. The fact was...

She had...

Trust issues...and...and...

In her dream, she was on a boat, its gentle rocking motion peaceful. In a few moments the boat changed to a cloud and she sank into it. Angels surrounded her, as sweet as baby Soul, and they carried away her shoes, then the rest of her clothes. One of the angels had an incongruously growly voice and it settled onto the cloud beside her. She patted its naked baby chest (it was one of those cherubs with the loose diapers) then snuggled up to it as sleep swamped her again.

From far away, she thought the grouchy cherub made another noise of complaint or frustration, but Cilla patted the baby again and settled her head onto its shoulder (that was now strangely adult-sized, as could happen in dreams).

In the morning, she awoke thinking of that peevish, cranky angel that had visited in her sleep. Weird! Then her brain registered the pillow beneath her cheek wasn't a pillow. Her lashes fluttered open. The pillow beneath her cheek was a man. Specifically, his chest.

Ren's chest.

Whoa.

She sat up slowly, striving not to jar the mattress. That's when she realized she wore only her bra and panties and that under the sheets and blanket her legs were tangled with those of the man who'd offered to be her sexual mentor.

She hadn't done the deed with him, though, she knew that.

Her stomach flipped, pancake-style, anyway. Because falling asleep beside him now seemed even more intimate—and more dangerous?—than sex.

Chapter 6

Through the pool house windows, Ren could see Cilla in the workout area. He saw her jump as he swung open the door and that sign of nervousness only served as fuel for his already crappy mood. "I'm not going to bite you," he said. It came out like a snarl.

Instead of answering, she climbed onto one of the treadmills. He took the other, hoping a challenging run would sweat the aggravation right out of him. They both started warming up at a fast walk.

"A good morning to you, too," he said, glancing over at her. Her tight body was wrapped in black-and-pink exercise gear that clung to her round ass and her high breasts. He'd been aware of both all night long. With her plastered so close against him he hadn't slept a wink until after dawn.

Instead of answering, she adjusted her speed and began an easy jog.

Frowning, he did the same. "Is there something wrong?" Unlike him, fatigue couldn't be her problem. Her relaxed breaths had bathed his chest throughout the night.

"Not a thing," she said, in that way women did when much was, in fact, wrong.

He ground his back teeth and depressed the button to kick the machine into gear. Let her have her mood. His own was enough to deal with.

They ran side-by-side, the thump of their shoes on the moving belts the only sounds. The room needed a TV, Ren decided, or he should have brought some music with him. Looking around to see if there was a distraction to be found, he stumbled and had to catch himself on one of the handrails. "Shit," he muttered.

Cilla glanced over. "You don't get to be in a bad mood."

"What?" He stared at her.

"You're not the one who woke up to find yourself undressed and with an unexpected bed partner."

He continued staring.

"Well?" Her glare could melt steel. "Your explanation?"

"I don't know what the hell you're so mad about."

"Undressed? Unexpected bed partner?"

Considering she'd asked him to be her mentor in a realm that involved beds and undressing, her ire didn't make sense. Particularly since the bed and the undressing had stayed remarkably G-rated—except in his head—which was why he'd been mainly sleepless and woken up totally frustrated. "Cilla..." He shook his head. "You make me nuts."

"You made me naked."

"For Christ's sake. Semi-naked. And I was doing you a favor."

"So that's what they call it," she said, with a roll of her eyes.

He wrapped his fingers around the handrails and

squeezed. "What's gotten into you?"

"I didn't expect to wake up next to an unclothed man."

"I was wearing my boxers. Did you even check?"

"I wouldn't look," she said, clearly on her high horse. "Not that I bet you can say the same."

"Oh, no, I'm not going to be made to feel guilty about that," Ren said. "Yeah, I didn't undress you with my eyes closed." All that sweet skin, pale and fragrant. "But you were dead to the world. I did it so you could be more comfortable."

"Or so you could crawl into bed beside mostly naked me."

"That was not my intention, sweetheart." Now it was his turn to glare. "I was planning on heading to the other room when *you* latched onto *me*."

Her head swung his way and her eyes went wide. "Um, what?"

"Yeah. I was pulling up the covers when you yanked me down to the mattress. And sorry, as your proposed sexual mentor, I didn't think that meant I had to sleep in my clothes for a second time this week." He gave her a hard look. "Not that I got any rest."

"Um, what?" she said a second time.

"You're a clinger, Cilla."

She looked shocked. "I am *not*."

He shrugged. "You were last night. A dead-to-the-world clinger, and because of that I scrounged up some gentlemanly scruples and lay there beside you playing platonic pillow for the most fucking miserable night of my life."

"It was so bad being my platonic pillow?"

"There's other ways I'd planned to spend a night with you."

"Oh." Her eyes were round again. "About that."

Something in her tone put him on alert. "Yes?"

A long moment passed, their feet a synchronized *thump thump thump*. "Um..." she finally said.

He tried to dredge up some patience. "Cilla—"

"I've rethought everything." Her words came out in a rush. "I don't want you as a sexual mentor."

Ren stared at her. Then he reached over and yanked out the red safety cord on her machine, halting the belt. Her feet stuttered to a stop and by the time she'd climbed down, he was on the floor too. "Say that again."

Her face was flushed from more than exercise and her gaze was trained over his shoulder. "The mentoring thing. That was a crazy idea." Her big blues shifted to his face. "Don't you think?"

He'd convinced himself it wasn't, so much so that now he felt...what was it? Disappointed? Wait, *that* was a crazy notion.

"Ren?"

"It was what you said you wanted. If that's no longer the case..." He shrugged, as if it didn't matter to him one way or another.

She worried the fingers of her hands. "It's just... I know you better now and it makes it weird."

"I see. You'd be more comfortable being sexually mentored by a complete stranger."

"No!" Her palms slid over her thighs. "It's that..."

"What?" He crossed his arms over his chest. "It's that now we're better acquainted you're no longer attracted to me?"

"Of course not. And how do you know I was attra—" She bit off the rest of the sentence as another blush bloomed on her face. "You're tying me in knots."

Seemed fair, after those long hours of torture the night before. But her embarrassed expression made him relent and he leaned near. "FYI, baby, you've got to know I'm attracted right back."

Cilla froze. "Um... Well..."

"But it's all good. You don't want my mentoring, it's fine by me."

"Ren..."

"Lady's choice," he said, and chucked her under the chin.

She swallowed. "So you're fine?"

"Perfectly." Or he would be, once he found some way to get rid of the sexual frustration pulsing in his blood. The anticipation of getting down and dirty with sweet Cilla had been building inside of him from the moment she'd mentioned it.

Or perhaps from the second he'd woken up and glimpsed her nipples pressing against a black cotton Byrds T-shirt.

"I wonder what the Speckleman twins are doing tonight," he mused.

"Ren!" She slapped at his chest with the flat of her hand and he caught it, holding it against him.

He had no idea why. Just as he had no idea why the thud of his heart against her palm made her gaze fly to his. They stared at each other and then her fingers were curling into his shirt, taking the fabric into her fist so she could drag his head toward hers.

Then they kissed.

At the first press of her lips to his, he felt that fire surge through him again. But he stayed still for the burn, allowing it to sweep through his bloodstream as Cilla's mouth moved on his. When her tongue delicately touched his bottom lip, Ren moved, curling his arm around her, sinking his fingers in the hair at the back of her head, sliding his tongue into the wet, heated cavern of her mouth.

She went boneless again, melting into him as she had before. He drew her closer, his arm sliding down to her hips to tilt her against the growing stiffness of his cock. Her free hand clutched at his shoulder and her tongue tangled with his as he deepened the kiss. A tremor ran through her and it made the flight of the blood in his veins more urgent. She was shaking with desire and something as simple as that unpeeled a layer from his hard, jaded soul.

His fingertips slid beneath her tight top at the small of her back and when he found her damp, heated flesh, he groaned into her mouth. Just that small touch made his cock throb. She squirmed in his hold, her belly rubbing against his hardness. With another groan, he angled his head to change up the kiss, this time sucking her tongue into his mouth.

Cilla moaned, her fingernails digging into his shoulder.

He shoved his hand farther up her shirt, so his entire palm covered the small of her back. The skin was silky beneath his rougher flesh and he pressed the heel of his hand into her spine, forcing their bodies closer as the kiss went wild.

Finally needing air, Ren tore his mouth away and lifted his head for a breath. Movement over her shoulder caught his attention. "Hell," he said scowling. Through the windows he could see the pool guy and his assistant, both of them staring through the glass in apparent fascination.

Cilla glanced back, saw what he did, and broke away from him. "Oops." Her face was pink and her clingy top was askew, giving him a glimpse of a slice of her pale belly.

He reached over, tugged it straight, then grabbed her

hand. "Let's get out of here."

The morning air felt cool against his heated skin. He gave a nod to the pool people, noting that Cilla was thoroughly inspecting the toes of her running shoes. She kept her gaze on them until they reached the entrance to Gwen's cottage. Inside, she broke free of him again and made her way straight to the kitchen where she filled a glass with water and immediately drained it down.

Ren leaned against the door jamb and watched her fill it a second time. Her gaze slid to his. "Uh..."

"Yeah," he said. "My sentiments exactly." He didn't know what to say or think beyond that. She didn't want a mentor, meaning she didn't want sex with him. No doubt it was a crazy idea. It *would* be weird. He got all that. But then why moments later were they going at it like they were horny teenagers?

"Really." Cilla set her glass on the countertop and turned to face him, her back to the granite bullnose. "It's better if we don't."

"Your decision."

Her fingers curled around the counter behind her. "Do you mean you want to?"

As she said, it would be better to forego it. He was leaving in less than two weeks, she didn't want a mentor now, and he couldn't be anything more than something so casual. Yeah, he'd considered he'd be doing her a favor, but now that he thought it over further, the idea of having him teach her about sex so she could find happiness with another man seemed arrogant. Or maybe asshat-ish. Definitely no longer to his taste.

He strolled forward to pick up her abandoned glass and suck down its contents. "You're right," he said. "We shouldn't."

When he set the tumbler down, his hand brushed her

forearm.

Then they were kissing again. He had her hips pinned to the lower cabinets with his, her face caged in his fingers, his tongue in her mouth. Lust had him by the balls and he gasped for breath even as his lips moved to her throat. She tasted salty and sweet at the same time and his fingertips tingled, remembering the feel of her damp flesh against them, anticipating the pleasure of the wet flesh between her legs.

It was going to happen, he was sure of it.

Until the loud whine of a leaf blower had his head jerking up. "What the—?" He stared out the mullioned French door to the courtyard, where a short man in a straw hat was sending leaves scurrying across the cement. The little guy waved with his free hand.

Ren looked down to see that Cilla was waving weakly back. "Is the universe trying to tell us something?" he asked.

She moved, and he instantly dropped his hands and stepped back. "Seems that way. I guess we really shouldn't do this."

"Yeah. Really." Ren pushed his hands through his hair. "Shit."

"Is this going to be awkward?"

"No," he said, instant and adamant, in case she thought again of kicking him out of the compound. He hadn't forgotten the two strangers scaling the wall. Gwen would have his ass for leaving Cilla alone with the empty houses and the deserted grounds. "Not for me."

Her chin lifted. "Not for me either."

He shoved his hands in his pockets. "We'll be friends."

She crossed her arms over her chest. "Exactly."

They stared at each other for a long moment, then Ren

shifted his focus to the gardener just outside. "We should get out of here." The whine of the leaf blower was giving him a headache. "Go somewhere."

She eyed him. "Together?"

"Why not?" He took another step back from her. "Somewhere with lots of people. And action. Things to look at."

"Hmm." She seemed to be thinking, then a smile broke over her face. "I have just the place."

"Good."

Her mouth pursed as she continued to eye him. "You're sure? You're sure this is okay? That we're friends. And that your mood...it's better now?"

"Friends." And fuck no, his mood was three-million times worse.

Cilla breathed a silent sigh of relief as she exited the passenger seat of Ren's rented Beemer and stepped into the late morning sunshine. Getting away from the compound was good. This time out would provide an opportunity for any residual strangeness from the nearly-naked-night, the mentoring-that-wasn't-to-be, and the-kisses-that-shouldn't-have-happened to fade. That attraction they'd both admitted to in Gwen's kitchen could slide from a boil to a simmer to a friendly warmth because that's the way they both wanted things to be.

By the end of the day, relations between them would be normalized. They'd be just a couple of pals.

As Ren rounded the car to the sidewalk, she sneaked a glance at his face. An unfortunate move, because then the memory of those kisses hit her like a sledgehammer. His mouth had been demanding, and she could still feel the burn of his whiskers around her lips as well as the imprint of his thumbs on the edge of her jaw. Champagne bubbles started speeding through her blood again, just thinking of that.

"Cilla?"

Her gaze jerked to Ren's and she realized she'd been standing, frozen, for some embarrassing number of seconds. Ordering herself to get a grip, she started walking, away from the side street where she'd instructed him to park and toward their destination. "Close your eyes," she said as they neared a corner.

"What?"

"Close your eyes. I'll lead you, but I want this to be a surprise."

With a shrug, he did as he was told, which was when she realized that "leading" likely involved touching—not such a great idea. They'd taken time to shower and change out of their exercise gear, so he was now in jeans and a chambray shirt, sleeves rolled up, tails out. To avoid skin, she grabbed the side of the shirt at his waist and tugged him forward for half a block, then stopped at the corner. "Ta-da!" she said.

His eyes opened and he looked out at the car-crammed intersection of Hollywood Boulevard and Vine Street, then back at her. "Uh...?"

"You wanted a distraction, right? Action, things to look at." She spread her arms in both directions. "The Walk of Fame."

He blinked and looked around again, this time his gaze traveling over the sidewalk crowded with people streaming by, some moving purposefully, others pausing every few steps to take note of the star-studded squares at their feet. "I've never stopped here."

"Just as I guessed," she said, grinning. "I brought an out-of-town friend to the Walk for the first time last summer and everybody from L.A. I've told about it since say they've never strolled the stars."

"So that's your plan? We'll stroll the stars?"

"Yep." She started forward. "C'mon, breathe deep of the auto emissions and breathe in all the Hollywood glamour you can handle."

Glamour was a bit of an exaggeration. The fact was, there was more kitsch than elegance to be found on the blocks that made up the Walk. Besides eateries and bars and Starbucks there were a zillion souvenir shops that sold *I Love LA* T-shirts, facsimiles of Oscar statues that ran from the size of a finger to the size of a Doberman, and maps that promised purchasers directions to the exclusive homes of actors, musicians, and supermodels.

Still, it made for an entertaining amble. Ren kept at her pace, even going along with the game of who could spot the stars awarded to fictional characters, the first to find three being declared the winner. Each of them had spotted two (Cilla scored with Godzilla and Donald Duck; Ren with Bugs Bunny and Shrek) when she saw him hesitate, glance down, then keep moving.

Cilla's gaze dropped to the star he'd dismissed. Another point! "Hey buddy," she called out. "You missed Tinker Bell. I win, three to two." When Ren turned back, her eyes narrowed in sudden suspicion. "Wait. You saw her, didn't you?"

He shrugged.

"Oh my gosh." She laughed. "What, do you think you're too macho to acknowledge Tink?"

"I don't just *think* I'm macho, squirt."

She stared up at him, the sun limning with gold the disordered darkness of his hair. It didn't surpass the brightness of his easy smile. Her last breath caught in her lungs and she had to cough to dislodge it. He was that beautiful.

"Anyway," he continued. "Tinker Bell isn't fictional. Don't you remember *Peter Pan*? 'I believe in fairies. I believe in fairies.'" He clapped three times, then reached for Cilla's hands. "Repeat after me," he said, his warm fingers guiding her palms together. "I believe in fairies and I didn't win the game. I believe in fairies and I didn't win the game."

"I didn't win the game," Cilla whispered. Oh, my. It really looked like she was losing the game, big time. Because Dark and Dangerous Ren, the bad boy of her dreams, had an entire other dimension to him. That would be Charming Ren, who teased about fairies and smiled at her in the sunlight and who could make her think "squirt" was as wonderful coming from his lips as "sweetheart."

His smile died and he dropped her hands. "What's up, Cilla?"

What's up was she was in trouble if she didn't get Charming Ren out of her head and Bad Boy Ren out of her fantasies and find Friend Ren in the next five minutes. "I'm hungry," she said. "I need food."

They settled along the rail of the outdoor seating section of a noodle bar. It was nearing the end of the lunch hour, and the people-watching was at its finest. There were business types returning to offices and the hucksters out hustling clients for the convertible tour buses. Superheroes—young men and women dressed like them anyway—stalked the sidewalks ready to pose for photos in hopes of a couple of bucks in tips. Families of tourists streamed by in their Disney-the-day-before sunburns and mouse hats.

Cilla and Ren used chopsticks to scoop up their noodle concoctions, from time-to-time idly pointing out the more outrageous-looking characters. She'd just drawn his attention to a buxom woman wearing a plush unicorn head and a braided tail when a man halted in front of them on the sidewalk.

"Ren," he said, with a big smile. "What the hell, Ren Colson." The stranger was thirtyish and wore casual slacks, a silk T-shirt, and beat-up loafers. He reached out a wide hand.

Grinning, Ren gave it a hearty shake. "Jaz. My God, how long has it been?"

"I ran into you in Amsterdam...three years ago, I think?"

"That's right. We went out that night and—" Sliding his gaze to Cilla, Ren put the brakes on the reminiscing. "Uh, let me introduce you. Cilla, this is Jasper Reyes, a buddy of Payne's. Jaz, Cilla Maddox, my, uh..."

Before he could say something close to "sister" (which she'd never been and never would be) Cilla reached her hand across the rail. "I'm Ren's friend."

Jasper Reyes ran his gaze over her. She had on her favorite cropped jeans, a waist-length blue cotton sweater, and a pair of striped platform espadrilles. A double-hairband kept her mess of half-curly, half-wavy hair off her face and she wore dark, celebrity-style sunglasses. His voice turned soft as he squeezed her fingers. "Hey, Ren's friend."

She gave him her best smile as he hung onto her hand. That is, until Ren cleared his throat in a somewhat-ominous fashion. Jaz's smile grew wider and he released her fingers as he looked back at the other man. "Speaking of Payne, I just finished up lunch with him."

"Yeah? I haven't had a chance to schedule a meet yet."

"He's doing good. Playing with his car parts, making money hand-over-fist, breaking hearts all over town."

Cilla was unsurprised by this last piece of info. Like all the rock royalty, word was Payne didn't have a steady lover, but that didn't mean women wouldn't wish to be his. Where Ren was dark-haired and Cami auburn, Payne was golden-haired and with a surfer's body.

Then Jaz turned to her. "While I, on the other hand, am looking for that one woman to end my sad, single existence."

From her right a sort of non-human growl emanated from...Ren's throat? She glanced over at him, but his gaze was on Jaz. The other man was smiling again, mischief in his eyes. "But I guess I'll move along on my search to find that special female."

They said their goodbyes, then Jaz was striding away. Several women he passed turned their heads to give him a second look. Ren snorted. "Looking for that one woman to end his sad, single existence, my ass," he muttered.

"I thought he was nice," Cilla said.

Ren slid a look at her. "Not nice enough for you."

He snorted again when she rolled her eyes at him.

Lunch finished, they started star-strolling again. They found the terrazzo-and-brass square dedicated to the Velvet Lemons and their long pause at it caught the attention of one of the sidewalk hucksters. When he extolled the virtues of the Magical Musical Mystery Tour to all the famous local music landmarks, their gazes met and Ren reached for his wallet. Two tickets later, they climbed into a ten-person convertible passenger van. Soon they were motoring down the Sunset Strip where various clubs were highlighted and then they traveled to home turf. As they wound through the skinny streets of Laurel Canyon, the guide pointed out homes purported to be the one-time (or current) residences of artists like David Bowie and Mick Jagger, Graham Nash and Joni Mitchell. Other homes he said were lived in by more recent musical stars like Ke$ha and Katy Perry. On a street narrower than any before, the tour bus paused in front of a Mexican villa-styled monstrosity. To their surprise, the guide informed them they were looking at the home of the Velvet Lemons and then he went on to relate several salacious anecdotes about lavish parties and rowdy weekends.

Ren whispered in her ear. "Stories true, address wrong."

Cilla couldn't help but like that address-wrong part—they didn't need any more unexpected fans showing up. And, if she was honest, she also liked Ren's warm presence beside her and his breath blowing against her ear. But she put that from her mind by starting up an inner chant, *FriendRenFriendRenFriendRen*, until the tour completed and they were strolling on the sidewalk again, moving down Hollywood Boulevard toward the car.

She pointed out a Marilyn Monroe lookalike across the street, the hem of her dress wired into a permanent subway-breeze upswing. As Ren half-turned to follow her finger, another tall man bumped into his shoulder.

"Excuse me," he said.

"No problem," Ren answered, giving the person a cursory glance before both men continued on in opposite directions.

It was Cilla who grabbed the passerby's arm to turn him back. "Payne."

He halted as the sea of people around them was forced to part. After a long moment looking at her face, he said, "Cilla?"

"And Ren." She took hold of his wrist too, and gave a little laugh as she drew the half-brothers together.

The two stared at each other a longer moment. Then they shook hands, hearty, but brief. Pleasantries were exchanged. Ren told about running into Jaz. Payne mentioned he was going out of town for the next few days.

Then the conversation petered out.

Payne cleared his throat. "Well...I have another appointment..."

"Sure." Ren gave a quick nod and held out his hand again. "It was good seeing you."

"Later," Payne said, and strode off.

"Later," Ren echoed, watching his half-brother walk away.

When he finally resumed walking himself, he shoved his hands in his pockets and trained his gaze on the sidewalk, a scowl on his mouth. Trailing a half-step behind, Cilla suspected he wasn't seeing a single one of the stars at his feet.

In the man's now clearly dark mood, she caught a glimpse of the brooding seventeen-year-old who had so fascinated her. She'd wanted to make him smile then. She wanted to do the same now. Noting where they were, she made a sudden decision.

"A last stop," she said, curving her fingers around his elbow and tugging him toward glass doors beneath a deeply recessed arch. "More Hollywood history."

"Cilla—"

"You'll enjoy this." She couldn't guarantee it, but she knew the good part of their day would be spoiled if she didn't try to lighten his gloomy frame of mind. Inside the building, it was shadowy, cool, and well, *cool*. "This is the famous Hollywood Roosevelt Hotel."

He was taking in the marble floors and the thick plaster walls.

"It was built in the 1920s with money from silent movie stars of the time. In 1929, its ballroom hosted the presentation of the very first Academy Awards."

His grunt wasn't encouraging, but she kept up the chatter as she led him toward her favorite spot in the hotel.

"Marilyn Monroe stayed here for two years when her modeling career was taking off. There's rumors of ghost sightings and mysterious phone calls to the front desk."

Then she led him outside again, and they were by the huge pool. On one side the twelve stories of the original hotel building sheltered the turquoise water. On the other three, two stories of cabana-styled rooms gave it an intimate feel. She led him straight to the bar, and perched on a stool, giving Ren a little push toward his own. "You have to have one of their mojitos."

He glowered at her. "Baby, men don't drink mojitos."

"Oh?" She raised an eyebrow. "The Roosevelt Hotel's mojito comes with jalapenos. Didn't you say you liked hot?" Before he could answer, she ordered two.

After that, she let him alone. The drinks were quickly delivered and she sipped at hers, letting her gaze travel over the bar area. Though she didn't recognize any famous faces, there were plenty of beautiful people stretched out on the white terry cloth-covered loungers. A knot of men in expensive suits sat under an umbrella with a mixed tray of appetizers before them. The bartender chatted with another patron about his other job on the staff of a company producing a new TV series. So very L.A.

Ren appeared aware of none of it. He stared into his glass, lost in thought.

Cilla took a breath, then put her hand over his.

He looked up, startled.

She squeezed her fingers. "Hey, what is it?"

Grimacing, he hesitated.

"Friends, remember?"

He went to stone for nearly thirty seconds, then he picked up his glass and swallowed the rest of the concoction down, taking some jalapeno slices with it, she supposed. Another grimace, then his gaze moved to her.

"Sure. Friends."

Oh, yay, Cilla thought, though the happy thought didn't really make it to her heart. "Friends share," she said, giving another encouraging squeeze of his hand before letting go.

His fingers forked through his hair. Then he half-turned on his stool to face her, his elbow on the bar, his free hand gripping his thigh. "I didn't recognize my own brother."

Ah. And that was eating at him. "You weren't expecting to see him—"

"I didn't recognize my own brother," he said, more adamant this time.

The dark note in his voice made her stomach jump. She rubbed the back of her knuckles against the edge of her jaw. "He has that grit thing going."

"It's wrong, Cilla." He leaned his forehead into the heel of his hand. "It's whacked."

Without thinking, she touched him again, placing her fingers over the ones on his leg. She curled the tips so they pressed briefly into his warm palm before letting go. This wasn't his fault. "It's the Lemons."

"So I should make lemonade, huh?" He lifted his head, his gaze boring into hers. "Make this better? How? I live in London and I travel all the time. But still, it's screwed that we're so distant. How can I fix this, Cilla?"

Her mouth opened, closed. For as long as she could remember, Ren had held himself aloof from his siblings and the other Velvet Lemon kids. And as they'd all grown and left the compound, every one of the nine had busied themselves pursuing their adult lives. She supposed that connections, even between siblings, had been a little loose of late.

Gwen hadn't wanted it to be like that for the rock

royalty, though. Was that why she'd sent Ren a key to her cottage? So that he'd have a second chance to bond with his brother and sister? Maybe with the others, too?

"Call Payne," she said, on a sudden inspiration. "Set up a lunch or something."

"He's going out of town," Ren reminded her.

"Oh, right." Instant letdown.

Ren rapped his knuckles against the top of the bar. "But I'm going to see Cami again. Tonight. She said she had another gig, right?"

"Right."

"She and Payne... I think they look out for each other. I want her to know she can count on me too."

The words warmed Cilla. She smiled at him and placed her palm over his knuckles once again, squeezed. "That's nice. Then maybe the two of you can start a dialogue about the Colson family."

She made to slide her hand off his, only to find it caught between his fingers. She glanced up, taking in his bemused expression. "Start a dialogue?" His lips twitched.

"You know what I mean."

He smiled.

Her lungs trapped air again. "Ren..."

"I'll start a dialogue," he said, amusement in his voice. "You'll come tonight too?"

What could she say? "Sure."

He gazed on her a moment longer, then nodded. "So, this friends thing might work out well after all," he said, and released her fingers in order to tug at a wisp of her hair that had escaped its band.

The little pain sent a wash of prickly bumps over her scalp that continued down her back. She still wasn't breathing as she fought a little tremble.

"Cilla?" he asked, eyes narrowing. "You all right,

squirt?"

"Great," she choked out. Except that clearly being his friend didn't make him one jot less attractive to her. And yeah, he could so make "squirt" sound as good as "sweetheart."

Chapter 7

Ren motored west on Sunset, avoiding the freeway traffic by taking the surface street route to the beach. Tonight Cami's gig was at a club close to the water in Santa Monica. As he drove, he chewed on what he was going to say to his half-sister if he could get her alone long enough for conversation. Would he ask for chatty emails? Demand she send regular selfies and convince Payne to do so as well? Somehow he suspected that wasn't the other man's style.

He sure as hell wouldn't do such a thing in return.

But Ren hadn't recognized his own damn brother when he'd passed him on the street. Payne had looked right through him as well. That couldn't be right.

From the corner of his eye, he caught Cilla's movement. It stirred the air in the car and he breathed in her delicate citrus scent. The good thing about the Colson sibling situation was it gave him something to think about besides her. If he was going to prevent death by blue balls, he needed another focus.

Her legs crossed and he took another look at her

chunky-heeled boots. His musings over his sibs weren't so all-consuming that he had forgotten her completely. She looked damn sweet in those boots, a pair of tight jeans, and a ladylike pale blue filmy blouse that she'd tucked into the pants and was unbuttoned to reveal a less-ladylike glimpse of cleavage. Hanging from a gold chain around her throat was a square-shaped polished blue stone wrapped in an intricate pattern of slender gold wire. A matching bracelet circled one wrist and square-shaped gold-wire earrings dangled from her ears. Their neighbor Jewel's work, she'd said.

As they neared their destination, he took a turn down a side street. Even though his gaze was aimed out the windshield, he sensed Cilla straighten.

He glanced over, noting she was staring out the window, her attention riveted on the neighborhood of small bungalows they were passing through. Huh. It was full dark, with just streetlights here and there offering dim illumination. When her head turned so she could stare out the side window, he slowed.

"See something you like?" he asked.

"Oh, no. It's just..." She made a vague gesture. "We passed my house."

With new interest, he inspected the area. Little stucco houses, probably built in the 1940s. Each had a tidy, tiny front yard. Most had some kind of decoration hung on the door. "Do you want to stop?"

"Um." There was a brief pause. "Well..."

That hesitation had him spinning the steering wheel.

"No, Ren. Honest, there's no reason..."

"We should at least make sure everything's secure. You haven't been living there in—how long?"

"A couple of weeks," she admitted.

"Which one is it?"

Her finger pointed at a place in the middle of the block. He pulled into the single-wide cement driveway, a strip of close-cropped grass running down its middle. In the glow of a metal-hatted porch light, he could see that it was white, with bright turquoise shutters on either side of the picture window. Beneath the glass, a wooden box dripped pink geraniums.

Curious to see Cilla's digs, he stepped from the car and made for the three steps to her front door that was painted the same green as the geranium leaves. Glancing around, he realized Cilla remained in her seat. Frowning, he returned to the car and opened her door. "What's up? Don't have your keys?"

Her hand lifted and a ring of them dangled from her fingers. "I'm coming," she said, a resigned tone in her voice.

"Hey, if you don't want to go in..." Her reluctance puzzled him, however.

"No, no. It's fine. I should pick up my mail."

It was delivered through a chute in the door and had made a small pile on the hardwood floor of the entryway. She scooped it up in her arms and as she walked it toward a small coffee table placed in front of a loveseat in the living area, he found switches and flipped them on.

Inside it wasn't any bigger than it appeared from the outside. To the left of the front door was a small living room and he could see a kitchen beyond that. The hallway directly beyond the entry led to a couple of bedrooms, he supposed, and a bath.

Instead of exploring on his own, he followed Cilla. She'd dumped most of the mail and with just a few envelopes in hand walked into the kitchen. It was tiled in old-fashioned ceramic of pale blue and pale yellow. The sink was spotless, the painted cabinet doors all primly closed. She took a glass from a cupboard and moved to the dispenser on the front of the fridge. "Water?" she asked, as she filled the glass.

He shook his head, running his gaze around the room. Something was off about the place, he thought, moving to take in the living room again. The rooms were clean, ordered, colorful, all things that didn't surprise him about Cilla's home. But...

There were no photos. Not one. Not anywhere in the public areas.

He'd been around. Dated plenty of women. And in his experience, they chronicled their lives by plastering surfaces with pictures of the people in their world. They tacked them to bulletin boards. Magnets held up more images on their fridges, along with mementos from various social events. Where were Cilla's BFFs? Did she toss out used concert tickets and theater programs unlike the majority of the females he knew?

Even Gwen had hung that big-ass, blown-up photo of the rock royalty.

"Mind if I look around?" he asked Cilla.

She was working on one of the envelopes. "Go ahead. If you get lost, just whisper. I'll be sure to hear you."

He grinned, then took the two strides that got him from the kitchen to the living room. Once he hit the hallway, he saw he hadn't been wrong about the rest of the house. There was more tile in an old-fashioned bathroom. Then two other rooms. One was tiny, filled by a daybed that was covered in a quilt and had two pillows propped on its headboard. The other was larger and held a four poster queen-sized bed. Stilling, he stared at the interior, that weird feeling ghosting down his spine once more.

Again, no personal souvenirs were stuck in the frame of the mirror over the chest of drawers. None sat on its wooden surface. Likewise, the top of the bedside table was only a repository for a light coating of dust.

His gaze skipped back to the bed and held there. The mattress was stripped bare. There wasn't a pillow in sight. Instead of sleeping in this larger space, Cilla rested her head in that narrow coffin of a bedroom.

Footsteps behind him had him turning. Keys in hand, Cilla wore an inquisitive expression. "That's the longest tour anyone's ever taken of my house."

He gestured toward that bare mattress. "You don't sleep in the master."

"You watch that TV show, don't you? The one where everyone thinks the detective is psychic, but he's really just figuring out things through observation."

"Don't watch much TV at all."

"You should. It's a good one." Lifting her keys, she shook them so they jangled. "Want to see my workroom? It's behind the house."

"Sure. But, Cilla..."

She didn't turn back to face him, just hesitated in the hall. "Yes?"

He was too curious to let it go. "Why don't you sleep in the bigger room?"

"I'm thinking about updating it. You know, new paint, new linens, new...new everything." She glanced over her shoulder. "My studio...workroom, whatever you want to call it, is this way. Coming?"

Hmm. Clearly ready to get off the subject of the space that needed new everything. He gave it a final sweep with his eyes, then shrugging, followed her.

In the kitchen, they slipped out a side door. Around back, another building, almost as big as her home, was a few steps across a miniscule lawn. She made quick work of the lock and then flipped on lights. It was essentially a single space. On the left, there was a long table with bolts of fabric stacked on one end. Two sewing machines were set up in separate corners. Full-length mirrors were installed just about everywhere and he could see another behind some curtains that delineated a changing room. Everywhere was more fabric, spangly trims, rolls of ribbon, and jars of what appeared to be sequins. A rolling tool cart held those of her trade: scissors, pincushions, several glue guns.

On another long table was a photo album. He idly flipped it open and wasn't surprised that this too held nothing personal. On the pages were shots of costumes, matching fabric swatches and trim samples attached. He went through it at random, and like when he'd visited her website, he was intrigued by the imagination and talent that she expressed with such skill. Each piece was intricate and fanciful and seemed to tell its own story.

He was also intrigued by Cilla, the woman, he admitted to himself. She was a conundrum with her photo-less house and her sexual unease, with her artistic gift and the way she'd melted under his mouth.

Something else to solve, he thought, like his sibling dilemma.

Across the room, movement caught his eye. Sketch book in hand, Cilla was studying a drawing, that small furrow back between her brows. As she continued to scrutinize the page, her other hand swept across a rack of bolted fabrics, her fingers caressing the different materials, absently enjoying them with clear sensual appreciation.

And she thought she was bad in bed. All she needed to bring to it was that tactile appreciation. He—no, some lucky man—should be able to do the rest. In his mind's eye it *was* him, though, sprawled naked on rumpled sheets. Cilla's head on his chest, Cilla's slender fingers tracing random patterns on his skin as she came down from the screaming orgasm he gave her.

Well, hell. That did it. He turned away from her to adjust the change in the fit of his jeans. Foolish to think of those stroking fingers, that smoking little body, and a bed at the same time. He was supposed to be focused on other things, right?

But he had a bad feeling, a very bad feeling, there was nothing that could distract him from this sexual ache that had started by waking up beside Cilla and that wasn't easily going away.

Ren had a Shock Top beer waiting for his sister at the bar. She joined him there between her first and second sets, hopping onto the stool beside him and giving a little grin. "You came to see me play again."

"Yeah," he said. "And in my not-so-humble opinion, you killed it again." True. Her throaty yet pure voice was eminently suited for the pop/rock/folk/country blend of her set list. Most songs she covered were known for their versions by female artists, but she snuck in a few surprises, including Jason Mraz's "I Won't Give Up."

She took up her beer, looking at him while she tipped back the bottle for a slug. He couldn't say for sure—he didn't know her well—but he thought she was pleased by the compliment.

The bottle hit the bar with a subtle *clack*. "So, we have business?"

He hid his wince. They were related, for God's sake, and she was looking for an ulterior motive for this meet-up. Damn Lemons. "Maybe I just wanted to listen to some good music."

"You were curious the first time and I can believe you liked what you heard. But to come back so soon? You want something."

And he thought *he* had a cynical soul. Shaking his head, he sighed. "Fine. Let's start with a request. How about you give me your cell phone number?"

She blinked, then ran her fingers through the long slide of her auburn bangs. "Uh, really?"

"Really. I can get in touch with Payne but somehow you're not on my contacts list."

"You want me to be on our contacts list?" Her eyes were wide with surprise.

Fucking Lemons. "Yeah." He yanked his phone from his pocket and handed it over. "Here."

When she was done, he called her cell. "Now you have mine," he said.

"Cool," Cami replied, picking up her beer.

He took a swallow of his own and thought about other biographical basics. "I don't know where you live, either."

As her eyebrows rose, he saw hints of russet in their dark brown. When she was tiny, her hair had been strawberry blond and her eyebrows so light they were almost non-existent. "Nearby," she said. "In Santa Monica."

That sent his mind straight to Cilla's small bungalow. "So...do you have photos at your place?"

"Photos?" Her eyebrows climbed high again. "What kind of photos?"

"The kind you put in frames and on fridges. Of you and your best friends, going to parties, hanging out. That sort of thing."

"I don't have a lot of time to cultivate friends, Ren, not with my work schedule and my music."

And because growing up rock royalty had made them all lousy at connecting with others. Ren supposed he was the worst offender, but to paraphrase Payne, not one of them knew much about normal relationships.

Cami tilted her head, studying him. "So what's with the twenty questions?"

"It was three."

She just kept looking at him. "It's because we're family," he finally said, giving in. "We should know how to get in touch with each other in case of emergencies."

"That's the only reason?"

He sighed. "Look, I ran into Payne on the street today. We didn't recognize each other."

Cami's expression went soft and her hand brushed her chin. "Well, he has that stubble thing—"

"That wasn't it," Ren ground out. "And it's just flat-out fucked that I walked past the man with whom I share a good portion of my DNA."

His half-sister was staring at him again. Then her lips twitched.

"What?" he demanded.

"Who would have thought big bad Ren Colson was sentimental?" she mused, appearing to fight a smile with little success.

He narrowed his eyes at her. "Cami—"

"You're an old softie. Who knew?"

"Be careful, kid," he warned. "I've well-earned my reputation for rough-and-tough."

His half-sister snorted, then tipped back her beer again. After she swallowed, she pinned him with those eyes so like his own. "So now it's my turn for questions."

He hesitated. "Okay..."

"What's up with you and Cilla?"

Ren kept his face blank and made sure not to glance back at the table where he'd left the other woman sitting. "Nothing."

"Oh, come on."

"If there was anything—which there is not—have you considered it might be a private matter?"

Her lips curved. "Word has it that this is exactly what people do who share DNA, Ren. Family members pry into each other's business."

"We don't know what it is that families do," he muttered.

Cami set her beer back on the bar. "But you want to, don't you? Isn't that what the cell phone number exchange is about?"

Shit, Ren thought. Maybe he *was* a softie. Still, he refused to start regretting that his half-sister had her own line on his contacts list.

She reached over to pat his knee. "I didn't say anything after the gig at the club on Sunset, but I saw you kissing her. A massive pheromone cloud was forming over your heads. It was freaky."

Maybe he did regret her having her own line on his contacts list. "You can forget all about that."

Her smile was mischievous. "Should we have The Talk?"

"Cami..." He shook his head.

"Really. I can tell you all about safe sex and how to pleas—"

"Who gave *you* The Talk?" he asked, suddenly struck by the thought. And appalled. "Surely not Bean."

"No." She waved that away. "Gwen, of course. And very tasteful it was, too, considering she probably boned more rock stars than there are eucalyptus trees in Laurel Canyon."

Boned. He winced, thinking that Gwen might have given tasteful Talks, but she'd been almost rawly open about her groupie past.

"I miss her," Cami said.

"Yeah." He'd put off locating the box she'd left him. Marked with his name on it, she'd said in her last letter. It was stored somewhere in her cottage and she'd written that he'd know what to do with the contents. "I should have found a way to get back before she passed."

Cami contemplated the label on her bottle of beer. "All of us could have done more for her." Her gaze drifted across the room. "From what I understand, Cilla was there a lot, though." Now his half-sister's brows met in a frown.

"What?" Ren asked.

"It's Cilla's former boyfriend again."

Tad. Ren glanced over his shoulder and saw, sure enough, it was the man he'd met the other night. The one who'd told her she was a lousy lay on they day they'd broken up.

No wonder her expression looked once again strained.

But could it be more than that? Ren thought. Though this was the guy who'd told her she was bad in bed and asked her to watch porn as a warm-up before date night, might she still be in love with him?

Or he, her? Otherwise why the hell was he back, this time sans the blonde with the yard-long hair? Was he following Cilla?

But none of this was Ren's business, he reminded himself. He was supposed to be putting her out of his mind, right?

Still, he couldn't drag his gaze from the pair. "You know anything about him?" he heard himself ask his half-sister. "Not her type, don't you think?"

"I've never met the man," Cami said. "He looks too starched for my taste, but how would I know Cilla's? I don't even know yours."

He looked back at this half-sister. "Easy and stacked." He actually didn't have a preference for big tits, though it was true that the women he came across behind stages while doing his business of shepherding mega-bands on mega-tours weren't there to make hook-ups hard.

If he was honest, the allure of that kind of female and those kinds of encounters had worn off years ago. He just hadn't found another variety to fill the empty side of his bed.

His gaze slid to Cilla again. Her ex appeared in earnest conversation with her. She was staring at the toes of her boots. Then she darted a quick glance Ren's way.

None of his business, he thought again.

At her second glance, he wondered if that was true. Last time she'd been conversing with the other man, Ren had laid a kiss on her. Was she expecting that sort of conduct from him again as a way to salvage her pride...or make the ex jealous? If so, didn't he have an obligation to meet those expectations?

With a muttered, "I've got to do something," to his sister, Ren slid off the stool and stalked toward his housemate.

His intentions were good, he assured himself. Read the situation, read what she might need from him. As he drew closer, he decided that might not be so simple. Cilla's closed expression gave little away and her big blues were again trained on her feet. The ex, Tad, was talking, and though he was bent close to her, Ren caught a fragment of the man's words, "...you made me crazy..."

Something about his tone made up Ren's mind. Screw it, he didn't care where Cilla's head was on this situation. The asshole was not getting a second chance with her. Not on his watch.

He slid his arm around her waist and pulled her against his side. "Baby," he said, and kissed her temple.

Cilla twitched and Tad's head jerked up. "You," he

said, a new interest kindling in his gaze.

Ren's brows rose. "That's right. Me."

Tad straightened to full height which meant he had a bead on Ren's nose. "The other night, Cilla didn't tell me you were Ren *Colson*. You're Cami's brother."

"True." Why was the ex talking about Ren's sister?

"One of the things Tad wants is an introduction to Cami," Cilla said, her body stiff against him.

And what other thing Tad wanted, Ren was just itching to know. "Is that so?" he returned, his voice mild.

"Yes." The other man dove into his pocket to pull out a wallet and then a business card. "I rep musicians. I'd like to talk to your sister about that."

Taking the small piece of tagboard, Ren gave it a glance. Okay. Legit agency. He jerked his chin to where Cami sat at the bar, her Shock Top in hand. "Not her receptionist. You want to talk to her, make your own approach."

Tad hesitated, glancing between Cilla and Ren. "I'm not through—"

"You're through," Cilla said, her voice firm. "And you wanted that meet with Cami." Then she transferred her gaze to Ren. "I'm ready to leave, is that okay?"

"Sure." He squeezed her closer and pressed another kiss to her temple, his eyes on You-Should-Watch-Porn Tad who was clearly torn between heading for the bar and talking further with Cilla. "Whatever you want, beautiful."

They made their getaway with a nod to the ex. Ren steered Cilla to the exit, sketching a wave at his half-sister. He could text her later, now that he had her number. As they pushed through the door, he saw Tad moving toward the bar. Second thoughts assailed Ren when he was outside, pressing the fob to open the car locks.

"Cilla."

Clearly pre-occupied, it took her a moment to glance up. "Hmm?"

Ren pulled open the passenger door for her. "Am I going to regret not playing Cami's receptionist?"

Her brows drew together. "What?"

"Is that guy okay? Why didn't he ask *you* to facilitate a meet?"

"He did, and I refused. I didn't want her to feel like I was foisting someone on her." She slid into the seat.

"Okay." With a nod, he shut door. But behind the wheel, he realized she hadn't answered both questions.

Pulling out of the parking lot, he asked it again. "Cilla, is that guy okay?"

Something pulsed in the silence and that cold prickle slid down his spine again. *Shit*. "Cilla?"

She cleared her throat. "Professionally, he's on the up-and-up. Very successful at what he does."

"But personally?"

"Personally?" Cilla repeated. Then she twisted in her seat and gripped his forearm with fingers that bit into his skin. "Would Cami be interested in him in that way?"

"Doubt it, sweetheart." Ren was getting an ugly vibe from Cilla's sudden concern. He no longer wondered if she was still hung up on the ex, that was sure. "Is there something more about him I should know?"

Her grip on Ren's arm relaxed and she sat back in her seat. "Just that personally...he's not so great."

Double shit, Ren thought, as resignation rolled over him. He glanced at Cilla's profile, her expression unreadable in the darkness of the car's interior. "When we get back to the compound," he muttered, "I'm going to make every last thing about you my business."

Chapter 8

I'm going to make every last thing about you my business.

Those ominous words echoed in Cilla's brain as she preceded Ren into Gwen's house. Even the familiar surroundings and the warm memories she had of the place couldn't prevent the shiver that rolled down her back. She didn't want to talk any more about Tad and Ren seemed determined to get additional information from her about him.

"Well, I guess I'll head off to sleep," she said in a bright voice, her feet taking her toward the bedroom. "I'll see you in the morning."

He hooked a finger in a belt loop at the back of her jeans, halting her forward movement. "I think we should talk for a while instead."

"We've talked all day, Ren. All that chat when we strolled the stars. Didn't we converse at the Roosevelt Hotel bar? Then we had words, I'm sure we did, when we visited my house." Her voice was getting higher as he used his hold to tug her toward the living room. Her feet encountered the carpet there and she dug in her heels. "Seriously, Ren. I'm tired."

"And I'm tired of you trying to slither out of whatever it is you should be telling me." He towed her another foot, then pushed her to the soft couch with a gentle hand. "C'mon, Cilla."

She glared up as he towered over her. "I don't know why you think you get to pry into me, Ren. If we're going to communicate some more, it should be a two-way street."

"Start a dialogue, you mean?" he asked, a hint of a smile turning up the corners of her mouth.

Her arms crossed over her chest. "Why not? What are you trying to hide?"

"Not a thing." He sat on the next cushion and stretched out his legs, crossing them at the ankle. "We can play this your way if you'd like. Ask your questions, I'll answer. But remember, I reserve the right to do the same."

Cilla scooted to the far end of the couch, pretending she wanted the corner as a place to prop her back. There was nothing holding her here, of course. Nothing to keep her from eluding his presence and his questions by escaping to the bedroom. But he'd given her an opportunity to do her own prying and it was a temptation impossible to resist.

She'd just stick to her corner while doing so, delaying her escape a short while. The minute he insisted on mining her secrets, she'd high tail it away from him.

"Well?" Ren asked, lifting his hands. "What is it you want to know?"

Swallowing, she ran her gaze from the black hair tumbled over his brow to the dark shadow of beard at his jawline and around his mouth. What she wanted to know was how she was going to get over this stupid crush she had on him.

As she watched, he moved to strip off his leather jacket and toss it on the adjacent easy chair. That left him in faded jeans and a knit shirt that fit tight to his muscled chest and biceps. On the hem of the short-sleeve was stitched a small British flag.

"Why London?" she blurted out. "Why did you choose to make that city your base?"

He was silent a moment, then one corner of his mouth kicked up. "Because of a man."

Her eyes flared wide. First a threesome, and now... "A *man*?"

Ren's laughter rang out. "You should see your face. God, you're adorable. You're making me want to kiss you again."

"No more kissing," she said, scowling at him. "We agreed."

"We could always revisit that agreement."

She ignored the soft-spoken remark. "I'm guessing I took the 'because of a man' comment completely wrong."

"Yeah." He started laughing again. "Your sexual instincts are crap."

"Hey," she protested. "That's why I was so surprised. I took you for...for straight-up hetero. Not that there's anything wrong with a man who likes other men or a woman who likes women or a person who likes both kinds or more than one at once—"

"Not the Speckleman twins again," Ren said, and there was more laughter dancing in his eyes. "Though from what I heard they also were the kind of women who liked their pony—"

"Stop teasing." Cilla scowled at him once more. "Enough about them. Now...London? The man?"

"My grandfather," Ren said. "On my mother's side."

The laughter was gone now, replaced by an expression of fond affection. "I looked him up the first time I was doing security for a Lemons tour."

Before he started his own business. "What did he think of the tough guy-grandson with long hair and piercings who appeared on his doorstep?" His mother had been less than welcoming. Had her father been any different?

Ren shook his head. "He didn't ever really understand who I was. He was living in a facility for disabled World War II veterans. Alzheimer's."

"Oh."

"He was a great guy, though. We—the people who cared for him and I—figure he saw me and thought I was one of his old mates. 'Reggie!' he'd yell out every time I came for a visit. 'We survived another day!'"

Ren's faked British accent made Cilla smile. "Ren...Reggie."

He nodded. "His hearing wasn't the best. But he was a talker. Told me about his childhood, his war experiences, his love life. Apparently he had quite a way with the ladies."

"The apple doesn't fall far from the tree," Cilla murmured.

"He enjoyed my visits so much, that when it came time for me to go out on my own, I decided to headquarter my business nearby. It gave me the chance to check in often. Fed him when I could—that man loved his bean soup but couldn't manage the utensils himself."

"He's gone now, though," Cilla said, catching up to all the past tense references. *Bad boy Ren had spoon fed the elderly man?*

"Yeah." Ren nodded. "He slipped away in his sleep almost a year ago. But while he lived, we had good times."

Good times that his grandfather had never understood were with his grandson, and not some old friend.

Ren frowned. "Now what's put that sadness on your pretty face?"

"He never knew it was you." Cilla slid down the cushions so she could place her hand on his thigh. "I don't like that he never knew you, Ren."

His hand covered hers. "I didn't mind being Reggie."

But she minded, because it was clear Ren wanted to have *family*. Surely it was so. This was the man who'd turned all moody when he'd failed to recognize his brother on the street. The man who'd gone "a little wild and a lot remote" when his mother hadn't brought him into her fold with open arms. Cilla's gaze caught on that half-heart on his wrist. He was *so* not Mr. Solitary, despite everything he'd been telling her.

"Cilla?" His fingers squeezed hers. "You're still wearing that sad expression, baby."

"I don't like you being sad either." She couldn't look away from his silver-green eyes framed by their spiky black lashes and her wish whispered from between her lips. "You should always get what you want."

"So sweet," he whispered back, and his eyes changed, going darker as the pupils dilated. His fingers tightened on hers and then he tugged, bringing her closer. One big palm cupped her cheek and his mouth descended toward hers. "I know what I want right now," he murmured, "and I know I'm lousy at resisting when I really want like this." His lips touched hers.

When it came to Ren's kisses, she had no defense. His tongue brushed her bottom lip and she opened her mouth so he could claim more of her. When his palm slid around her back to urge her nearer, she pressed against him, bones gone and muscles as pliant as warm candle wax.

Her hand curved around his neck and the silky strands of his hair tickled her fingers. He made a sound, low in his throat, and then he pushed her back, into the cushions, coming over her with his delicious weight. Her breath stuttered in her lungs as he lowered between her parted thighs. One leg pressed into the back of the couch, the other she wound over his hip.

His mouth lifted and he stared down at her, his hands brushing the hair away from her face. He shook his head, a small smile curving his mouth. "What you do to me."

What *he* did to *her*. Her heart was pounding, her breathing was shallow, and she couldn't look away from his lips.

They dipped lower and he pressed them to her chin, his tongue touching the very center. Then he drew his mouth along her jaw, so his burning breath tickled her ear. She shivered, a hot tremor that sent goose bumps tumbling over her skin. Her hips lifted into his, all on their own, and he groaned, the sound muffled against her neck. But she felt it all the way to her belly and beyond.

Between her legs she was already hot and swollen. Wet and needy.

"Ren," she whispered.

Raising his head, he gazed into her eyes once again. "What, baby?"

She hesitated, unsure of anything beyond how good it was to be this close to him.

He ran the back of a finger along her flaming cheek. "You want to talk now? You ready to give up your secrets?"

Anything but that. So when he moved to straighten away from her, she tightened the leg wrapped around him and pulled his mouth to hers once more. "Kiss me again," she demanded against his lips. "That's what I want."

With another low groan, he complied, taking over just as she liked. His tongue thrust against hers, the wet friction causing the muscles at her core to clench. She tilted her hips and he ground against her there, the heat building between them. When his hand palmed her breast and then moved to the buttons of her blouse, she was desperate for the fabric to part. He ended the kiss to glance down as he pushed aside the edges of her shirt.

She looked too, not surprised to see her breasts quivering in the lacy cups of her bra.

"So pretty," Ren murmured, then he drew his mouth down her neck. Her fingers clutched at his shoulders and she closed her eyes, squirming on the cushions to bring his mouth lower.

His tongue swept over a hard, lace-covered nipple. She gasped, then gasped again when he tucked a finger in the fabric and drew it down. He stared at her bared breast, his half-lowered lashes hiding his expression. Then he drew her into his mouth, sucking in long, tender pulls.

She thought she would lose her mind.

One hand tangled in his hair, the other clutched at the fabric of his shirt. Ren didn't appear to notice her desperate groping. He continued with that delicate suction, all teasing and zero relief.

Her back arched, offering more of herself, and his only response was to tuck the stretchy fabric beneath the other breast. When his lips merely brushed over the neglected peak she swallowed a frustrated moan. The place between her legs throbbed with a fervent ache and when he finally, finally suckled the nipple, she felt another rush of wet there.

Her fingers scrabbled at his shirt and she managed to yank up the hem to find the sleek, hot skin of his back. At her touch on his bare flesh, the pressure from his mouth became greedy, and she groaned in relief as her hips lifted against his.

He kept sucking, his heavy body and the hard bulge in his pants just more provocation. Still lifting into him, she squirmed, pressing denim to denim. His big hand curled around her breast, plumping the swollen flesh and feeding it between his lips.

Her neck arched as she rubbed against him, the friction beautiful and almost right, almost there, and then she felt the sharp pain-and-pleasure edge of his teeth.

Ecstasy exploded like a glitter bomb, detonating low in her belly then expanding outward, sparkling sensation spreading through each cell. Her toes curled into the soles of her boots and she cried out, her fingernails digging into Ren's scalp and skin as she rode out the waves of hot delight.

That moments later washed back, bringing with them a flood of embarrassment.

Which Ren didn't make any better. "So now I know your deepest secret of all—maybe one you've even been keeping from yourself," he said, his expression bemused as he gazed down on her.

Cue more mortification. "What's that?" she had to ask, closing her eyes.

He pressed his forehead to hers. "Honey, you're as hot and ready as a firecracker."

Ren stared down at Cilla, her eyes closed, her cheeks flushed. "And sweet," he said, lowering his voice to a whisper. "A sweet, sexy little firecracker."

Without lifting her lashes, she struggled in his hold. "You should let me go now," she said.

"In a minute." He pushed up, bringing her with him, then holding her close until they were seated upright on the couch, Cilla in his lap. She still wouldn't look at him.

Smiling to himself, he went about adjusting her clothing. Bra back in place, he re-buttoned her blouse then took her hands in his, squeezed. "Hey, squirt," he said, trying not to laugh. "Though you can't see me, that doesn't mean I'm not here."

"Please. Have it be that *I'm* not here, okay?"

Now he did laugh, and hoped it didn't sound as smug as he felt. "You're here, I'm here, it happened, babe." He leaned close to her ear. "You know, the big *it*."

"Just kill me now," Cilla moaned.

He lifted a hand to draw his knuckles over her hot cheek. "What's the problem?"

"First I was a no O-er and now I'm a premature O-er."

He relaxed back into the cushions, vastly entertained. His mood had been all over the place that day. There'd been the sexual frustration—back, but now greatly tempered by his satisfaction over Cilla's responsiveness— the pissed-off feelings he'd had about Payne, and then those strange, angry twinges he'd experienced when seeing Cilla with another man. But now he had her in his arms, he'd set her off in record time, and the only thing he needed to do at the moment was savor this new, mellow mood of his.

He'd been edgy all his life, worse since his grandfather died followed by Gwen. But something about Cilla seemed to knock off his sharper corners. His personal Fay Wray, taming the beast.

His knuckles traced another path over her cheek. "There's no such thing as a premature orgasm when it comes to women."

"I think I could maybe have waited for one item of clothing to come completely off, Ren. And certainly what happened wasn't the least bit...polite to you."

"I'm fine, Cilla."

She finally opened her eyes and slanted a look at him through her lashes.

He could read her thoughts. "Nobody's keeping score."

Her aggrieved expression made him stifle another laugh. If she wanted to share a few more kisses—and whatever that led to—with him, he wasn't going to worry about it. Like his father, he was that selfish. He'd wondered if he'd be too much for her, too rough, too demanding, but now he knew he had soft and gentle—surprise, surprise—in him.

Settling deeper into the sofa, he sifted his fingers through her hair as tension continued to seep from him. It was like that first night on Gwen's patio when they'd shared the quiet night and again at the outlook on the trail that gave them the primo view of L.A. Maybe it was home, maybe it was Cilla, in any case he felt deep in his skin and deep in the moment. All good.

Not the usual whatsoever—when he was all about making up time by hurrying someone else along. There wasn't the typical impatience he felt with the world either. Or dissatisfaction with it, like life had let him down.

Shit, and didn't that just sound fucked. He'd had a crappy family life but still a damn entitled one.

He rested his chin on the top of Cilla's head and dialed himself back to chill. Breathing in her fragrance, he draped one arm around her waist and used his free hand to play with her soft hair. The curls and waves of it clung to his fingers as he combed through the soft stuff. Her body was heavier against his than before and he enjoyed her slow slide into half-slumber.

"Great hair, Cilla," he said, watching it drift down as he released a lock and it floated toward the rest. "So many twists and turns to it."

"Then maybe I shouldn't be so mad at Tad," she replied, her voice drowsy, "for cutting it."

Her words took a moment to sink in. Then tension shot into his muscles. *Tad had cut her hair?* No. That couldn't be what he'd heard. Her body was soft and warm and he made his voice the same. "Say again? Tad encouraged you to cut your hair?"

"No." She ran her fingers through the stuff and tucked it behind her ear. "After we broke up... I sleep like the dead."

He'd seen it for himself, the two times they'd shared a bed. "Yeah...?"

"I'd given him a key to my house. You know, how you do."

Ren had never lived with anyone nor had he ever given a woman access to his house, let alone his heart. "Okay. And...?"

She took in a breath, seeming to come completely out of her half-doze. "I don't know why I'm telling you this."

On heightened alert, he tightened his hold on her. "Because I'm asking."

Another moment's hesitation, then she spoke. "He was angry when I broke up with him. He said he wanted to get back together, even though he'd also said I needed to work on...well, you know." She flicked Ren a quick glance.

"And now you know that part of you is just fine."

She grimaced, then slid off his lap. Ass on the cushions, elbows on her knees, she put her head in her hands. "When I was sleeping one night..."

Fuck. "Cilla? When you were sleeping one night...what?"

"He came in and cut off my hair. Left the hank of it on the bedside table along with the scissors and his set of keys."

His blood pressure rocketing, Ren's jaw dropped. "*What?*"

"When I was asleep—"

"I heard you." He leaped to his feet, feeling as if the top of his head might explode. His hand shoved in his pocket for the car fob. "What's that asshole's address?"

Cilla's head twisted and she stared up at him in silence.

Every second of it felt like a century as his blood coursed beneath his skin, lava-hot. "Damn it, Cilla, where does he live?"

"Um...Why?"

"Why?" Now it was Ren's turn to stare. "So I can go kill him."

"Ren..." A little laugh petered out to nothing and her eyes got bigger. "You can't do that."

"I don't know why the hell not." Anger buzzed through him like a hive of hornets. "Address, Cilla."

Her gaze trained on him, she rose from the couch. "Ren, no. That isn't necessary."

"Fuck it isn't." The hornet wings vibrated even faster, making him feel itchy all over and jacking up his temperature. He wouldn't be surprised to find his flesh smoking. "I've got to get to him."

Cilla walked toward Ren, palms out, a placating gesture. "Calm down."

"I'm going to kill him." The bastard had dared to hurt Cilla. First he'd slashed at her confidence in her sexuality—advising her to watch porn, good God—then he'd taken away what she considered her crowning glory by stealing into her house, uninvited.

"No, Ren." She put one small hand on his chest, over his heart. The other wrapped around his forearm, a cool touch that did nothing for his temper. He was vibrating with the power of it.

"It's just hair," she said. "I probably should have done something with it long ago."

"You didn't want to cut it. You never wanted to cut it. I remember you saying that."

Cilla looked down. "Partly because of you. You once told me how pretty it was and how you liked it long." She glanced up at him, a little smile quirking her lips. "I didn't get a lot of male attention when I was young and...and I kind of took that compliment to heart."

He stared at her, picturing that quiet child she'd been, with her big blue eyes and her long fall of hair. "Oh, Cilla."

She touched the short ends of it now. "I'm glad to hear you like it this way, too."

"It's very pretty, but that doesn't mean I'm not going to kill the man."

Her expression turned alarmed. "Ren—"

"Look, I have to do something," he said, still infuriated by the idea of what that fucking sneak had done.

"Then kiss me," she whispered.

"Not now—"

"Kiss me, Ren." She stepped into his body. "That's the something you can do for me."

He gritted his teeth, his cock going hard despite his temper as she pressed her hips to his. "It's not enough."

"It's what I need."

"Cilla—"

"Make me feel desirable," she said, her voice sweet temptation. "Show me a man finds me sexy. That *you* find me sexy."

"Of course you're sexy," he muttered, trying to ignore the hand that stole around to the small of his back and slid beneath his shirt. "But right now—"

Her mouth muffled the rest of the sentence. On tiptoe, Cilla kissed him, her small tongue sliding between his lips as he groaned. His body was stiff against hers, his rage had infused his muscles with cement, it seemed, but she didn't appear to notice as she wrapped an arm around his neck, and kept kissing, kissing, kissing.

She maddened him. He wanted action, his temperament compelled him to redress the wrong done to her. "I need to teach him a lesson," he said against her mouth.

"Teach me instead," she said, sliding her lips along his jaw. "Teach me everything you know about sex."

God. Her tongue was painting a wet design on his neck. His hands closed over her hips, in preparation for pushing her away. "We both know you don't need a mentor."

"I need a man, Ren. Right now I need you."

I need you. The vessel that contained his anger broke then, shattering like a glass container to release new emotions, a tangled rush of them: inevitability, dread, yearning, lust, some feeling that was an uneasy precursor to loss. With sudden disquiet, Ren stepped back.

He should go! Find Tad and make him pay!

Cilla moved into him again, her body fragrant and her hold firm. On tiptoe, she whispered in his ear. "Fuck me. Take me to bed and fuck me."

He shuddered, those raunchy words out of her sweet mouth laying waste to his violent intentions as well as his Galahad hesitation. This was the result of being rock royalty—of being String Bean Colson's son. No will power. If Ren wanted something, well, he took it.

Later, he'd get to the asshole. Later, he'd deal with the insult and his anger. Now it was time for Cilla. *Fuck me.*

She'd said that. *Take me to bed and fuck me.*

Galvanized, his arms banded her body and he hoisted her up so he could take her lips the way he wanted to. As he slanted his head her legs came around his hips and he kneaded her ass as he made for the closest mattress.

He tossed her to the one where they'd first slept together and followed her down. She giggled, the sound so sweet that he attacked the fastening of her jeans to make her understand this was no laughing matter. "I'm going to do you," he said, yanking denim and silky panties down her legs to just below her knees. Good God. She was completely bare down there and the top of his head threatened to explode again, but for a completely different—better—reason. "I'm going to show you what you do to me."

In the low glow from the bedside lamp, he saw she was up on her elbows, her chest heaving. Her big blue eyes were trained on him as he licked his thumb then insinuated it along the groove of her intimate flesh. She jerked at the first touch and he sucked in a breath as he felt her juicy wetness spread over his skin.

"You're drenched," he said, flicking her a glance.

Her cheeks turned even pinker. "Ren."

"Say my name just like that," he whispered, nudging her clit with the pad of his thumb. "I like that plea in your voice."

She moaned, her head dropping back as he circled the knot of nerves. "I still have my boots on. You're still dressed."

Pushing up the hem of her blouse, he circled her navel with tip of his tongue. "You come again and I'll take off all your clothes."

"Ren..."

"You come *again*, and I'll take off mine."

Her skin was like nothing he'd felt before, smelled before, tasted before. He continued to play with her, his thumb rolling, pressing, teasing as he kissed her belly, scraped his beard against her hipbones, sucked the skin below her navel to mark her.

She squirmed in his hold, her breath coming fast, her whole body trembling.

"Good, baby?" he asked.

Her only answer was to draw up her heels, her legs widening as far as her pants would allow. He knew the restraint would only ratchet her desire higher and as he leaned up to take her mouth, he pressed his free palm on her shoulder, anchoring her to the mattress. More masculine control.

It made her wild.

She sucked on his tongue, she made low noises at the back of her throat, her hips tilted into the hand that played with her sex. He took his thumb from her and she froze, then jerked her mouth from his. "Ren," she said, sounding peeved.

"Be still then," he advised, stroking his knuckles along the inside of her thigh, in a light, calming caress. Down. Up. Her flesh quivered.

"*Ren*." This time it was breathy and sweet.

To reward her, he returned to the liquid-glazed flesh with more caresses. Her body was swollen and heated there, and the layers were opened like a lovely, luscious flower to his gaze. The tips of two fingers pressed into the soft entrance and when she squirmed again, he stilled them, sending her another quelling look. Her gaze trained on his face, she instantly stopped moving and then he said "Good," and slid the long digits into her, all the way, until his palm cupped her smooth and soft labial lips.

Her moan wrapped around his hard cock and tugged.

"Pretty girl," he said, watching his hand start a gentle rocking action. "You're so pretty all over." An image of her breasts came to mind, framed by the stretchy lace of her bra that he'd tucked beneath them. Her pale nipples had drawn hard against his mouth, poking like berries against his tongue as he sucked on them.

Glancing up, he saw her gaze was fixed on him, and he could feel the tension invading her body. But she didn't move except for the quivering of her belly and the fluttering of her internal muscles against his pulsing fingers. *God*, he thought, *so damn sweet*. He reached with his free hand to cup her hot cheek. She turned her face to kiss his palm.

His heart spasmed against another punch of mingled dread and longing, leaving a painful ache in his chest.

"Cilla," he whispered, his voice rough. *Oh, shit*. What was happening here?

Her lips touched his hand once again and he drew it away to run his thumb over that valentine-shaped mouth. She ducked her chin, taking the digit into its heat and when she sucked, all his muscles steeled and his cock went so hard he nearly lost his mind.

Focus, he told himself. *Focus on her pleasure*.

His fingers moved in the wet clasp of her body, twisting, thrusting, establishing a rhythm as he toyed with the engorged nub of her clitoris, swollen for him. Her hips rose into his touch and he didn't stop her or stop himself this time. Her little gasp was his final warning, and then she was crying out as the crisis came over her. There was no way he couldn't watch. His gaze shifted to her face as her cheeks flushed pink and her lashes drifted down. She rode out the long orgasm on his hand, her muscles tight around his fingers, her flesh wetter than ever. *God*, he thought. *Beautiful. So beautiful.*

When she opened her eyes, he was tugging off her boots and socks. "Ren," she said, holding out a hand.

"In a minute, kid," he said, as he drew off the rest of her clothes. Then he gathered her delicate nakedness into his arms, the armor of his own jeans and shirt necessary while he attempted to gain some control.

"You now," she said, her voice husky. "Come on. You promised to teach me everything."

He turned them to their sides, her back to his front, to hide the doubt and concern that surely showed on his face. How could he give her any further instruction when he couldn't say for sure what had just happened? When he didn't understand how a closed-mouth kiss on the palm of his hand—that he could feel even still—seemed so dangerous. It was something he had no experience with.

None at all, and he was afraid it might go wrong for both of them.

Chapter 9

Spooned with Ren, Cilla wiggled in his hold. His arm tightened around her and she wiggled again, secretly enjoying the scrape of denim against her bare bottom. It brushed the bulge behind Ren's zipper too, and she was ready to get a closer look at that, even as she still tingled from her latest orgasm.

Wow. Renford Colson had given her an orgasm. A *second* orgasm. And it had been fabulous, she thought, feeling a cat-with-cream smile curving her mouth. Absolutely fabulous. She wiggled deeper into his body.

But this time Ren shifted his hips away from hers, and drew her hair to the side to press a kiss on her neck, right where it joined her shoulder. "Cilla," he started. "About the hair incident—"

"Oh, no," she said. "We're done with that." Going over it again would only rile Ren and she'd more than half-believed he was actually prepared to hurt Tad when he'd first learned of it. Since then they'd moved on to newer, more pleasurable pastures and she planned on staying there.

"I think—"

"It's my business," she said, turning to face him. Her ex wasn't going to intrude here. "Promise me we're done with that."

He was already shaking his head. "No promises."

Okay, time to try another tack. "What about the ones you already gave me?"

His eyebrows drew together. "Which?"

She lowered her voice in a Ren-dition of his. "'You come again and I'll take off all your clothes. You come *again*, and I'll take off mine.'" She wanted that, badly. She wanted to be able to see and touch, kiss and caress the sinew and bone and skin that was all sexy Ren.

His lips quirked. "I probably shouldn't have said that." A look of regret entered his eyes. "And Cilla, we probably shouldn't have..."

The look, the words, felt like a stab in the side. She was in the middle of living out a fantasy and he was filled with remorse? Except... "Um, Ren, you *did* take off my clothes. If this was such a bad idea in your mind, why am I naked right now?"

He blinked, then let out a low laugh. "Christ, Cilla." His big hands ran down her back to cup her behind and a delicious shiver rolled over her skin. "The lizard part of my brain can't resist you, I guess. You're one hell of a temptation."

"You're a temptation to me, too. What's wrong with two consenting adults giving in to mutual enticement?" She gave him her best smile. "Please?"

His fingers tightened on her bottom and he adopted a mock-stern expression. "I should spank you for trying to break my will."

Her lungs seized even as an imp took over her mouth. "Maybe...maybe I'd like that." She could feel a blush bloom on every inch of her skin.

Ren's eyes closed as if he was in pain. "What am I going to do with you?"

"Anything," she whispered in the imp's seductive voice and she saw his eyes fly open. This breaking of Ren's will was getting to be fun. For obvious reasons, sex had never before been a playful subject with her, but now... "Anything your heart desires."

He groaned, then caught her fingers as they moved to his fly. "Now what did we say about the next order of events?"

And with that he turned her again, returning her body to the cradle of his with one big hand cupping her breast and the other splayed across her belly. His mouth was at her ear. "Prop your top leg on mine," he said, sliding his knee between hers.

The position slightly spread her labia, the room's air cool on the fevered, still damp flesh. Cilla's chest tightened and a hot chill ran down her back. "Um, Ren..."

He tenderly kneaded her breast as the other hand crept lower. "Your clit's very sensitive right now, isn't it?"

Cilla shivered again, finding the question both highly embarrassing and incredibly erotic. *Clit.* She'd never even thought the word in her head, but hearing it in his dark male voice made her nipples go hard. He laughed as if he knew, tweaking one, then plucking the other.

"You're sensitive all over," he continued. "So I'll be careful with you, princess. So careful until you come once more in my hand."

She didn't breathe as Ren's questing fingers drifted past her bare mons. "I like that you wax," he said. "I like how there's nothing between me and your skin."

On a moan, Cilla buried her hot face in the pillowcase. She caught the fabric with her teeth when he used his thumb and forefinger to expose the nub of flesh at the top of her sex. It throbbed, the whole area below her belly button super-sensitized. Her inner muscles clenched on nothing and she ached to be filled there.

His free hand shifted from her breast to her mouth. "Wet my fingers, baby. Lube them up for me."

She might climax just from listening to him! But when his fingertips pressed between her lips, opening her there, too, she drew them into her mouth and rolled her tongue along and over them.

"Yeah, girl," Ren praised, then pulled them free. In an instant they were rolling over her sweet spot in very light, lazy little circles. And in an instant she was moaning, pleading, so turned on she could barely hear herself over the fast *whoosh whoosh whoosh* of blood in her ears.

"Ren." She needed him to give firmer pressure, to kiss her, to do something more. Her hands grasped his forearms, trying to communicate the fervency of her desire. "*Ren.*"

"Baby," he said, scolding a little. "Take your hands away...or do I need to tie them up?"

Cilla froze, her heart pounding against her breastbone.

His whisper was hot against her ear. "I did promise you an education, didn't I?"

One-by-one, her fingers loosened their hold. She'd die, just die, if he took control that way.

Die of passion-overload.

He laughed. "Next time." And then he was kissing her neck and toying with her sex with his clever hands and she was rocking against his big body behind hers, his jeans and shirt grazing her nakedness. The sound of her panting filled the room and she was reaching, reaching, but her senses were charged to such a degree that they held her up on a wave of pleasure so strong she thought it would prevent her from tipping over into bliss.

"Let go, baby," Ren whispered in his dark voice. "Let go, baby, because then I'm going to fill you up and fuck you good."

His teeth closed over the lobe of her ear and she tumbled, falling into a breath-stealing, pulse-pounding, oh-yes-I-am-dying orgasm.

Stunned by the force of it, she lay boneless as Ren rose to stand near the end of the bed while he efficiently undressed.

It was enough to rouse her. Without a qualm, Cilla ogled him shamelessly. For so long she'd considered herself not a highly sexualized being, but as Ren was revealed to her she discovered she'd been all wrong in her thinking. His body fascinated her. He stripped off his shirt and her belly fluttered at the sight of his dark tattoo, its primitive design only highlighting the strength of him, the male architecture of his shoulders and pectorals and biceps. Her gaze dropped to his flexing forearms, the long muscles of them moving as they worked at his jeans then pushed both the denim and his boxers away.

Her gaze took in his penis. With her past few lovers—okay, two—she'd politely kept her gaze trained away from that area, but with Ren...with Ren she didn't feel polite at all. She stared at the stiff column of flesh, the veins that traced over it, the large cap, heavy and swollen. His testicles were fascinating to her too, she realized. So full and potent-looking. Manly.

All of him completely...male.

His right hand gripped his shaft, his thumb ghosting over the head. "Like what you see, princess?" His fist swept down, to the root, then below, his fingertips tracing his balls.

She shivered and she knew he could see it because he

laughed, low and wicked while he caressed himself again. Then he stalked closer, his knees brushing the end of the mattress. Without conscious thought, primal instinct sent her scooting away until her shoulders hit the headboard.

With one knee on the bed, Ren paused, his gaze trained on her face, his eyes narrow. "Baby...we can halt everything right now."

Cilla stared at him, the bones and the muscles, the lean power in his body. Hers, if she wanted it. To touch, to kiss, to take into her body. The prospect nearly rendered her speechless. Maybe she'd always held back with her previous two lovers because she didn't know how to reach out, how to connect, how to actually be *with* someone. But fear or shyness or inexperience wasn't going to stop her this time. Not when it was Ren.

"Yes," she said.

"Yes, we should stop?" His voice was soft.

"No. I mean yes." Cilla shook her head, aware she was confusing him. Her arm lifted. "Yes, I want you," she said, pointing to him. A gleam came to his eye and his smile was that delightful, wicked, thrilling, dangerous Ren smile. From somewhere, a condom appeared in his hand.

Cilla shivered as he rolled it down his erection. Cock, she admonished herself. That's Ren's *cock*. "And I want that," she said, aiming her finger a little lower. "Definitely that."

He laughed again. "Oh, baby. You'll definitely get that."

Then he was on the bed with her, crawling between her legs which sprawled to invite him in of their own accord. Her heart pounded, her mouth was dry, but as she drew in ragged breaths she drew in Ren, the salty, spicy smell of him, the assurance of him, the absolute gorgeousness of him.

The head of his cock brushed the wet and willing entrance to her body. "What are you thinking?" he whispered.

"Gorgeous," she whispered back. "You're so gorgeous."

And then he buried his face in her neck as he pushed into her body. She sucked in a breath—he was big and she was still swollen from her orgasms—and willed herself to open for him. Her body's protest was token, because the slow slide, the thick pressure of his entry felt so good.

He groaned, his breath hot on her skin. "God, Cilla."

Yes, they both wanted this.

She forked her hand in his hair and wound one leg over his hips. He slid in another crucial distance and they both moaned.

"Are you good?" he whispered against her ear, his body still over hers.

Hot tears pricked as she realized he was waiting for her to adjust to him inside her. "Oh, yeah," she said against his hard, bristly cheek. "I'm very, *very* good."

Then he began to move. It was an age-old rhythm, she supposed, but it felt wholly new to Cilla, because it was Ren rocking into her body, Ren's cock she squeezed down upon, Ren's flesh that went hot and damp under her hands as they roamed his back.

She tilted her hips, an instinctive move to take him deeper, and his next moan was low and dark. Her eyes closed and she reveled in the feel of him against her skin, inside her body. One hand stayed in his hair and the other squeezed his shoulder as his palms slid under her bottom to cradle her.

His strokes went from glides to something harder. Faster. More desperate.

Still, it all felt magical to Cilla. Her fantasy. Ren

Colson in her bed and in her body. She was a woman who worked her imagination—or her work *was* her imagination—each costume make-believe. And this was just like that...she was in the dream zone, floating on the awesomeness of it. She tightened her arms and legs around him.

Then Ren moved his mouth from her neck to bite her lower lip.

Cilla's back bowed. Dream became urgency. Floating became striving. She lifted into his driving body, taking, taking, taking. Accepting the masculine penetration with every cell. From somewhere far away, she heard a whimper.

It was hers. Needy. Needing.

Ren lifted up, repositioning so her thighs were over his and he could still plunge into her but he had access to more of her. That knot of nerves.

Catching her gaze, he wet the fingertips of his right hand with his tongue. Then, planting his left palm to the mattress, he hovered over her, fucking her like she'd asked, while he played with her clit like it was his favorite toy. She felt the pleasure gather, and her inner muscles clamped onto his cock. He groaned, but didn't change a thing.

Kept driving.

Kept toying,

And then she shattered, her body jolting upward to take everything she could get of Ren.

She saw the fingers of his left hand clench the sheet and then he was jabbing in short strokes, never quite leaving her body.

Thank God.

His jaw went tight, his eyes squeezed shut, and then he found his own pleasure on a groan that sounded pulled from his soul.

When it was over, when he'd pulled out of her while kissing her shoulder, then gone to the bathroom—condoms, what a PITA—he returned to gather her into his arms. Cilla let her eyes drift close, skipping over the PITA-condom issue to return to the fantasy world of Cilla and Ren together in bed.

She sighed, snuggling her cheek into his chest. Probably there were consequences, but not now. Not when her body was sated and her senses so full.

"Tomorrow," Ren murmured into the hair at the top of her head.

"Mmm." She dismissed whatever he meant by that. There was no tomorrow. Only tonight. This moment. This fanciful, pleasurable instant in time. Why couldn't a rock princess adopt some of the hedonistic ways of her rock 'n' roll father?

Ren wrapped his free hand around his mug of coffee and stared out the kitchen window as his assistant chattered in his ear. It was late morning in L.A. and since London was eight hours ahead, he'd caught her at home when her official work day was over. Still, Raina sounded much more energized than he felt. Of course, she was the antithesis of the cool Brit stereotype and ran his office in Pimlico with cheerful verve and not a small amount of cheek.

"...if you would only take the time to read the company Facebook page—"

"Raina, you know I hate social media."

"Yes, but it's all right there. Where the bands are, which of our operatives are traveling with—"

"Operatives?" He laughed. "You've been reading too much spy fiction."

On the other side of the line was a long pause. "Hmm," Raina said, and he could picture her short dreadlocks twitching as she tilted her head as well as the speculative gleam in her dark brown eyes. "You laughed. You almost sound...relaxed. What's going on?"

"I don't know what you're talking about." *Except last night I got laid.*

"You got laid," Raina announced, a wide smile in her voice. "You found some starlet and stuck it to her good."

"I didn't find any starlet."

"A surfer girl, then."

"No."

"One of those rollerbladers that skate on the beach boardwalk. What's that famous one—Vienna Beach?"

Ren shook his head. "Venice Beach. And whether she rollerblades or not—" Lack of sleep had made him sloppy, he thought with a mental groan.

Raina cackled in delight. "Well, enjoy yourself, luv," she said. "You've got nine more days before you're on a plane heading back home."

Grimacing at his own stupidity, he signed off to the sound of her continued laughter. He took a long slug of coffee. "Home" in nine more days.

On their own, his feet moved him down the hall to the room where Cilla still slept. She was belly-down in bed, her arms under the pillow and her face obscured by the fall of her beautiful hair. Her shoulders were bare and he remembered pressing a kiss to one as she lay on her side nestled in the curve of his body.

Uneasiness crept over him, tightening his neck muscles. He massaged them with his free hand, trying to dissipate the vague sense of impending doom that he'd also experienced the night before. Damn, this wasn't his typical morning-after attitude.

Post-coital worries were new to him.

But they shouldn't surprise him, because he was post-coital with *Cilla*.

Cilla, who'd proved beyond the need for mentoring.

Cilla, who'd come apart in his arms, her blue eyes going wild, her face flushing a gorgeous pink, her body trembling against his.

Cilla, who'd pressed a kiss to his palm and shaken something loose inside him.

Maybe she felt the weight of his gaze, even in sleep, because she stirred now. He leaned against the doorjamb and let himself enjoy the process of her coming awake. Under the covers, her toes stretched toward the end of the bed. One hand crept from beneath the pillow to push the hair off her face.

Her lips were rosy and still swollen from his kisses. Beard burn appeared as a faint rash around her mouth and along her throat and Ren ran his hand over his now-smooth jaw, wishing he'd taken the time to shave the night before. Yet his dick was going hard at the sight of how he'd marked her, primal beast that it was.

She opened her eyes and they stared, unfocused, at the vicinity of his knees. Then her gaze traveled upward—shit, over the growing bulge in his jeans—to finally land on his face. He saw the awareness of all they'd done the night before dawn over her.

Her eyes widened and she grabbed at the sheet to pull it close. It was too late for modesty, everything about her body, from her pale nipples to the tight clasp of her slick pussy, was etched forever onto his brain, but he wisely kept his mouth shut. She looked spooked enough as it was.

"Um, good morning," she said.

"Time to get up, sleepyhead," he returned. "You slept through breakfast." While he, on the other hand, had barely closed his eyes as he struggled with a dilemma nearly all night long. "Home" in nine more days.

Her gaze shifted to his hand. "Is that coffee?" she asked hopefully.

He put the mug behind his back. "Not until you get up and at 'em. I'm taking you someplace for lunch, so you need to start moving."

Places to go, baby. People to see. Problem to solve.

In an hour they'd made it to a beachside neighborhood. He pulled into a free spot in a narrow public lot that looked out onto sand, with houses on either side. It was foggy here at the coast and a weekday, so they shared the parking with just two other cars.

Cilla sipped at her extra-large latté as he dug into the bag for the roast chicken-and-veggie wraps that he'd purchased for their lunch. As he handed one to her she stole a quick glance at his face—she'd been avoiding his eyes. "Is this someplace special?" she asked, gesturing toward the beach on the other side of the windshield with her paper cup.

He shrugged. "I wanted to get a closer view of the Pacific," he half-lied. It was a dramatic sight that day, the waves slamming into the steep shoreline with angry vigor. Two surfers were out beyond the break, sitting up on their boards in black neoprene, their dangling legs shark-bait.

Ren and Cilla both watched the action, eating their food in silence. When one of the men took off on a ride, from the corner of his eye he saw her suck in a quick breath, then hold it until the surfer cut right and slid back down the lip to paddle out again.

"You used to surf," she said, her gaze still trained ahead.

"Still do," he said. "I prefer it without wearing a wetsuit...so I hold out for warm water most of the time."

Another silence welled between them.

Her wrap dropped to the white butcher paper in her lap. "I feel like an idiot," she blurted. "A gauche idiot."

Shit. "Cilla, no." He'd wanted to make things better for her by taking her to bed, not worse. It was his rationale for last night. It was his reason for today. The fixer in him coming out again, he supposed. A habit from all the years handling thorny issues that came up on the job.

Turning to her, he gazed on her profile, noting the clear distress in her expression. "Can't you look at me?"

"I'd rather not," she confessed, though she flicked him a quick glance. "This part is weird for me."

"What part?"

"The morning-after thing."

"Maybe we should think of this as that 'afterplay' you wondered about." He noted another stolen glance. "You know, to take any heaviness out of the situation."

"I don't want heaviness."

"Me neither," he said. "We're both on the same side of this, right? Neither of us has illusions about the future."

"Right."

"So for afterplay, we can re-hash the night a little bit. It was fun, don't you think? I had fun." Shit again. Because when he thought back to it, "fun" didn't quite cover those hours, her pleasure rising and peaking three separate times.

But Cilla's mouth was moving upward in a smile. "I suppose. Especially when I stole that pillow out from under you. I'm sorry, but I do need three to get truly comfortable."

Despite her being a pillow hog, they'd managed to find a very comfortable twining of limbs. He could have slept that way if her vulnerability and his temporary status at the compound hadn't gnawed at his peace of mind. But he didn't share that. Instead he drew a knuckle over her warm cheek. "You can have as many pillows as you need."

And the smile she turned on him should have been warm enough to burn the fog from the sky. "Thanks, Ren."

He caught her hand and brought it to his lips. "Any time, baby."

A knock on the driver's side glass startled him. He glanced over then dropped Cilla's fingers and pressed the button to unroll the window. Salty air rushed in, as well as the voice of one of her brothers. Bing or Brody were nearly identical and Ren couldn't tell them apart after all these years. "This looks cozy," one of the twins said.

His brother stood at his shoulder, an eyebrow rising. "Hey, sis," he added, but his gaze was on Ren.

She made a little sound of surprise, then she was out of the car, running around the trunk to practically leap on her brothers. "What are you guys doing here?" she demanded.

Ren exited more slowly. With the door shut behind him, he leaned against its cool metal side.

The twins allowed Cilla's hug, squeezing her in return, though their attention was still trained on Ren. When she moved a little away, he held out his hand to each of them in turn. Their grips were strong, their eyes cool. "Colson," one said. The corner of the other's mouth lifted in a half-smile. "Renford."

He appreciated their watchfulness—it was what he was counting on, after all. "Good to see you, Brody, Bing."

They were big men, about the same size as him, and their rugged bodies and tanned skin he assumed came from their careers in construction. Though they ran their own business now, he figured they'd spent plenty of time with carpenter bags slung around their hips.

"What are you doing here?" Cilla asked again, tugging on the sleeve of one's shirt with a logo reading "Double B

Construction" embroidered over the left pec.

"Uh..." A twin's gaze moved from his sister's face, to his brother, to Ren.

"I was gathering the nine's contact info," Ren put in, lying like a rug. "Once I got Cami's, I figured I should get the rest of the rock royalty. When I talked to your brothers, we cooked up this surprise for you. They said they hadn't seen you in a while." He'd actually told them it was imperative they get together because Cilla was having a problem they needed to be made aware of.

But her eyes were shining with the pleasure of the meeting, so he didn't let a shred of guilt enter his conscience. "It's definitely been too long," she said. "Weeks."

Ren couldn't fault the brothers for it, though he wanted to. He was just as bad with his sibs. Much worse, actually.

"But why the beach?"

Cilla hadn't let go of her brother's sleeve, and damn if that didn't do something to his chest. His ribs were squeezing down on his heart. "They're working on a house nearby," he said, nodding to the place next door. It was in the throes of construction, with red tiles stacked on the roof and scaffolding covering the outside walls. "Thought I'd get my Pacific fix and see them at the same time."

"Will you show it to me?" Cilla looked from one twin to the other. "I'd love to see your work."

"Yeah?" Brody smiled down at his sister. Ren remembered now that he had a scar under his eye, an accident involving a feral cat and a boy's love for animals. "Well, come see then."

She linked elbows with her brothers as they led her out of the parking lot.

Once through the fence surrounding the property, they

picked their way around construction debris and into the frame of the large, two-story house. "Wait until you get a load of the view from the upstairs deck," Brody said, pointing toward a set of stairs that at the moment were mere plywood treads without newels or handrails.

As she mounted the first step, Ren managed to catch Bing's eye. The other man glanced over at Cilla, still moving upward, and back at Ren. With a lift of his chin, he indicated the great room beyond the foyer. "Show me around the first floor, Bing. We can catch up with them later."

His brows shot up, but he followed Ren toward a large space that he assumed would ultimately be the kitchen. It led to another expansive room with a wide glass door leading to the backyard. They halted there, both looking out across a scruffy patch of grass that was littered with more construction detritus.

Unsure how to begin, Ren shoved his hands in his pockets. "Business good?"

"Business is great," Bing said. "You're doing well in London?"

"Yeah. Just here for another week or so."

"At the compound with Cilla."

Ren glanced over, but couldn't read Bing's expression—did he suspect something was going on between them? "Like I told Brody when I called, Bean wanted me to check over the place and when I got there, I found Cilla in residence. As I said, I'll be leaving soon, and I'm worried about her staying there alone." He went on to tell him about the two Lemons fans who'd scaled the wall.

Bing shook his head. "Shit. I'm glad you could handle that. We'll see about talking her into returning to her place."

Ren now knew why she didn't sleep in her small

house's master bedroom. That's where she'd been when the ex let himself in. "She might not be easy to convince." He hesitated. "There's more that concerns me."

"Like what?" Then Bing put up a broad hand. "I should warn you, we don't make a habit of sticking our noses into each other's affairs."

Yeah, Ren got that. The rock royalty were all similar in that way. But this needed to be said. "It's about the man she was seeing."

Bing frowned. "I really don't want to hear about that."

Ren looked him straight in the eye. "Too bad. You're hearing it." His fury rekindled as he told him about Tad. Not all of it, of course, not the porn suggestion or the bad-in-bed thing—which was crap as Ren well knew—but he explained how the ex didn't accept the break-up and how he'd let himself into Cilla's bedroom and cut her hair while she slept.

Bing snapped straight and he stared at Ren, his blue eyes going hot. "*What*? I thought it was just a new style she'd chosen. He cut her *hair*?"

"Shh." Ren glanced over his shoulder to ensure she was nowhere in sight. She'd not appreciate him spilling her secrets.

Bing lowered his voice to a furious whisper. "Who the fuck does something like that?"

"A guy I'd be happy to kill, but Cilla's not so much in favor."

"She doesn't still care for him, does she?"

"No." Ren shook his head. "But I don't trust him not to come sniffing around again. So you gotta keep your eye out for that once I'm gone too."

"Okay." Bing blew out a long breath. "Right."

"Good." Relief was a cool balm over Ren's smoldering anger. *Problem solved.*

Bing turned his gaze out the sliding door, then looked back at Ren, his eyes assessing. "So what's your stake in this?"

He blinked. "Uh..." What the hell could he say? Since forever, he'd kept himself distant from the other Lemon kids and their concerns. "Well—"

"Ren?" Cilla's voice called from upstairs. "Where are you and Bing?"

Saved by the bell. Ren turned back and hurried through the almost empty space in her direction. She was coming down the steps, one hand trailing along the unfinished sheetrock wall. Preoccupied with his "surprise," he hadn't noticed what she was wearing until now. Another vintage band T-shirt, somehow looking feminine and Cilla-sized, with a denim skirt that flared at the top of her knees and revealed an old scar on her right leg. The size of a half-dollar, it was slightly raised and a tone or two darker than her creamy skin. A bit of road rash, he thought, from a fall or a bike accident.

Her voice sounded in his head. *I barely learned to ride a bicycle.*

Because Mad Dog couldn't stir himself to be a father. Because her brothers were occupied with their own interests. Ren hated to think of this beautiful rock princess being ignored, being overlooked, doing without. The image of her falling, hurting, being unhappy for one damn minute was suddenly more than he could bear. His ribs did that new trick of theirs, contracting until his heart was squeezed toward his throat. A ridiculous, dangerous drive to protect her surged through him.

"Ren?" Her voice sounded uncertain

He sure the hell didn't know how to control the raw emotion that was likely showing up as a savage expression on his face. He felt wild with...with something.

His gaze lifted toward her.

She caught his look, mid-step. It must have startled her, because she seemed to be trying to move back at the same time as her body was in forward motion. The conflict put her off balance and he saw her wobble, begin to pitch.

She wasn't far from the ground, but she wasn't going to take a spill. Not when Ren rushed forward to capture her in his arms. Her fingers bit into his shoulders, he heard her sharp intake of breath, and he sensed her pounding heart with her breasts just inches from his face. For a long moment they held each other like that, close, too close, then realizing the audience, he let her slide down his body until her feet touched down.

Clearing her throat, she stepped back and sent him a vaguely aimed smile. "Clumsy me," she said. "Thanks."

"Welcome," he muttered, turning away so he could no longer see the pretty flush on her face. Instead, he caught the identical suspicious expressions on those of her brothers'. *Fuck.*

Now he cleared his throat. "We should get going, Cilla. I bet Bing and Brody have things to do."

She seemed just as eager to make a getaway after doling out another quick round of hugs to the twins. Then the other two men walked them back to the Beemer. Brody held her door and bent down to say a few words to her through her open window.

Bing rapped a peremptory knuckle on Ren's. As the glass slid down, the other man got in his face. His voice was quiet, but deadly serious. "I heard what you said about her ex, Ren. But we better not have to protect her from you, too."

Ren kept his mouth closed and merely released the brake to drive away. Because he could only hope the same damn thing.

Chapter 10

Cilla fought her fidgets the entire way back to Laurel Canyon after their beach lunch and then a grocery run. Although Ren had eased some of her new-lover nerves with their "afterplay," the idea of being alone with him in the compound again remained unsettling. Where did they go from here? He had several days (and nights) left in California and were they going to spend them sharing a bed...or no?

Asking that question aloud was not an option. She couldn't risk looking foolish or presumptuous so she was just going to have to live with her discomfort until she could figure it out from his signals—or lack of them.

It was somewhere between four and five o'clock in the afternoon when they turned off Laurel Canyon Boulevard and wound through the streets toward the gated entrance that led to the Lemons' houses. As they neared, Ren swore, and Cilla took her gaze off her lap and looked up.

A cute little green Mini Cooper sporting a black racing stripe was parked on the shoulder of the narrow road. Two slender, dark-haired teenagers, one a boy, one a girl, had their hands curled around the wrought iron rungs and were peering through them.

Ren steered to the side, braked, then jerked the car into Park. "Wait here," he murmured, then vaulted out of his seat, to take brisk strides toward the pair. They spun to confront the clearly annoyed man.

Through the windshield, Cilla tried to read the situation. He appeared to bark out something and the teenagers looked at each other for a beat, then the girl stepped forward. Whatever she said had Ren jolting back.

New concern poured a dose of adrenalin into Cilla's bloodstream and she put her hand on the door. But Ren was already stalking back. The kids moved toward their car.

The air inside the Beemer seemed to crackle as he slipped inside, bringing with him a dark energy. His hands gripped the steering wheel, but he didn't say a word to her, just stared out the windshield. Then, in a flurry of movement, he started the car and swung back into the lane as the gate to the compound slid open.

Their car nosed through and wide-eyed, Cilla took in that the Mini Cooper was following. "Who's that?" she asked, gesturing over her shoulder with her thumb.

"My mother's other kids," he rumbled, his expression stony. "They want to talk."

Ren didn't appear any happier about the situation as they walked into Gwen's house, the teens at their heels. Cilla dropped the bags of groceries she carried on the kitchen counter beside the ones that Ren set down. "Um..." she said, looking at his still-tight expression. "If you don't mind unloading the food," she began edging out of the room, "I'll just go to my bedroom."

Ren's hand clamped around her wrist. "You stay," he said. Then he pointed to the kids. "Cilla, that's Nell and

Clark Holzman. Nell and Clark, this is Cilla Maddox."

They sketched a couple of waves. Since her right arm was still commandeered by Ren, she gestured to the kitchen table with her left and smiled. "Would you like to sit down? I can get you something to drink."

With low murmurs of assent, Nell and Clark took the few short steps to the chairs. The girl was older than her brother, sixteen or seventeen to his fifteenish. Each looked both shy and excited and they kept darting glances at the brother they'd never met before today.

Once they were seated, Ren let her go so he could fold his arms across his chest. He leaned against the countertop. "First," he said, gazing at them with cool eyes. "Does your mother know you're here?"

"Um..." Nell glanced at Clark.

"That's it," Ren said, straightening. "You need to go back where you came from."

"Our dad knows," Clark said quickly. "He said it was okay."

"And it was Mom who told us about you," Nell added.

One of Ren's brows rose. "Really?"

"After that lady, Guinevere Moon, died," she said. "Mom was crying at the breakfast table one morning—she'd just read the obituary in the paper—and it all came out."

"I guess they knew each other back in the day," Clark put in.

Cilla busied herself putting ice in glasses and pouring out soda. When she placed the drinks in front of each kid they immediately gave their thanks. Studying them, she caught their resemblance to Ren. It was around the eyes and in the angle of the chin and it made her send them another reassuring smile.

On her way back to the grocery bags, she trailed her

fingertip along Ren's forearm. "Can I get you anything?"

He shook his head, though his focus remained on the young people. "How'd you find this place?"

"Dad knew that too," Clark offered. "And we thought you might be here because on the Facebook page for your company it said you were in California."

Ren muttered something that might have been, "Damn Raina."

"But we didn't have your cell number so we decided to go for a drive," Nell said.

"Why today?" Ren asked.

Clark set his glass of soda down on the table. "Because of my class project for social studies. I have to do a family tree."

"Let me give you some advice, kid," Ren said, grimacing. "Your mom won't want my name to show up on any of her branches."

The boy nodded. "Dad explained that." His head ducked down, then he looked up again. "'Youthful indiscretion,'" he said, making air quotes with his fingers. Then he grinned, looking so much like his big brother that Cilla's heart rolled over like a puppy.

"My mom sure doesn't seem like someone who hung out with rock 'n' rollers," the boy continued. "Now she listens to opera and shit."

Nell knocked her younger brother on the shoulder. "Don't swear. What's he going to think of us?"

Clark looked unrepentant as he rubbed at the spot. "I bet he knows his share of four-letter words." He transferred his gaze to Ren. "Right?"

Instead of answering the question, the man had one of his own. "You care what I think of you?" he asked, in a bemused tone.

Cilla glanced over, understanding his puzzlement. It

had to be weird to have these unexpected family members actually reaching out to him. But weird in a good way, she hoped, for his sake.

"Sure we care," Clark answered with a nonchalant shrug. "I mean, we're related."

"We don't have another big brother," Nell said. "It's just you."

Cilla's heart did another roll.

Clark picked up his glass. "And you're, like, famous."

"I'm not the Lemons," Ren said immediately.

"No. Because of your company," Nell said. "We've been reading all about it on Facebook. Those tours you manage. The operatives that work for you."

"Raina," Ren muttered again. "Operatives."

"It sounds cool to us," the girl said. "You should tell us everything about it—I know you organized Heartbeat's latest tour." A flush crawled up her neck. "Not that I'm into boy bands anymore."

Their big brother's lips twitched and his body seemed to relax. His arms dropped to his sides, then he paced to the table and pulled out a chair. "Instead of talking about that, what do you know of your grandfather? Your mother's father?"

The teens looked at each other. "He died," Nell said. "We never met him."

Ren smiled at them. "Let me tell you about the first time I did..."

It was then that Cilla tiptoed away, determining the situation was stable. In the master bathroom, she filled the oversized tub and threw in bath salts. Immediately, the scent settled her down. It was a combination of sweet lavender and lemon and reminded her so strongly of Gwen that she smiled at her reflection in the mirror while she undressed and gathered her hair at the back of her head with a flat clip.

The older woman would love Ren meeting with his mother's other children. She was all about connections, being part of a group, and the nine, frankly, had in ways large and small failed her in that.

As Cilla slipped into the hot water, she sighed, willing the day to float away. But as she rested her head against the porcelain, she decided she didn't want to lose everything about it. There'd been that moment in the car at the beach when Ren kissed her fingers after she'd confessed her discomfort.

Then her brothers. It was great to see them, and she resolved to not allow so much time to pass between visits. Yes, they weren't extremely close, never had been, but thinking of Ren with his two brand new siblings...well, it reminded her she shouldn't squander the ones she had.

And before the lunch and the twins...there was waking up in the bed where she'd spent the night with the man she'd fantasized about since she was old enough to dream about boys. How amazing was that?

Not to mention the amazement of the night before. The bathwater swished, bubbles popping as her legs moved, restless with memories. Truth, she was a little sore between them, but it only served to make her memory sharper and her more aware of how lovely the warmth felt against sensitive tissues. Sensitive tissues that Ren had mastered.

She shivered, noting the way her nipples tightened and were poking above the level of the water. Without thinking, her hand moved, her palm rubbing against the nub of flesh. The gentle graze felt good, and she squeezed her thighs together to savor the sweet spasm that occurred between them at her own touch.

Closing her eyes, she imagined Ren in the tub behind

her, her back against his broad chest, her body bracketed by his long, muscled legs.

His hand plucking her nipples.

His fingers sliding into that hot cove where he'd entered her the night before.

The water rippled as she shivered again.

Then, suddenly self-conscious, her eyes popped open and she moved her hands away from erogenous zones. If anyone could see her face, surely her cheeks would be fire-engine red.

But no one could see her.

Who would know if she indulged in a bathtub shared with a fantasy-Ren? Her hips tilted, her bottom sliding against the foundation of the tub. Even that sensation—slick against skin—made excitement shiver through her. She closed her eyes again, let her legs part, and feathered her fingers down her ribs and over her belly, intent on stroking away the last of her tension.

But when she touched herself, her mind flew back to the night before. To Ren's big hand, his sure way of handling her—and to the thought that it might be him in her bed again this evening. Did she want to enjoy this spike of desire alone, or...

Did she want him?

Without answering the question, Cilla finished up in the bath. Wash cloth in hand, she swept her skin clean with efficient movements and then she was out of the water and onto the mat, drying herself with a thick towel. She studied her reflection in the mirror again as she gently abraded her flesh. Her whole body was warm, sensitized, and her eyes looked huge.

With the towel hung to dry, she pulled on a pair of panties and her short terry robe then gave herself a last inspection. She looked flushed. Ready. Wanting.

Yes, wanting Ren.

Exiting the bathroom, she tilted her head, listening to determine what was happening in the rest of the house. It was preternaturally quiet. The teenagers were gone, she decided. And Ren? Perhaps he was kicking back with a beer, enjoying the memory of talking with his previously unknown sibs.

Or maybe enjoying the memory of being with her the night before.

Stomach fluttering, Cilla padded out of the bedroom toward the kitchen. All was dark. Hmm. Had he left the house as well?

But as she made her way into the kitchen, she saw him, a darker shadow in the shadows. He swigged a beer as she crossed the threshold. Something about the vibe in the room made her pause and her belly tighten. "Are you all right?"

"No," he said, his voice low, and there was an aggressive edge to it.

All the tension that she'd tried to release was back, big time. "What's wrong?"

"Go away, Cilla. You don't want to be around me now."

Chilled by his dismissive tone, Cilla was halfway back to the bedroom before she paused. Should she really leave him alone? Retreat was always her first choice, but what had hiding away given her? A pretty lonely existence.

Maybe this time she should take a cue from those kids and reach out. Ren had done her a favor last night, after all, so shouldn't she at least attempt to find out what was wrong and make him feel better?

Acting on the impulse, she quickly returned to the kitchen and without a word flipped on the light.

"Turn that off," Ren said, putting a shielding hand to his eyes.

"It's time to make dinner," she said, wrapping the butcher-style apron over her robe.

"I'm not hungry."

Oh, she knew this brooding mood of his. Ignoring him for the moment, she went about taking things from the refrigerator: cheese, green onion, avocado, tomato. From the small pantry she grabbed the tortillas. "Quesadillas coming right up," she said.

"I said I'm not hungry," Ren growled, getting to his feet.

She stepped close, and pushed him back to his chair with a hand on his chest. "Sit down."

His brows met over his nose as his ass hit the seat. "Bossy."

"Mmm." She opened a drawer to find the grater. "Now tell me what's going on."

"I'm a moody son-of-a-bitch."

"Tell me something I don't already know." She glanced over at him, saw he was picking at the corner of the label on his beer bottle. "Really, Ren. Am I going to have to track down those Holzman kids and give them a Cilla take-down?"

He looked up, a faint, almost-smile on his face. "What the hell is a Cilla take-down?"

An idea that made him look vaguely less unhappy. "You jumped to my defense over the Tad incident. Maybe I want you to know I have your back when it comes to Nell and Clark."

"They're not remotely the same thing, and this isn't about those teenagers."

"No?"

"No." He got up from his chair and went to the

refrigerator for another beer. Without asking, he pulled out a bottle of chilled wine and poured her a glass. "They're good kids. Liars, but good kids."

She sipped at the wine as he returned to his chair. "What did they lie about?"

"Their dad didn't give them permission to come to the canyon today, they confessed that just before driving home. He did say he'd make arrangements for us to meet some time if I agreed, but they weren't prepared to wait for that 'some time'."

"Or your agreement?"

He shrugged.

"Would you have said yes if contacted by their dad?" she asked, as she began grating the cheese.

Silence welled. "Probably not," he finally admitted.

"But you're glad you met them? You like them?"

"It sounds as if they have a good life. A good family. Clark made the junior varsity water polo and soccer teams as a freshman. Nell is vice-president of the dance club and runs cross-country. They vacation together, all four of them, and have been to eight countries. At their house in the 'burbs they have two dogs, two cats, and a pond with goldfish."

Cilla's brows rose. "You learned all that?"

"They apparently like to share."

Then he lapsed into another heavy silence. Biting her lip, Cilla continued dicing vegetables, unsure how to proceed. Maybe making dinner was enough.

She put the chopped tomatoes, chopped green onion, avocado slices, and grated cheddar in separate bowls. After locating the griddle, she slid it onto the burner. Then she looked over at Ren.

"Hey—" she started, but before she could get out another word, he was on his feet and exiting through the

French door to the adjoining courtyard.

Grr. Cilla looked down at her bare legs and then into the night darkness. He was out there, standing on the patio, hand in his pockets, head bent as if contemplating his toes. Alone, so alone.

With another glance at her naked legs, Cilla dashed down the hall to the bedroom. There, she pulled on a pair of cropped yoga pants and yanked some thick socks over her bare feet. Once she scurried back to the kitchen, she grabbed a jacket that hung on a hook by the door and let herself out into the night.

Ren made no comment when she stepped up beside him. Digging in her mental heels, Cilla continued to stand there, even as the cool temperature started to penetrate. She zipped up the jacket and shoved her hands in its side pockets.

The movement seemed to alert Ren to her presence. He half-turned, gave her a quick glance, then did a double-take. "What the hell do you have on?"

Cilla looked down at herself. Bulky socks. Flared-at-the-calf exercise pants under the short hem of her terry robe that was covered by the longer hem of the bib apron. Over that, the jacket. Now that she took a good look at it, she realized it was a puffy, silk, bomber-style favorite of Gwen's, with Mick Jagger's face printed across the front.

All right, fashion disaster, but she'd not come out here to be pretty. She'd come out here to find out what was troubling Ren.

"What's going on, huh?" she asked, touching his arm.

Instead of answering, he put a hand on each of her shoulders and turned her to face him. In the weak light coming from the kitchen, she couldn't read his expression, but his voice was soft. "I liked what you were wearing this afternoon, Cilla."

Her pulse skipped a beat. "Um, thanks."

"I like *you*, Cilla," he added, his hands tightening a moment. Then he spun her toward the French door and gave her a little push. "But right now I'd really like to be alone."

She took a forward step, then halted again. All their lives, he'd been much too solitary. Sucking in a bracing breath of the cool air, she turned around. "You can't get rid of me that easily."

"I can't seem to get rid of you at all," Ren said, his voice dry.

"You're right."

"Fuck, Cilla." He threw up his arms in an impatient gesture. "What do you want from me? What the *hell* do you want from me?"

"Show me what's behind that handsome mask of yours. Tell me about that dark place you go to and what drives you there."

Ren pushed his hands through his hair and folded them on top of his head. "Why?"

The zillion-dollar question. She hesitated and her heart started pounding in a fast, erratic rhythm. Her mouth felt dry and she had to blot her damp palms on the skirt of the stupid apron. "Because..." she started, and then had to swallow to lubricate her voice. "Because last night you gave something to me I needed. Maybe this is what you need. Someone to confide in. A sympathetic ear."

"Sympathy?" He barked out a sharp laugh. "You think *sympathy* will do me any good? You're wrong. Flat wrong."

She ignored her unsteady heart. "What will do you good then?"

With angry strides, he paced the courtyard. "A slap upside the head. A kick in the ass. Some fucking thing that will sweep all this shit out of my brain."

She swallowed, watching his agitated movements. "What shit is that, Ren?"

On his next turn, he stopped in front of her, glaring down. "All these unmanageable, infuriating, useless emotions swirling inside me."

"Name one."

He stared at her. "What?"

"You heard me. Name one." Her voice lowered. "I dare you."

"Fuck!" Ren spun away from her, spun back. "Grief," he ground out, bending close so they were almost nose-to-nose. "God damn it, I've been wallowing in a black hole of it for the last eleven months. How stupid, how pitiful is that? I've been grieving for a man who never even knew who the hell I was."

His grandfather. Oh, God. Oh, *Ren.*

Sucking in a breath, she held her ground. "All right. Name another."

His fingers curled into the collar of Gwen's Stones jacket and he gave Cilla a small shake. "Damn you," he said, then let her go. "Okay. Regret. Are you happy now? I'm filled with regret that tastes like acid on my tongue and burns like an ulcer in my belly because I didn't bother to make it back to say goodbye to the woman who was more a parent to me than anyone else."

Somewhere, Gwen was tearing up over this latest confession. Cilla felt a sting behind her own eyes. Blinking rapidly, she looked up at Ren's still-tense figure and told herself to stay strong. "Name one more," she said.

There was a long moment of charged silence. "Anger," Ren finally answered, and there was bitterness in his voice and fury radiating from his body. "I'm angry at the woman who gave birth to me."

"Of course you are."

He continued speaking as if Cilla hadn't uttered a word. "She gives those kids all that good stuff, stable home, nice vacations, family time. You know what she gave me?"

"What?"

His head dropped back and he stared at the sky. Then he returned his gaze to the ground. "When I was twenty, when I made that visit?"

"You went to her house in Pasadena."

"Yeah. After our little chat, after I realized she wasn't too thrilled about our reunion, as I was getting ready to leave she told me to wait." He took in a breath, let it out. "I was standing on the stoop, she'd already hustled me out of her house, and then she came back with a box she shoved into my arms."

The night seemed to quiet, waiting for him to continue. "What was in the box?" Cilla asked at last.

His back to her, he laughed again, a sharp, almost broken sound. "Dumb shit. A baby blanket. Some infant clothes. A rattle. I didn't even look at all of it, to tell the truth. I didn't need to examine all that was there to realize she didn't want a single reminder of me."

Cilla closed her eyes and Cami's mournful singing voice echoed in her head.

Motherless children have a hard time
When their mother is gone

Except Ren's mother wasn't gone in the same sense that Cilla's wasn't in her life. She supposed that on some level she held the comforting (and possibly deluded) idea that her mom might have returned to her if she'd lived. But the woman who'd given birth to Ren had chosen to keep herself apart from him.

Without a second thought, she took a step forward and put her arms around his waist from behind. Her cheek went to his spine as she felt him stiffen in her embrace. "Ren," she said, and turned her face to press a kiss to his shoulder blade. "God, Ren."

He remained rigid in her embrace for a long minute, then, in a lightning move, he turned, breaking her hold. Next, he yanked her to her toes and against him so his hot breath was on her cheek and his words were low and dark in her ear. "And you know what else I feel, Cilla?" he asked, clearly still in the clutch of that aggressive, bad mood. "I feel like another night of fucking you."

Though she knew what he actually wanted was to use sex as a way of feeling nothing at all, her defenses were shredded, her heart was aching, her body was already softening against the strength and heat of his.

"All right," she said, even knowing that another night with him risked making her feel much too much.

Ren's sharp edges had returned and the beast inside him was beating its chest, eager to work off the raging maelstrom. Cilla had said "all right," but he wondered if she really knew what she was in for.

Because he was going to screw her. Screw her good, as a way to get her out from under his skin.

Using his body, he herded her toward the house, even as he thrust his tongue in her mouth, his kiss heated and assertive. She responded like a fucking dream, her neck arching and her hands clutching his shoulders.

It didn't soften his mood or his intention.

Damn her for her digging and damn him for giving up what she'd demanded. Saying all that aloud, talking about his grief, his regret, his anger, had only served to wreak havoc with his ability to contain those feelings. She moaned as he ran his hands down her back to cup her ass, and she crowded closer, her belly rubbing against the hard cock behind his jeans. His hips responded with a involuntary thrust.

Fuck. The lust he had for her wasn't contained either.

Taking one hand off her ass, he twisted the knob and pushed her inside. She stepped backward into the kitchen. He followed, continuing to explore her mouth, then shoved the door shut with his foot. When he lifted his head to allow them breath, she tried to turn.

Ren caught her arm, jerked her close again. "Where are you going?"

Her mouth was wet, her breathing heavy. "The bed—"

"No bed." No bed, no bedroom, no more sleeping together. Ignoring her widening eyes, he unzipped the two halves of Mick's face and shoved the jacket from her shoulders. The apron went next, and he let it fall to the floor as well.

Underneath all that was a simple white robe, belted at the front. The sides had edged open, from his height giving him a partial glimpse of her breasts. He sucked in a breath, then crouched at her feet, his hands going under the terry cloth to find the waistband of her stretchy pants. Fingers tucked under the elastic, he pulled, catching a pair of panties along the way.

Her hand went to his shoulder for balance, and as he bared her lower half beneath the robe her lemon-sweet, bath-fresh scent hit him. There was another note to it— something more flowery—as well as the distinctive, creamy perfume of female arousal.

More lust crawled over his skin as heat surged through his veins. Her pants, panties, and socks were bunched at her ankles and he just stared at them, head bowed, the rest of him unmoving as he breathed in her lusciousness.

Perhaps she was even less patient than he, because she lifted one leg, stepping on the other's ring of clothes to free her foot. The action opened that knee and parted the lower edges of her robe. He could see it then, that dainty, denuded female triangle, at the moment all its mysteries closed to him. At the sight, he dropped to his knees.

Then, reaching out a hand, he cupped her, hearing her gasp as his long middle finger parted the soft groove. She gasped again, and a rush of wetness spilled. He used the lubrication to ease his penetration and his cock ached as her inner muscles clamped onto the intrusion.

"Ren," she breathed, his name a note of desperate desire.

"Draw up the robe," he ordered softly. "Bare yourself for me."

She made another sound, half-distress, half-acquiescence, and then reached down to pull at the fabric so it bunched at her waist. "Oh my God," she said, as he leaned forward.

His tongue met smooth, hot flesh and then it wiggled between the soft lips of her labia. They opened for him, unfurling in welcome, and he explored the petals with his mouth, the other hand cupping the curve of her ass to keep her in place.

Her taste flooded his mouth, both lemon sweetness and salt and cream, and he savored it, closing his eyes. He felt her fingers sift through his hair as he began to lap at her, tapping the nub of her clitoris at the top of her sex then dancing away from it. The scrape of her nails set goose bumps rolling down his back and he shuddered even as he flattened his tongue and pressed against the pink tissue.

She moaned, clearly wanting more, and he gave it to her by sliding his finger out of her hot channel then pressing another beside it before gliding back in. His light and easy rhythm had her legs trembling—or maybe that was the continued pressure of his tongue. With another little sound, she broke, her body moving against his mouth, pushing and grinding with her hips.

God, it was hot.

But more so when he went into new action, his tongue moving to her clit in a flurry of light, lashing strokes. Cilla made a strangled sound and her inner muscles clamped down on his fingers. He shoved them deep and held them there, then made his mouth go still too.

"Ren." She sobbed out his name and started moving once more, trying to get herself off on his tongue.

His fingers dug into the skin of her ass and then he withdrew his other hand from her and used it to cup the other cheek. Holding her in place, he let his mouth slide down the slippery furrow of her body and then he was fucking her with his tongue, spearing inside that hot, wet channel, her juices deliciously coating his lips and his tongue. He swallowed down her taste and his cock ached, the head throbbing.

His dick wanted to be in the paradise his mouth was now enjoying.

But first...Cilla.

He lifted his head, giving a little nudge to her clit with his nose, and then he went to town, lapping, toying, licking, playing. The tension gathered in her body, he could sense her muscles tightening, and then it was upon her and she made a low, keening noise. Her body quivered, once, twice, and then she was coming, as he pulsed his tongue against her sensitive knot of nerves.

Her hips were still rolling against his mouth when her

fingers fisted again in his hair. "Bed," she said in a hoarse voice. "I need you inside me."

But she didn't get to make the demands. She'd already gotten so much—too much—from him.

He jerked to his feet, taking in her flushed face and darkened eyes. Sometime during the oral play she'd flung away the robe. The terry cloth lay several feet away and he stepped over it as he lifted Cilla and boosted her onto the kitchen counter.

She made a surprised sound as her bottom met granite. He ignored it as he wrenched open his jeans and freed his cock. His fingers fished a condom out of his wallet and rolled it on. "Get your ass to the edge of the counter," he said, at the same time pulling her there himself. Her thighs widened to make room for his hips and he took one mind-blowing moment to look at the sight of her spread for him, her pink pussy lips open and glistening with wetness. Then he drove inside her in a single stroke, his hands tightening on her hips so she had no escape from him and his possession.

"Oh, God." His head dropped back as her swollen tissues encased him, so hot and so tight that each flutter of her inner muscles rippled down the length of his dick.

Her hands were tugging on his shirt and he lifted one hand to grasp the cotton between his shoulder blades and yank upward. When his chest was bared she leaned into it and kissed a trail along his collarbone and up his neck.

He drew back his hips, shunted inside her again, and felt the scrape of her teeth along his jaw.

That did it.

He speared his fingers in her hair at the back of her head and tilted her mouth for his kiss. The advance-and-retreat of his tongue and his cock were near-brutal, uncompromising, but she didn't protest. Instead, she wound her ankles at the small of his back, pulling him back to her each time he withdrew.

This was great. This was working, he told himself. Screwing her like this would put emotional miles between them. When he treated her like a mere toy for his pleasure, she'd distance herself from him. Crawl out from his head, separate from his skin.

Of course, he didn't need for her to make that move.

Detachment was what *he* did best.

But he couldn't think straight with his dick in the heavenly vice of her body and it was about to blow in three...two...one.

His hips pistoning, he tore his mouth away to suck in air. Pleasure rose high, twisted sharply, burned bright as it ripped through him. He groaned and yanked her tight against his groin as the climax pulsed...pulsed...pulsed.

When his brain could function again, her forehead was resting against his shoulder. He pinched her chin to take a look at her face, and at the flushed, slumberous expression a disconcerting, unwelcome surge of tenderness swept through him.

Fuck!

"Can we go to bed now?" she murmured.

"No," he said, adamant. "We've got more to do."

He had to keep her tentacles from winding around him.

"Okay," she said, drowsy but agreeable, and her fingertips brushed his bottom lip. "Whatever you say."

So he said they needed a shower and he let the water wake her up a little so he could do her again, his favorite this-is-just-fun position, her hands on the tile, her bottom pushed out, his cock once again tunneling within her. When she winced a little as he reached around to touch her clitoris, he gentled his caress until she was pushing back into his hips in clear sexual demand. Her mouth closed over her own forearm as she came, but he still heard the muffled cries.

After that round was over, his dangerous mood hadn't dissipated. Cilla was limp as a fading flower, however, so he decided they needed provisions before starting the next operation in extricating her from his psyche. With Cilla rewrapped in her terry robe, he deposited her in a kitchen chair. Barefoot and wearing only his jeans, Ren made those quesadillas she'd half-prepared.

Once he turned with a plateful of triangular pieces, it was to find her asleep in her seat, her head cradled on her arms braced on the table.

"Oh, Cilla," he murmured. She didn't stir and he just continued staring at her, the vicious feelings that had been riding him earlier evaporating. How could he possibly have found her some kind of threat? Why was he so worried she was a danger to him? With her tousled hair and her swollen mouth, she looked impossibly sweet and incredibly ravished.

He'd done that to her—ravished her, and all for the sake of putting distance between them, something that was going to happen anyway. Home, after all, in just nine days.

With quick movements, he stored the food. Tomorrow, he'd serve her mountains of calories to make up for what she'd lost out on tonight.

She was light in his arms. Her head went to his shoulder as one arm curled around his neck. He experienced that weird constriction once more in his chest, but he ignored it, telling himself it didn't matter because everything would be all right when he was on a big flying machine and heading to London courtesy of Richard Branson.

In the master bedroom, he placed her on the mattress,

then pulled back the covers on the other side and nudged her onto the sheets. He had to bend close to make that happen, and she did it again, she somehow had her arms and then her legs wrapped around him.

Cilla, you're a clinger.

I am not!

She sure as hell was.

Resigned, Ren let himself roll to the mattress beside her. He could fight her hold, he supposed, but he was tired too and it didn't seem worth it to summon the energy. Despite her hold on him, he managed to shed the jeans and then she settled with one arm and leg thrown over him. He reached to turn out the bedside lamp and then linked his arms around her and breathed in the citrus-blossom scent of her hair. His head settled into the pillow and he realized the sex bouts had done him some good.

With Cilla wrapped around him now, he felt mellow. Edginess only came about when he tried to resist her, he realized.

Right now, his emotions were not so loud in his head.

But the Cilla situation was not fixed. Not at all.

"I'm going to want you every night," he admitted to her sleeping form on a sigh.

Every night...but only until he was gone. Home in nine days.

Funny, how that certainty didn't dispel the getting-to-be familiar sense of loss.

Chapter 11

Cilla woke to the twittering of birds, to the pale yellow light of morning filling the bedroom, to the knowledge that she was in bed with Ren, cuddled close. Her cheek was pillowed on his chest, one of her arms was stretched across his abs, and her legs were tangled with his.

Oh, God.

She was *clinging* to him.

The undeniable fact of that sent a chill over her, starting from her naked shoulders and traveling all the way to her bare toes that were pressed to his warm shin. Her stomach folded in on itself and Cilla could only think of one thing: retreat.

The operation took long minutes. She held her breath as she eased away from him, raising her arm as if it went weightless, sliding her legs from his in miniscule increments, scooting her booty across the soft sheet one centimeter at a time. He slept on and she wanted to keep it that way.

When the soles of her feet found the carpet, she

tiptoed around, gathering fresh clothes, her toothbrush, toothpaste, and comb. At the doorway, she glanced back at Ren. He hadn't moved and she allowed herself a few seconds of silent admiration. One long arm was thrown over his head, his glossy hair lay disordered on the pillow, the sheet was gathered low on his belly to reveal more rippled muscles. In sleep he didn't look any less dangerous, especially with that gunslinger-stubble of dark whiskers around his mouth and jaw, but she felt a jot safer with those silver-green eyes closed. Unseeing.

After last night, she was afraid of what he might read on her face.

It had been crazy. Wild. She'd recognized his mood the instant he'd said he wanted to have sex again and what proceeded after that...she could still feel his kisses on her mouth, his mouth between her legs, his body thrusting inside hers.

But she was afraid he might have touched her even deeper.

Which was why retreat was imperative. Time to regroup. Get perspective.

She rushed to the hall bathroom and washed and dressed there, then made a pot of coffee. Steaming mug in hand, she let herself out of Gwen's house, trying to decide where to escape. Her eyes drifted across the compound and caught on the tower of the Castle—the name they'd given the house where she and Bing and Brody had grown up. The turret had been both playroom and refuge, and it called to her now.

But she'd have to go back inside the cottage to hunt up the key. The one to Gwen's storeroom was on the ring in her pocket and she had work to do there.

The space was quiet and again she was struck by the sense of the older woman's lingering presence. Cilla breathed deep of it, turning in a circle to run her gaze over the shelves of shoes and the racks of vintage costumes. Giving in to her need to touch, she picked up a pair of rhinestone-encrusted platform stilettos and ran her thumb over the bristly, "diamond"-studded surface. Then she walked them over to the room's single side chair and set her coffee onto the small adjacent table. On a whim, she kicked off her flat-soled TOMS, and indulged herself by strapping the sandals around her ankles. They wobbled as she stood, but she grinned as she caught sight of herself in the free-standing mirror propped in a corner of the room.

Paired with her jeans and a vintage Three Dog Night concert tee that she'd redesigned and reconstructed to womanly lines, the shoes made her look more hooker than musical act.

Of course, after last night...

Shoving those hours once more from her mind, she removed the shoes. But instead of replacing them on the shelf, she slid hangers along one of the racks, searching for the perfect pairing. It showed up in a polyester jumpsuit with stripes of white, black, and silver. A costume made for the Motown sound. She remembered that Gwen had showed her a stack of flat cardboard dress forms and she found them in another corner of the room, piled on top of a plastic bin. When she shifted them, she saw that Gwen had inked "REN" across the top of the box.

His inheritance.

Without allowing herself to speculate, she dragged the forms into the middle of the storeroom. Each had a kickstand of sorts, so that once dressed, the costume could be displayed upright. Motown was slipped over a form and then propped with the rhinestone platforms peeking out from the stovepipe pant legs.

Something about the sight lifted her mood. What

could be wrong when she had clothes to play with? She put together several other outfits, until the empty space in the middle of the room was peopled with a half-dozen forms dressed in pop-music chic. A "rocktail" party, she decided, grinning a little.

Going back to the racks, she did more exploring, the slight screech of metal hangers against metal pole like nails on chalk, raising the fine hairs at the back of her neck. Then she froze, her fingers clutching the clear plastic covering a beautiful, maxi-length vintage dress.

Gunne Sax. Gunne Sax *black label*. That meant it was from 1969, the year Jessica McClintock took over.

Cilla swooned. It was Renaissance-inspired, with a high, lace-edged collar that circled the back of the neck but was open at the throat to accommodate a square-shaped, low neckline that would offer a deep glimpse of décolletage. Made of a delicate, off-white cotton, the two halves of the gown's bodice was fastened by thin cord. A fall of lace trimmed the cuff of each long sleeve and another fell from below the bustline as a second, shorter overskirt.

What rock princess could resist trying it on?

On her just-over-average frame, the ruffled hem dragged on the ground like a train but that didn't mar the overall effect. Cilla swished back and forth in front of the mirror, admiring her reflection. It was an awesome dress. Nearly bride-like.

From its place by her mug, her cell phone rang. Cilla started, almost-guilt washing through her.

Guilty about what? she wondered, crossing to her phone.

The screen said it was her brother Brody. "Hey!" she greeted, in pleased surprise.

"Cill," he said. "What's up?"

"You called me," she answered, slightly puzzled. "Is something wrong?"

"Why would you ask that?"

"I just saw you yesterday," she pointed out.

"Yeah." He hesitated. "About that. Uh...Ren?"

In an instant he appeared in her mind's eye, lying naked in the bed. Then another image flashed, this time of Ren at her feet, drawing away her yoga pants and underwear so he could—

"Cilla?"

Blinking away the vision, she brushed her hair away from her hot cheek and avoided her own gaze in the mirror. "What did you say?"

"Bing and I...we're concerned about you getting in over your head with Ren."

Another wash of heat crawled up her neck. "I don't know what you're talking about."

"He seemed a little too interested in you yesterday. That's not good. Because really, let's face it, he's, uh, not your style."

Cilla bristled. "You mean I'm not *his* style, don't you?"

Brody's sigh gusted over the phone. "Look, I'm not an expert on the heart or anything..."

Rolling her eyes, Cilla tightened her fingers on her cell. "Yeah, Brody, you're no expert. How're things between you and your best pal, Alexa Alessio?"

"Lex? Why are you bringing up Lex?"

Because it only took a person with eyes in her head to understand that Alexa, her brother's running partner, next-door-neighbor, and the woman he treated like an asexual chum, was more than a little interested in the man. You could see it on her face when she was anywhere within Brody's vicinity.

You could see it on her face...

Stomach tightening into more origami folds, Cilla slowly slid her gaze back to her reflection, half-afraid to inspect her own features.

A new voice came over the phone, distracting her. "Cilla, it's Bing. First, leave Lex out of this. Second, we're trying to get a bead on this thing between you and Ren. We didn't even know you knew him before yesterday."

"I didn't know him, not really, not until he came back to the compound," she said. But now...now she knew so much. The severed connections in his life—with his siblings, his mother, with Gwen—all weighed so heavily upon him. Cilla thought of him feeding his grandfather bean soup. Of Ren sitting down with Nell and Clark, the children their mother was raising with such care. Of how after they'd departed, the grief and regret and anger had torn through him.

He'd turned to her...

Then turned her on.

Gave her the best night of her life, because...because...

He'd let her into his pain and because he'd given her pleasure and because due to both of those...

She'd tumbled into love with him.

Oh, Lord.

She was in love with Ren.

No! She thought instantly, rejecting the notion. It couldn't be that. This rock princess wouldn't be that foolish.

"Cilla?" Bing's voice sounded impatient. "Cilla?"

"I'll talk to you later," she said slowly, ignoring his sputters as she pulled the phone from her ear and ended the call.

Her gaze went to her reflection in the mirror and she met her own wide eyes. *Oh, hell. Have you done it?* she asked herself. *Have you gone ahead and fallen in love with Ren Colson?*

No, she answered. It couldn't be. Maybe halfway, if anything at all. But never the entire salami, right?

Wrong.

Before, when she was young and he was as remote as a movie star on the big screen, it had been girlish infatuation and teen fantasy. But then she'd woken to find him in her bed and he'd looked at her with those sage-and-silver eyes and, just like that, she'd begun her free-fall.

There'd been other accelerators to her descent: The I-believe-in-fairies episode at the Walk of Fame. The way he'd appeared at her side both times she'd been confronted by Tad at the music clubs. The surprise trip he'd arranged to re-connect her with her brothers (even though she found their meddling, at the moment, more than a bit annoying).

The times she'd made brooding Ren smile and even laugh.

The creak of hinges had her spinning toward the storeroom door. It wasn't latched, she realized. Her hands found each other at her waist, gripping tight. *Ren.*

Would he see it on her face?

For a brief moment she considered hiding in the racks of clothes. If there was a window, she would have dived through it, because she needed time to reverse the course of events and get her back to a solid place, where her two feet were planted firmly on the cliff of Not-Falling-For-Ren. But both were impossible, so she braced, pressing her lips together so as to not inadvertently blurt out the truth. She wouldn't tell him. She could never tell him.

A man stepped into the room.

Cilla jumped, her eyes going wide as she took in the man she'd not expected.

"Good morning, sweetheart," Tad Kersley said, and

let the door slam shut behind him.

Though cowardly instinct screamed at her to back away, Cilla didn't retreat and instead gave her ex a cold glance. "What are you doing here? How did you get in?"

His hands slid in his pockets and he sauntered into the room, taking a curious look at the clothes. "You told me about Gwen's collection. The other night when I chatted with Cami Colson at the bar, she happened to mention you were staying here."

"So you climbed the wall?"

He glanced down at his impeccable loafers, slacks, and starched dress shirt. His palm caressed the silk tie he wore, it was his favorite Gucci. "No. I came through the gates behind a truck hauling a wood chipper."

She remembered Ren speaking to the gardeners about some downed eucalyptus limbs he'd noted on the compound property. Lucky her, she thought wryly, they took their responsibilities seriously.

Tad cruised about the racks of costumes, then turned his back to study the shelves of shoes. "This is quite something."

"I don't want you here," Cilla said. "I told you I don't want to see you anymore."

Turning, he let out a sigh. "You're miffed, I get that—"

"I broke up with you months ago," she said from between her teeth. "We're over."

"That's not how I want it to be."

Her fingers curled into fists. "You cut off my hair, Tad."

He waved a hand. "My bad. I apologize for that. But look, you can grow it out again. It's already longer than it was."

Her eyes felt hot as they stared in his direction. She'd

tried being calm during their break-up. Reasonable, even when he pushed to get back together. Though a temper tantrum seemed warranted after he cut her hair, she'd elected to hold her outrage in.

All her life she'd been the quiet one tucked away in her tower, so maybe that's why Tad hadn't heard her loud and clear when she'd told him they were through. Perhaps she'd just not been direct enough.

"You came into my house uninvited. In the middle of the night." She advanced on him, and it was gratifying to see him back up, retreating into a corner of the room, almost disappearing between two racks of clothes. Her voice lowered, but it sounded deadly to her. "*And then you cut. Off. My. Hair.*"

Cilla was standing five feet from him when she again heard the distinctive creak of the storeroom door's hinges. Her head whipped in its direction as Ren stepped through.

His gaze instantly snapped to her, and she knew he wasn't aware that Tad was in the room. "Hey," he said. "You weren't in bed when I woke up."

An explosion of movement came from Tad's direction. Then he was on Ren, letting fly a sucker punch that plowed into the taller man's ear.

Horrified, Cilla could only stare, frozen, as Ren stepped back, shaking his head. "What the—?" He blinked at Tad who'd retreated a few feet and was bouncing on his toes, his fists hugging his chin, pugilist-style.

Then Ren looked over at her, his expression unreadable, his voice low. "Did you invite him here?"

"No! He—"

"I'm going to take you apart," Tad interrupted, scuttling in Ren's direction. "Are you sleeping with my woman?" He glanced toward Cilla, then looked back at

Ren. "You're sleeping with my woman."

"*Your* woman?" Ren said in icy tones.

Without responding, Tad rushed forward. Cilla did too, throwing herself in front of Ren. "Leave him alone," she told Tad, pressing her back to Ren's chest and holding her arms out at her sides like a human shield.

Her ex came to a halt. "Get out of the way, Cilla."

"Baby." Ren's hands clasped her shoulders and it sounded as if he might be smiling. "Stand down."

"He hit you," Cilla said, twisting her neck to look at his face. He *was* smiling! "He shouldn't have hit you."

"And we'll be taking that up," Ren responded, "as soon as we discuss this habit he has of breaking into places where you sleep."

"I followed the gardener through the gates," Tad said. "I didn't *break in*."

"Well." Ren's tone was conversational now. "So you know, I'll break your face if I ever see you around Cilla again."

The threat had Tad bristling and he danced forward again. "Like I said, Cilla, get out of the way."

"Move, baby." Ren's hands tightened on her shoulders, but she dug in her heels.

"Tad, it's time for you to go," she said.

"Not until I teach this guy a lesson."

At her back, she felt Ren's chuckle. "Cilla." His hands moved to her waist to usher her away. "I've got this."

Then it happened. Before Ren had her completely out of range, Tad moved in. She guessed he was trying to facilitate putting distance between her and the impending *mano a mano* exchange by giving her an extra push or something, but the outcome was more of a shove. Her feet tangled in the too-long ruffled hem of the dress.

One minute she was upright and being directed to the

side, the next she'd fallen onto her butt. Hard. The jolt reverberated up her spine. The sting of pained tears pricked her eyes.

Silence fell like an anvil in the room. Ren leaped to help her to her feet. "Are you all right?" he asked, his voice tight with new tension.

There was a thick, scary vibe in the room. "I'm fine," she said, and didn't rub her tailbone because he looked mad enough as it was. Over his shoulder, she could see Tad was backing toward the door, his expression reading *oh, shit*.

Ren guided her a few more feet away, then, moving slowly, he rounded on Tad. "You took one shot, now I'll take mine. You can leave after that, or..." And in a lightning move, he was in Tad's space. His fist was in Tad's face.

The sound of the impact was more splat then thud and Cilla saw blood spring from her ex's cut lip. "Now you go," Ren said, "or you take me on."

Tad took him on.

Or tried to anyway.

Cilla backed behind the chair as Ren got in blow after blow. Each time he connected, he'd ask, "You done?" and each time Tad would launch himself back into the fray.

Five times this went on before Tad landed on *his* butt on the hard floor and stayed there, face bloody, eyes dazed.

Ren bent over to lean in close to the other man. "You understand me, yes?"

"I jus' wanted to talk to her," Tad said, sounding sulky through his swelling lip.

"You never get to talk to her again, asswipe. For God's sake, *you cut off her hair*."

"I jus' wanted her to pay attention."

Ren straightened and shot Cilla a hard look. "Baby, it's time to take out the trash." His hand reached for Tad.

"Wait," Cilla said. "I've got to do something first."

He glanced at her again. "Cilla, I'm sorry."

"You don't have to apolo—"

"I'm not sorry I hit him. But I'm sorry that I'm not going to let your soft heart into this equation. You are *not* patching him up. You are *not* offering him a bag of frozen peas or even a paper towel. He gets nothing but the lesson that you are done with him, finally and forever."

"Please, Ren."

He sighed. "Be quick about it."

Realizing his patience was nearly at an end, Cilla dashed from the storeroom and into Gwen's kitchen. After locating the implement she wanted, she dashed back.

Ren eyed the scissors in her hand as he yanked Tad upright. "Uh, baby..."

She ignored the warning note in his voice and marched right up to her ex, who was swaying on his feet. Grasping that favorite tie of his—now askew—she used the kitchen shears to cut it right beneath the loosened knot. A rush of power filled her veins as she dashed the pieces to the floor.

Then looked at Ren. "*Now* you can take out the trash," she said.

Ren was still a moment. A smile broke over his face. "As you command, princess," he said.

And that's when she knew that resistance was futile. Retreat was not longer an option. Time rewinds were never going to work. Cilla Maddox was irrevocably in love.

Chapter 12

In a lighter mood than he'd felt in days—hell, years—Ren returned to the storeroom, his gaze going from the broken skin on his knuckles to Cilla's flushed face. "The bastard's gone..." he started, but then his words faded away as he took his first real look at what she was wearing. The romantic dress revealed the delicate rise of her breasts, then clung to her slender torso until it flared at her hips and fell to the ground. A garment fit for Sleeping Beauty. Cinderella at the ball. Rapunzel.

"Wow," he said, with a sweeping hand indicating the fabric and lace.

"What? This old thing?" she asked with a cheeky grin.

The brilliance of that smile set him back on his heels. Images of the night before flashed in his mind. In the kitchen. In the shower. His mouth on her sex. His hands on her hips, his body bent over hers as he took her without holding anything back.

In return, last night she'd given him everything. No suggestion was too intimate, no position too raunchy. Cilla proved herself to be the best, sweetest, sexiest lover ever.

This morning she was five-plus feet of princess and she was looking at him with that brilliant smile that was only eclipsed by the stars in her eyes. *Shit*, Ren thought, rubbing the heel of his palm over his forehead as a terrible knowledge suddenly struck. *Shit*.

Maybe it was leftover adrenalin, he tried telling himself, that bright look the natural result of her taking her power back from the asshole ex. Or it could be surplus lust, he supposed, though after last night he thought she'd be at least temporarily sated.

"Ren?" she said, her voice gentle.

Her expression matched it, her face so soft that his heart jerked, waves of both tenderness and remorse rising up to batter the thing. *Oh, shit*. The evidence was too strong to ignore.

Cilla Maddox fancied herself in love with him.

Before he could move away, her hand brushed his arm, a brief, warm touch. "Hey," she said, with another smile. "Let's start over. Good morning."

"Oh, Cilla," he murmured, a hunger welling in his belly that had nothing to do with food or sex. He cupped her smooth cheek and stared into her beautiful eyes, wishing he could articulate how sorry he was.

Wishing he had words to explain that if he could, he would be the man to deserve those sparkling eyes, that open smile. What irony, that when Cilla finally dropped her armor it was to Ren, of all people.

What irony and what misery.

Because he was best at detachment. Wasn't he already as good as gone?

Stroking her face with his knuckles, he frowned, noting the faint streak of blood his broken skin left on her perfect flesh. Didn't that just say it all? If Ren wasn't careful, he'd wound her.

"Cilla..." What would he say? What should he do? How could he walk this back? "We should—"

"Check out your inheritance from Gwen," she said.

He blinked. "What?"

"I found the box. Or at least I think I did." With a nod of her head she indicated a large plastic bin nearby. Sure enough, his name was penned on top.

His inheritance. For days he'd avoided searching for it, and now it sat eight feet away.

It's good, Ren told himself now. *Perfect timing. Once I take care of that obligation, I can leave. I can go back to London as soon as tomorrow and then these glittering stars in Cilla's eyes will die a swift and easy death.*

Still, he approached the box on lead feet. At his side, Cilla practically hummed with curiosity, and when she grabbed his free hand to draw him toward the bin at a quicker pace, he barely resisted the urge to spin them both in the opposite direction. Then run.

Dismissing his odd misgivings, he hunkered down, and on a deep breath unlatched the lid.

What had he expected?

It certainly wasn't a set of photograph albums, neatly sandwiched by the plastic. He and Cilla exchanged surprised glances. "Have you seen these before?" he asked.

"Never." She wrapped her arms around herself as if suddenly chilled.

He felt cold feet tap dancing down his spine too. "Let's get these to the house. Have some coffee while we check them out."

Even the sun streaming through the kitchen windows didn't dissipate the dark cloud he felt hanging over him as he deposited the box on the table. Cilla disappeared for a moment and came back without her princess garb. But in jeans and a hoodie she didn't look any more comfortable than he felt.

"I don't remember Gwen with a camera," she said, eyeing the box as warily as he.

Ren shoved his hands in his pockets. "Maybe they're not filled with photos. Could be newspaper clippings about the Lemons—"

"Why would Gwen leave those to you?"

He shrugged, keenly aware neither one of them had yet to pull out an album. There were ten of them, their bindings dust-free leather. Feeling foolish for hesitating, he yanked his hand from his pocket and reached into the bin.

The first book made a solid thunk as he set it on the table. "It's heavy," he said. Then, like ripping off a bandage, he flipped open the cover.

Photos. Photos of babies, without identifying names or dates.

He and Cilla stared down at them. "That's got to be you," she said, pointing to an infant with a dark shock of hair lying on a blanket. "And the slightly bigger, bald one beside you is Beck, I'll bet."

Ren squinted, trying to see his grown-up features on that tiny face. "Maybe," he said, then flipped to another page.

More lying-on-blanket poses. This time he thought he recognized Beck in the one without hair. Farther along in the book, other infants joined the first babies who'd graduated to sitting up, then toddling about. "Walsh and Reed," Cilla said, pointing to tiny persons who did resemble Beck's younger brothers.

Why would Gwen leave these to me?

Cilla pulled out the next album and then he paged through the one after that. In shot after shot were photos of the Lemons' sons: Beck and Ren, Walsh and Reed, Bing,

Brody, and Payne. First, as babies staring at their toes, then as toddlers sitting beside each other in a sandbox, finally as small children surrounded by towers of colorful wooden blocks.

There was nothing particularly unusual about them as pictures of growing, playing children.

But something about them niggled at Ren.

"Oh, look!" Cilla exclaimed. She'd delved into yet another album. "All you boys dressed as skeletons for Halloween."

Seven small figures in black fabric printed with anatomically correct human bones. Between the ages of two and five, he guessed, they all mugged for the camera, displaying various amounts of little kid teeth.

"That must have been so fun," Cilla said.

He didn't recall anything about it. Each of them carried a round plastic pumpkin overflowing with wrapped candy. Puzzled, he continued to scrutinize the photo.

If you'd asked him, he'd have said he'd never trick-or-treated with any of the nine.

Cold trailed down his spine again, even as Cilla continued paging through the albums, pointing out more moments where the gang of little boys cavorted for the camera. They chased one another with sticks, they kicked bright soccer balls on the grass, they paddled in a kiddie pool shaped like a whale.

Ren didn't remember any of that either.

He didn't remember ever playing with the other Lemon kids.

At the base of his skull, pain began a low throb. Taking a step back from the table, he ignored the remaining albums and let Cilla peruse the collection all by herself. As she uncovered more evidence of the Lemon boys' good times, her delight was palpable. "Look how cute you were at Christmas, all of you dressed alike."

He grunted.

"And an Easter egg hunt!"

Over her shoulder, he saw an image of him and Beck, carting a full basket of candy between them, their grins gap-toothed.

"Oh, I wish we'd played like that when I was little."

Somehow Ren had forgotten that he had. Weird. Those photos were like images of someone else's childhood.

Cilla pulled the last album from the bin. "Maybe I'll be in this one," she said, glancing at him with eyes glowing with anticipation.

His gut tightened, and instinct screamed at him to yank that from her. They needed to put those photos away. Hide them. Bury them.

Oblivious to his uneasiness, Cilla continued turning pages. "What?" she murmured, as she landed on a blank page. "Oh," she said, clearly disappointed as she ruffled through the rest, all of them empty. "I guess Gwen got bored before I showed up."

Ren's heart twisted. "*You* didn't bore Gwen, baby."

Cilla tossed him a sad little smile, so sad that he wished he could snap his fingers and a chronicle of her childhood would appear—a happy childhood filled with Easter egg hunts and kiddie pools and a tribe of other kids to share them with.

But he couldn't do that. He couldn't give her anything beyond goodbye and the good intention to get out of her life as soon as possible.

Rising to tiptoe, she peered inside the bin. "Envelopes," she said. One was of the manila type and fat with whatever it contained. The other was letter-sized, and she offered it to Ren. "This has your name on it."

With reluctance, he took it from her hand but deferred opening it to watch Cilla dump the contents of the other onto the tabletop. Loose photos spilled onto the wooden surface.

Ren's sixth sense started screaming at him again. But when Cilla pounced upon a picture with a little crow of pleasure, he couldn't help but step close to see what she held in her hand.

"You," he said, drawing his hand over the back of her hair. It was definitely infant Cilla with her delicate features and a few candy-floss curls on the top of her head.

She didn't respond, but began sifting through the snapshots piled on the table. When she found another showing her sitting up in a tiny pink dress with a big bow tied around her topknot of curls, she went still.

"Hey," Ren said, tucking her hair behind her ear to better see her face. "What's up?"

"I've never seen myself as a baby before," she said, her voice low. When she glanced over at him there were tears in her eyes.

She was killing him. "Cilla—"

"Someone—Gwen, I guess—cared enough to want to remember these moments."

"Of course people cared," Ren said. "People *care*." Damn the Lemons! And damn himself for being just like them...unwilling—unable—to be anyone's anchor.

She ignored his reassurance. "I wonder why Gwen quit putting together the albums." With a fingertip, she spread the remaining photos until they were a single layer. As she studied them, Ren watched her lovely face, punishing himself with her beauty because he was going to walk away from it instead of giving her everything she needed—a man, a home, a family.

Cilla plucked a photo from the table. "Who's this?"

He gave it a cursory glance. A toddler dressed in pink. "If it's not you, Cami, I guess."

"No. This girl has dark hair, Cami's the one with the carrot top."

Ren gave the picture a second look. Pain surged into his head. His stomach churned. His knees weakened and he grabbed for a chair to keep himself upright.

A cold voice sounded in his pounding head, its stark tone making his whole body quake. *You can never speak of this. You can never speak to each other about this.*

Another voice sounded from far away. "Ren? *Ren.* Are you all right?"

He blinked, his gaze focusing on Cilla. "I'm..." His throat was so dry he had to swallow twice. "Fine. I'm fine."

"You look like you've seen a ghost."

"No!" The word spilled from his mouth. "I didn't see anything. Nothing at all."

There was a frown line between Cilla's downy brows. "Okay. But you look kind of pale."

Each passing moment lessened the pain and soothed the nausea. He took in a deep breath, blew it out, and nearly felt normal. Nevertheless...

"Let's put the photos away."

Cilla was already gathering them up. "I wonder if the rest of the nine would like to see them," she said, her voice pensive. Ren's wistful rock princess, still longing for ties that had never been...or had they? At the question, he felt a resurgence of his earlier pain. Fighting against it, his hands tightened into fists. The envelope crumpled in his grip.

At the sound, Cilla looked over. "Aren't you going to read what's inside?"

Staring down at it, Ren weighed the pros and cons. In a morning full of ups and downs, did he need to potentially surf another emotional wave? No.

But until he took care of business here at the compound, he couldn't leave for London. He couldn't leave Cilla and those stars in her eyes behind, and both were a must.

Without allowing himself time to have second thoughts, he tore into the envelope. A single folded sheet was tucked inside.

A single sentence was scratched onto the paper. He stared at the words, instantly understanding what Gwen was asking of him. Oh, sweet irony again, that she'd present her appeal to the member of rock royalty who'd left the compound first. Who'd stayed away the longest. Who had settled the farthest away.

But who now had one sweet reason to fulfill this last request.

Dear Ren: It's time to bring everybody home.

He stared down at the line, breathing deep. All right, Gwen, he thought finally, ignoring the heavy weight in his gut. He was going back to London, but before he left he'd gather a tribe for Cilla.

Ren had wrought a miracle. All but one (Beck) of the nine Lemon kids were going to be at the compound for an afternoon barbecue. So, two days after finding the inheritance box, Cilla rose from the bed she'd been sharing with Ren, leaving him to continue sleeping. In order to make the rock royalty reunion perfect, she needed to start early.

Two steps down the hall, her feet turned around of their own accord. In the bedroom doorway she ran her gaze over him as she'd done before, this time etching him into her memory. He lay on his back, the sheets in a tangle at his waist to reveal his olive-toned skin and chiseled chest. If she wasn't afraid it would wake him, she would love to smooth back the hair tumbling over his brow. She longed to press a secret kiss to his soft lips surrounded by that rough beard.

They hadn't discussed the decision to continue sleeping together (or the hot pleasure they shared before sleep). When darkness fell the past two evenings, he'd held out his hand to her and she'd put her fingers in his, allowing herself to be drawn to the bed.

She was in love with him and though self-preservation might dictate otherwise, she couldn't deny herself further intimacy.

If—when—he left, she'd have to deal with heartbreak, regardless of whether or not he delivered more orgasms (which he did, in ways that were almost scarily raw but always searing with passion).They'd gone to sleep the night before, his head pillowed on her bare breasts. She'd stroked and toyed with his hair until she'd felt all rigidity leave his muscles and he'd relaxed into sleep.

His continued tension was another reason she went so readily into his arms. Ever since they'd gone through Gwen's box, during his waking hours he often lapsed into heavy silences. She'd turn to catch him staring at her, his expression troubled until she skipped over to cajole a kiss or a smile from him.

Nope, she couldn't resist keeping him close.

"Whatcha doing, baby?" Ren murmured now, his eyes still shut.

She frowned. "How do you know I'm standing here?"

His lashes lifted and he gazed on her with his sleepy, silver-green gaze. "Wishful thinking," he said. "Because you're not *here*." He patted her side of the bed.

Oh. *Sweet.*

As if he wasn't the Ren of the charged silences and the

brooding moods, he sent her a lazy, easy smile. "Come on back, honey."

A woman had to have some will-power. "Can't," she said. "Things to do, baked beans to start, brownies to bake. I want everything to be just right for this afternoon."

His smile died. "Cilla. Promise me you won't expect too much. Promise me you won't expect too much from *anyone*."

"Sure," she said, reading between the lines. *Don't expect too much from me*, Ren was saying. "I get it."

And she did get it, she assured herself, as she made her way to the kitchen. She knew that maybe too much time had passed, that they'd all gone their separate, adult ways for so long that a new closeness between the Lemon kids might not be forged, despite the hope that had blossomed in her once they'd accepted the invitation. They might fail at forming those stronger, lasting connections that Gwen had always wanted for them. Still, Cilla would do her best to make this afternoon a special one.

By four in the afternoon, she was a mass of nerves.

"Cilla, baby," Ren said. "You've chased down those napkins three times now. Find a rock, put it on top of the stack."

He stood with his back to her, tending the fancy barbecue. They'd commandeered Bean Colson's house and its elaborate outdoor kitchen for their Lemon kids' reunion.

"It gives me something to do," she muttered. Some way to work off her anxiety. "What if they don't come?"

"They'll come. They said they would."

"But what if they don't?"

He turned around and put his hands on his hips. "We'll pack up lots of leftovers and we'll hit the sack early. See? Win-win."

It was *his* turn to make *her* smile. "You'd like that,

would you?"

His arm stretched out and he snagged her by the belt loop to haul her close. He smelled like soap and that exotic aftershave of his. "I—"

Whatever he was about to say was lost as he went on alert. "Car at the gates, baby." Turning her around, he swatted her on the butt. "You've got yourself a party."

He was right. Within fifteen minutes, their guests had arrived. Walsh and Reed first, with no new news about the missing Beck, though they seemed certain he would eventually turn up no worse for wear. When Cilla prodded them about providing his email address so she could at least try making contact, Walsh shook his head at her.

"Silly Cilla," he said. He had nut-brown hair and deep brown eyes that crinkled at the corners when he grinned. "Beck doesn't do technology."

"Complete Luddite," Reed confirmed, who was taller than his brother by an inch and had eyes a startling blue. He crossed to the under-counter refrigerator that they'd stocked with beers, waters, and sodas. With an easy underhand, he tossed a Negro Modelo to Walsh and then sent another Ren's way. "Anyway, his travels don't take him to internet-friendly territory."

"If he's lost, he's probably enjoying the hell out of it." Walsh wrapped an arm around Cilla's shoulders and drew her close. "Wipe that worry off your face, sweet pea," he said with an easy smile. "You're far too pretty to fret."

"Walsh," Ren called, his voice sharp.

The other man looked up, his lips still curved. "Yo."

"Truck at the gate. Go greet the new arrivals, will you?"

"Sure." His hand slid down Cilla's arm to capture her fingers. "Coming, hon?"

"Uh, no," Ren answered, snagging her other hand to

pull her free of Walsh's hold. "She stays here with me."

His brows shot up, then he glanced from Ren to Cilla. "Uh, sure, man." Then he strolled away, whistling.

Ren thumbed her chin. "Remember he's not your brother either," he murmured. "Now what would you like to drink?"

By the time he'd poured her a glass of wine, the rest of their guests joined them. Cami had hitched a ride with Payne. Bing and Brody had shown up right behind them and they'd brought Alexa Alessio.

"I hope I'm not intruding," the young woman said. She was petite, with nearly black hair highlighted with copper and gold threads. Her eyes were heavily lashed and a warm brown. "I know it's a family thing—"

"We're not all really family," Reed said. "Not in the way you mean, anyway."

As she crossed the patio to pass Cami and Alexa the glasses of wine they'd requested, Cilla felt Ren's gaze on her and heard his voice. *Promise me you won't expect too much.* "Each one of us might not be related," she said, unable to help herself, "but we've shared experiences—"

"Yeah," Payne said in a sarcastic tone. "So many happy times."

Ren narrowed his eyes at his brother. "Bro, come over here and help me get this food off the grill. Cami, can you get the condiments from the fridge?"

Under Ren's direction, they all pitched in to put together the last details of the meal. Drinks refreshed, they gathered around the large patio table, plates filled with barbecued chicken, potato salad, baked beans, and servings of the monstrous green salad that Alexa had contributed.

Cilla was the last to find her seat and before they dug in, all heads naturally turned to Ren, who'd been given the chair at the head of the table. His brows rose as he took in their expectant expressions. "Uh..."

"Say a few words," Cami encouraged, sending him a small grin.

He shook his head. "Really?"

"Toast!" Reed called out, and then the rest of them joined in the chant. "Toast, toast, toast."

"Okay, okay," Palms out, Ren quieted the gathering. He lifted his beer. "To all of you, who responded to my not-so-subtle arm-twisting when I said I wanted to get together after eight years away from the States."

"To us!" the group responded.

"And to Gwen," Ren continued, "who I think we all miss very much."

"To Gwen!"

Then his gaze shifted to Cilla. She held her breath. "And to Cilla, who..." He looked away, looked back. "Who made the gallons of baked beans and potato salad we're about to enjoy, and who reminds me...who reminds me..."

An awkward silence developed. She felt her face go hot. Then she jumped to her feet and held her glass aloft. "Who reminds you, who wants to remind all of us, that when life gives you the Lemons you—"

"Make lemonade," the others finished for her. Some said it with a groan, some said it with a grin, but familiar glances were exchanged around the table and Cilla decided it was definitely a Moment.

There were others as they enjoyed the food. Reed bouncing a balled napkin off Payne's forehead when the other man maligned his favorite basketball team. Bing and Brody thumb wrestling over who was to get up and retrieve more beers. It was even a Moment when the eye-rolling (from the women) trash talk (amongst the men) evolved into a challenge over a game of horse shoes. The six Lemon boys divided into teams which left the women with the detritus scattered on the table. Still, Cilla couldn't help but smile as she rose to clear it away, ignoring Ren's command to leave it until the horse shoes competition was over.

It wasn't a hardship to clean up when she had the company of Cami and Alexa.

The three chatted as the men began their competition around the sand pits they could see in the distance. Alexa mentioned an upcoming wedding in the family, some big Italian thing that required her to be one of the wedding party. When Cilla tried prying by asking who she'd be taking as a date (hoping to get some greater insight into her relationship with Brody) the other woman turned red and mumbled something unintelligible. Then Cilla turned her attention to Cami. She was focused on the horse shoes game, a stack of paper plates in her hands. Cilla joined her, also taking in the gathering of good-looking males. "Nice to see almost all of them together, wouldn't you say?"

"A surprise," Cami responded. "Frankly, I didn't think I'd ever see Ren in Southern California again."

"Perhaps he'll come back more often now." *Or stay*, Cilla's hopeful heart whispered.

Cami sent her a skeptical glance. "Maybe he's mellowed a bit. Maybe he's mended some of his wild ways. But I don't see him suddenly becoming the chummy sort. Not with the other Lemon kids. He was always a loner."

But he was chummy with them once, she wanted to protest. It was on the tip of Cilla's tongue to tell Ren's sister about the photographs and how delightful it was to see that evidence of a childhood filled with simple pleasures and camaraderie.

But Ren had spirited the box away the day they'd

discovered it and she supposed he wanted to put the contents on view when he deemed the time was right.

After horse shoes, the party re-gathered under two patio heaters. Flames leaped in the outdoor fireplace adding an intimate atmosphere. Dessert and coffee were passed about and then someone produced two decks of cards and began teaching the rest of them a cutthroat game that had half the table laughing in triumph and the other half uttering dire threats.

Cilla's cheeks hurt, she was smiling so widely. *It's like a family*, she thought. *This is what a real family would be like.*

But as the afternoon wore into evening, she worried Ren might miss his opportunity to share his inheritance from Gwen. Her concern edged toward anxiety when she realized he had removed himself from the group altogether. He stood at the edge of the patio, in the shadows where the lights couldn't reach. His back to the noisy party, he stared out into the surrounding canyon darkness.

As she crossed to him, in the distance a wild animal yipped in pain.

Cilla's skin prickled with chills even as she told herself to ignore the bad omen. She touched the small of his back, then let her hand drop when he didn't turn toward her or even acknowledge her presence.

"Well," she said, a defiant note of cheer in her voice. "I think it's a success. Everyone seems to be having a wonderful time." *Everyone except you.*

He grunted, his gaze never leaving the black night.

Cilla wrapped her arms around herself, trying to keep warm. "People are making sounds about leaving soon, though. So you might want to get them out now."

"Get out what?" he said, sounding puzzled.

"The photos," Cilla said. "Don't you want to give everybody a chance to see them?"

She didn't have to be touching him to sense his sudden stillness. "Those were left to me."

"Yes, but you should share them," she insisted. "Don't you think? Share the tangible proof of those good times that seem to have been forgotten."

"No."

"Ren—"

"I told you not to expect too much," he said, and then strode off into the darkness with quick strides.

Leaving her behind.

At the rebuff, a sting of tears pricked Cilla's eyes. But she squared her shoulders and dredged up some of her father's showmanship. Mad Dog Maddox was known for his onstage antics and she attempted her own display of theatrical ability by returning to the others with a smile affixed and held there by sheer force of will.

It remained pinned through the goodbyes. Ren had returned—his expression cool and his body stiff—but he stood nearby as she doled out farewell hugs and cheek kisses. Packages of leftover brownies were met with sincere appreciation. Payne was the last to head out.

Wearing a faint smile, he accepted his packet of goodies. "Gwen would have loved this," he said.

"Yeah." Cilla nodded.

He glanced in the direction of his half-brother. "You and Ren—"

"There's no me and Ren," she hastened to say.

Payne smiled. "I was going to say you and Ren did good today—making this happen. Thanks."

"Oh." Cilla felt her face flush. "You're welcome."

Then he bent to kiss her hot cheek. "Stay happy."

It was hard to follow that command as she returned to

Gwen's cottage. Ren had disappeared altogether. Cilla prepared for sleep, trying to ignore the knowledge that for the first time since he'd arrived, she was going to bed in an empty house. And for the first time in days, she was going to bed alone.

Apparently the attempt at togetherness with the rest of the Lemon kids resulted in a separation from the man that she loved.

Chapter 13

Bleary-eyed, Cilla made her way from the bedroom to the kitchen. It was nearing ten a.m., but she'd stayed awake long into the night, listening to the silence. Ren hadn't come home during the hours she stared at the darkness, but she figured he was once again in residence.

She smelled coffee.

It drew her forward, and she didn't hesitate. She needed caffeine more than she needed to tiptoe around Ren.

Anyway, she'd already decided how she was going to handle the man. If he was offhand, she'd be unruffled. If he was cool, she'd be ice. If he was distant, she'd be Antarctica (which had the benefit of being both a faraway and a frozen land).

He stood by the French door, his back to her, mug in hand. Broad-shoulder, lean-hipped, and a complete bastard.

Without a pause and without a word, she continued toward the coffee maker on stocking feet. At the splash of brew into the bottom of her cup, he turned.

She kept her focus on the dark liquid.

Ren cleared his throat. "Good morning."

"Is it?" she asked, moving to the refrigerator for the half-and-half.

Taking a seat at the kitchen table, she ignored him as she took in her first few sips of caffeine. When he sat in an adjacent chair, she pretended not to notice, only watching the way his palms cupped his mug from the corner of her eye.

He had beautiful hands. Long-fingered and strong. The rest of her life she'd remember them touching her face, removing her clothes, stroking her skin. Closing her eyes, she took another swallow of coffee.

"I made my plane reservation," he said. "I take the red eye to London tomorrow night."

Her eyes remained closed as she willed herself not to flinch. This was the way it was always going to end, he'd said that, she'd accepted that (sort of), and any dream of another outcome was on her. He'd never lied or implied differently.

"I know it's a few days early, but my duty's done here."

Wait. What? *Duty?* She felt her temper begin to rise. Remain unruffled, she tried reminding herself. Be ice. Antarctica.

"I'm sure you'll be glad to get me out of your space," he added, in a stranger-to-stranger tone.

Cilla's eyes popped open and there was a red haze across her vision. "Really?" she said, before she could stop herself. "That's the way you're going to play this? Pretend nothing happened between us? Freeze me out like you did last night?"

"You knew—"

"I suppose I did," she snapped. "But what about

everybody else who was here? You invited them, and in case you didn't figure it out, they saw that as an invitation into your *life*, Ren. Then, before a couple of hours passed, you pulled away."

"Yeah," he said, his expression set, his attitude unrepentant. "I do that."

Cilla shoved back her chair and stomped to the bread drawer. Maybe if she ate something, the acid burning a hole in her belly would be neutralized. Unfortunately, the bag inside was filled with a green and hairy penicillin experiment. Slamming it into the trash, she crossed to the pantry to stare at the shelves, fuming all over again. No sweetened cereal, and she'd be damned if she'd swallow down steel cut oats on a morning such as this.

From the fridge, she yanked the bowl of leftover potato salad. With a soup spoon in hand, she dropped back into her seat and dug in.

Ren caught her arm before the mound of mayo, celery, and spud made it to her lips. She jerked up her chin to glare at him, ignoring the traitorous roll of warmth traveling through her at his touch.

"Let me take you out to breakfast," he said, his voice low. "Let me at least do that."

Sucking in a fast breath, she tried steeling her spine. This was no time to say yes to the man. This was the time to tell him to take a dive into the fiery depths of hell.

But damn it all, he had hold of her heart, and she didn't want to consign it to the incinerator along with him.

She wanted to get it back.

His thumb brushed across her inner wrist. "Please, Cilla."

What a sap she was. What a silly, soft-spined, *fool*. But maybe during these few last hours with him she could find some way to reclaim what she'd so unwisely given.

"Fine," she said, with little grace.

Because they arrived at the small café she'd selected between the breakfast and lunch rushes, they nabbed a window seat. Cilla stared through it as she sipped from her oversized latté cup. The shops she could see across the street—a florist, a candy shop, and a lingerie boutique—bustled with business. She watched the parade of customers instead of paying attention to the man in the seat opposite hers.

"Hey," Ren finally said, breaking into the silence. "I don't like leaving with this friction between us."

She slid him a look. She didn't like him leaving with her heart.

Both his hands speared through his dark hair. It fell back to his forehead, the glossy strands a perfect frame for his high cheekbones and unusual eyes. "It was a mistake—"

"Let's talk about something else," she put in. She couldn't take talk about mistakes. Next up would be apologies.

He studied her face for a long moment, then he sighed. "Hell, Cilla, you know I'm sorr—"

"*Let's talk about something else.*"

Further conversation was halted by the appearance of the server with his eggs Benedict and her brioche French toast. After the woman topped off Ren's black coffee and moved away, Cilla gave her full attention to the flow of hot maple syrup she poured from a tiny stainless pitcher.

"All right," he said. "We can talk about something else. How long do you plan to stay at the compound?"

She placed the syrup onto the table and began cutting bites. "I managed to pack up most of Gwen's collection over the last couple of days and I've got fitting and design appointments at the beginning of next week. So I suppose

I'll move back this weekend."

"Okay. I'm sure that Tad the Turd—"

"What?" Cilla's head jerked up. "What did you call him?"

"It's Brody's name for your ex."

The corners of her lips twitched. "Say it again."

He shook his head. "Really?"

"Really."

"Tad the Turd."

Cilla's laugh might have been more of a giggle.

Ren seemed to enjoy it, whatever its classification, because he smiled as his fingers reached to cover hers. "There she is," he murmured. "I like that sound and those bright eyes."

Without making a big deal of it, she reclaimed her hand and went back to her meal as if she didn't want to fling herself into his arms and beg him to stay. "What were you going to say about Tad?"

Ren picked up his knife and fork. "He won't be bothering you again."

"I don't need your assurances. I can handle things myself."

Glancing up, he caught her eyes. "Yeah, baby, and I think you can handle *him*." With two fingers, he mimed a scissors action. "You're tougher than you look."

At his words, warmth glowed in her belly. Being at Gwen's cottage had restored Cilla's sense of self. Being with Ren had made her realize that losing eighteen inches of hair didn't mean *she'd* lost anything.

"But in any case, after our run-in with him, yesterday Brody and Bing told me they paid him their own visit."

She stared. "What? Ren—"

"It was just a conversation, okay? They'll be talking to you more often, too. As a matter of fact, I managed to have a quick word with everyone."

Before he'd disconnected, isolating himself away from her and the others. "A quick word about what?"

"In the future, there'll be check-ins via phone, text, and email. Face-time, too. You all live close enough to have regular contact. You can get together, have each other's backs. Be a tribe."

A tribe without Ren. Looking down at her plate, she swirled her fork in the syrup. "The rest are interested in that?"

"I think so," he said. "Everyone respects it's what Gwen wanted. And the idea appeals to them, it seems. It's the least we can get out of being the damn Lemons' kids."

The "we" that wouldn't include him. "What about you? Who'll have your back?"

"I've got my office manager in London. She keeps me on my toes."

They finished their breakfasts in relative silence. The notion of more rock royalty reunions warmed her, but it couldn't distract Cilla from the knowledge that Ren had little more than a day left in L.A. And that he'd never be part of the new closeness she and the other Lemon kids would (hopefully) establish.

As they left the café, across the street she noted a man on the sidewalk whom she'd been watching from her window seat. He'd started at the florist, moved on to the candy store, and now was approaching the lingerie boutique with bags from the other places in hand. He looked slightly harassed around the eyes, but his mouth was turned up in a faint smile. She imagined it was a big day for him—his partner's birthday? an anniversary?—and he was going to turn up tonight with pretties for the woman he loved.

"Ready?" Ren asked, as she paused to watch the

shopper disappear into the small store. He gave a cursory glance in that same direction then refocused on her. "Did you want to do some shopping?"

Hadn't he realized the kind of merchandise sold there? In the boutique's front window, a trio of headless forms were dressed in skimpy lingerie sets: one black satin, one peach lace, another outfit was leopard print with risqué cutouts.

As if she'd shop there with him! Why, she, of her pastel-colored, cotton-knit underwear would be mortified, and he....

An earlier snippet of Ren's conversation replayed in her mind. *Yeah, baby, and I think you can handle him. You're tougher than you look.*

Maybe she should give a try at handling Ren, too. Low at her side, Cilla made a scissors movement with her two fingers. It had been good to deliver Tad's final comeuppance. Would it work again? Would she bring up her mood if she meted out a little revenge? Surely she was tough enough to make Ren squirm.

Of course she was.

Beaming him a brilliant smile, she tucked her hand into his elbow and steered him toward the lingerie boutique. "Well, if you really wouldn't mind..."

She figured he felt so guilty for going to bed with her and then going bye-bye that he'd agree to just about anything. "Sure, baby."

It might not be a way to reclaim her heart, but perhaps she could prove (to them both) she still retained her pride.

As he sipped an after-dinner cup of coffee, Ren reminded himself he only had to get through this last night in Gwen's cottage. Tomorrow at this time he'd be gathering his belongings in preparation to fly free of Cilla and return home to London.

Except London had never been home.

It had been his base. But now that he'd returned to L.A., he realized *it* was his true native soil. During that hike near Mulholland he'd taken in a view—mountains to ocean—that encompassed land to which he felt he truly belonged. At the party the night before, he'd experienced that same sense of connection to the other Lemon kids.

There'd been pain attached to it though, the source of it something he couldn't put his finger on; something buried deep in his soul. He'd recalled his deep unease when studying Gwen's photos and heard again that sinister voice whispering in his head.

You can never speak of this. You can never speak to each other about this.

The tightening vise around his temples had made him withdraw into the shadows.

Hurting Cilla by the distance he put between them.

But it had to be done!

He dropped his mug to the kitchen countertop and ran his hands through his hair, trying to scrape away the guilt and gloom he felt at the thought of leaving her.

It was what he did, he reminded himself.

Detachment was what he did *best*.

"Ren!" From somewhere in the house, he heard Cilla's voice.

"Yeah?" he called back.

"Can I get your opinion on something?"

He closed his eyes, thinking of the other times she'd appealed to his judgment that day. His mind mostly elsewhere, he'd agreed to go into that shop with her. He'd actually suggested it himself. Idiot! Not until they'd stepped through the door had he paid attention to the kind of store it actually was.

His body would have beat an instant and hasty retreat, but Cilla still had hold of his arm and she continued sending out that blinding smile that made him stupider than usual. So he'd sat his ass on the upholstered chair she'd shoved him into, then survived an hour of torture as she flitted about the racks of filmy negligees and scandalous bra-and-panty sets.

"What about this?" she'd asked, holding up something made mostly of strings. "Or this?" In her other hand was a flesh-colored see-through corset that made the skin of his scalp prickle and heat pool in his groin.

"Why are you asking me?" he'd said in a hoarse voice.

"For the male point-of-view, of course," she'd replied, more smiles and good cheer. "What would a man—I mean, my next man—like to see me wearing?"

He groaned, just remembering the way that question had tied his gut in knots. *Her next man.*

Fuck.

"Ren?" She was getting closer now. "Where are you?"

"I'm in the kitchen," he said, in an unfriendly tone. "And busy."

She came around the corner. "Too busy for this?" she asked, striking a pose.

Ren stared at Cilla, now dressed in one of the little-nothings that had gone into her overstuffed bag from that boutique. Curling his fingers around the cool granite countertop, he tried telling himself it wasn't that revealing. The one-piece, slip-like garment was of midnight-blue lace and reached a couple of inches beyond the top of her thighs. But the neckline was a deep V, exposing the rise of her breasts and the valley between. Swallowing, he tried to think of something to say beyond *Go away, don't tempt me like this.*

Because he wasn't going to take her to bed again...or

do it with her anywhere else for that matter.

It wouldn't be fair to Cilla.

And he was self-aware enough to know it would only make it harder to get his goddamn libido on that plane tomorrow night. He wasn't the one for Cilla—for any woman, long-term—but his sexual hunger for her apparently didn't concern itself with right and wrong.

She gave a small bounce on her bare heels. "I guess this doesn't make much of impression," she said, then spun on her way back out again.

He nearly swallowed his tongue. The reverse side of that sweet little number was lethal. There was a strap at the back to keep the bodice in place, then a long, low dip that nearly met the crack of her ass. From there to hemline it was row after row of lacy ruffles, sending the nightie straight into naughty territory.

Sweet Jesus. His hands tightened on the countertop instead of reaching out to halt her departure.

She came back while he was still clutching that unyielding surface like a lifeline. Ren instantly closed his eyes, rejecting the sight of her in another alluring piece of lingerie. Its image was already burned onto his retinas, however. Another shorty gown in lilac-colored fabric, another V-shaped neckline, and then a fall of tiny pleats. A big satin bow of the same soft color tied right below her breasts. She looked like spring. Like sex.

Sexy Cilla.

He was *so* screwed, because he wasn't going to screw her.

"It's a pretty color, don't you think?" she asked.

Steeling himself, he opened his eyes and focused no lower than her face. But damn, that wasn't any better because her blue eyes were like jewels against her flushed skin. Her mouth was rosy too, as if he'd been at it already.

He wasn't going to go at it at all.

Fuck.

"What do you think you're doing?" His voice sounded rough. Almost mean. Because he felt that way. Rough and mean. And desperate, damn it.

"I want to model them for somebody," she said, apparently unfazed by his surly tone. "And you're convenient. You're here, and you're kind of like a brother—"

"I'm *definitely* not your brother." It came out like a growl.

Her eyes widened and he saw the first sign of nerves. "Um, well... I have another."

She escaped.

He thought he should too. The best course of action would be to grab his keys and go out like he had the night before. Have some drinks. Attempt to drown the clamoring voices in his head and the insistent lust in his body.

Turning, he got as far as reaching for his keys in his pocket when he smelled her scent in the room. It waved through the air, the delicate citrus-blossom-and-water fragrance that drifted from her hair whenever she was near. His senses went on high alert as he detected a note of yet another captivating perfume. Her personal perfume. Female arousal.

Cilla was turned-on.

His dick went instantly hard. "What do you think you're doing?" he asked again, his back still to her.

"I want to know I have something my future lover will like."

Future lover.

Ren spun to face her.

His head did a second spin as he took in what she was now wearing. "Fuck me," he muttered. "*Fuck me.*"

It was the flesh-toned, see-through corset, which boosted her breasts and cinched her narrow ribcage. The hem of it was a flirt of narrow ruffles that met the matching panties. Through the transparent fabric, Ren could see her bare pussy, the dainty line of her lips a shadow behind the sheerness. A pair of pale pink stockings were snapped to frilly garters.

His dick throbbed and he promised it that no one, no one beside him, was ever going to see her in something so decadent and so delicious.

"Get that off," he ordered.

Her eyes went wide. "What?"

"Get that off. I have to burn it."

Glaring, she slammed a hand to her hip. "You are *not* burning this."

Ren advanced a step. "I told you. Take it off."

Her eyes narrowed. "Then I'd be naked, Ren."

That halted him. "Right. Can't get you naked."

A sly smile turned up her mouth. "Unless you want to."

"I don't," he lied.

"It could be a goodbye fu—"

"We're not going to say goodbye. I don't do those."

She rolled her eyes. "You go, it's goodbye whether you say the word or not."

Her logic was making no sense to him, not when he was battling his lust and his agitation. *Future lover.*

"You can't wear that for anyone else," he said, adamant.

A sassy expression overtook her face.

Shit. Cilla. Sassy. He was done for.

"I'm not letting this go to waste," she said, drawing her fingertips from her cleavage to her mons. She rested her palm over the slight mound.

Ren's blood burned as it raced through his system. "Why are you doing this?"

Her brows rose. "I thought that maybe, just maybe, you might have something left to teach me."

He groaned.

"Do I take that as a no?"

Ren wasn't aware of moving. One moment he was standing there, resisting taking her into his arms, and the next she was up against his body and he was bending her over his arm so he could string kisses from her breasts to her throat to her dimpled chin. He tongued her there, hearing her moan as she trembled in his arms.

Then his lips met hers and his tongue slid inside the heated wetness of her. When he lifted his head to allow them breath, he looked into her half-closed eyes and read the triumph there. Temper joined the flames of desire licking over his skin. "Damn you," he whispered. "Damn you for this."

Cilla's hands speared into the hair at the back of his head and dragged his mouth back to hers. "You have all night to make me pay for it."

Fine. He would. And his anger would prevent any other, more dangerous feelings from finding their way in. He turned her, his hands hard on her shoulders. "Get to the bedroom," he said, and when she hesitated, he reached down to snap one garter against the back of her thigh.

She yelped, but the look she sent him over his shoulder was mischievous.

He didn't let it soften him. "When I get in there, that outfit better be off."

Breathing deep, he gave her a five-minute head start. Okay, he was going to do it one more time. Give it to her because she was asking for it and because his goddamn cock was clamoring for it and because tomorrow night he was leaving and London was so many miles away that his detachment would be guaranteed.

Still, he felt furious with himself and with her as he stalked down the hallway. Then he saw her, stockings off, panties off, as she struggled with the fastenings that brought the two halves of the corset together at her midline. She glanced at him standing in the doorway. "This is easier to get into than out of," she said. "Don't be mad."

But he had to be. So he stalked toward her and brushed her hands away. "I've got this," he said, taking over the task.

Once undone, he tossed the garment onto a nearby armchair and stood staring down at her bared body. "God, Cilla," he said, stunned by her beauty all over again.

"Are you angry?" she asked, a playful gleam in her eye.

"Yeah," he said gruffly. "How're you going to make it up to me?"

Her hands went to the sides of his waist and she steadied herself there as she dropped to her knees. "I have an idea," she whispered.

His head fell back while her fingers worked to unbutton and unzip his jeans. His cock practically leaped out as she bared him, pushing down the denim and his boxers before she drew her fingertips over his heated skin. He gritted his teeth against the delicate pressure, and his own hand came out to sift into the hair at the side of her head.

She gave him a kiss then, a string of them, wet and sweet from hip bone to hip bone. Pursing her lips, she blew air along the damp line, causing him to shudder. Next she tickled his navel with the tip of her tongue and then the devilish instrument brushed the swollen head of his dick.

His pulse leaped and his fingers flexed against her scalp. She tortured him with gentle flicks and long licks and slow swirls that made his muscles tense and his balls draw close to his body. She touched him there as she took him into her mouth, running her short nails over the tight flesh. Then she sucked, bobbing up and down on his shaft. Ren felt another flash of fire roll over him and he almost lost it when he glanced down to see her eyes trained on his face.

Those big blue eyes, that tousled blonde hair, her rosy mouth pulling on him, pulling on him, pulling on him—

He yanked out, almost coming at the sight of his engorged flesh wet from her hot mouth. "Get on the bed," he ordered. "I have things I want to do to you."

For the last time.

And he was going to do them, all of them, without attaching anything sentimental or romantic to his performance. That way, in the morning he hoped his libido would be so exhausted that it wouldn't have the energy to make an argument when he left.

So he went to work.

Cilla soon lost any vestige of playfulness. Her mischief was nowhere to be seen. As he tasted her, touched her, opened her, had her, her face took on a drugged expression. Her body moved as if in a dream, her limbs acquiescent to where and how he moved them. He arranged her for his pleasure and then made sure she experienced it too.

Finally, he could take no more foreplay. Cilla had come twice already and it was his turn. Working quickly, he positioned her on her hands and knees, not even thinking why he chose to finish this way until he pushed inside her and she turned her head to look at him over her shoulder. He'd wanted to avoid her eyes, he realized. He'd wanted to avoid this exact look on her face.

Sticky.

That's the only way he could think to describe it. That expression—willing, yielding, open, giving—was going to stay with him beyond the night. He braced one hand on the small of her back, the other buried in the bedclothes as he powered into her, thrusting, with each plunge trying to make himself believe this was just a body, a wet, heated glove of any woman. It was just an ordinary climax that gathered low in his belly then exploded, bursting from his cock in powerful spasms that rocked his world.

Afterward, he lay in the dark, Cilla spooned in his arms, the covers pushed to their knees. She breathed, soft and even, and he ran his hand over her flank, committing her shape to memory as she slept on.

She was like no other woman, and a wash of shame went through him that he'd even tried to convince himself otherwise.

Cilla was his sweet, passionate, rock princess and he'd had her for a time. For a time, she thought she loved him.

Lucky Ren.

Undeserving Ren.

Her feelings wouldn't last, of course. He'd leave and she'd realize she could have a man who could give her everything... His hand swept over her hip again and even in the darkness he could make out the black shape tattooed on his wrist. Yes. She'd find a man who could give her it all—including a whole heart.

He buried his face deeper into the pillow beside her, her scented hair beneath his cheek. "Baby, I'm not good enough for you, okay?" he whispered, knowing she didn't hear him. "But think of me...fondly, yeah? And I'll think of you always."

Chapter 14

Cilla lay naked and still beside Ren in bed, keeping her breathing even, as his words echoed in her head. *Baby, I'm not good enough for you, okay? But think of me...fondly, yeah? And I'll think of you always.* He was stroking her with his warm hand and through her half-closed eyes she watched his fingers caress her, that dark, partner-less tattoo on his wrist the reminder of something else he'd once said.

I suck at anything other than solitary.

But that just wasn't true! He wasn't a loner by nature—those photos from his childhood were testament to that—but then there'd been a change. Some occurrence, or simply the strain of growing up with such disreputable and infamous fathers perhaps, had made him turn inward.

If anything, she decided, Ren's need for bonds was greater than for the rest of the nine, as proven by his reaching out to his mother and then to his grandfather. Yet he'd been cut off from true connection with them in both instances. No wonder he'd stopped seeking out such ties.

Cilla could give one to him, though. The idea had

come to her as he continued with that light, gentle touch.

She could give him a solid, real connection that was permanent. That would let him know, forever, that he was a part of a whole.

The rest of the rock royalty would have a place in this too, she decided, setting her mental alarm clock to early. Beside her, she sensed Ren finally sliding into sleep. And relishing his closeness, she allowed her eyes to close too.

Late that next afternoon, Cami Colson returned Cilla to the compound gates, driving her Volkswagen Beetle. They'd been together for hours, as Cilla had contacted the other woman by phone first thing in the morning. Fortunately, Cami had the day off from the salvage yard and there was no musical gig on her schedule for the evening, which left her free to pick up Cilla while Ren was still sleeping.

Together, they'd concocted plans and worked their phones and once that was finished, they'd made a momentous stop. Now that the last detail was complete, they both stared at the closed metal gates. This near to Ren, Cilla's heart started thudding hard in her chest and a thousand doubts crept in.

"Are you sure about this?" Cami said, voicing Cilla's uncertainty.

She grimaced. "It's a little too late for second thoughts, don't you think?"

"Yeah," the other woman agreed. "So you know, I think you've inspired me to write a song."

"Tell me it won't be a country tune like that one about grandma getting run over by the reindeer."

Cami's lips twitched. "I'll make sure it doesn't have a holiday theme."

Still, Cilla didn't move a centimeter toward her door

handle. "I don't know what I expect him to do," she whispered.

"Didn't you say the point was that he didn't have to do anything?" Cami reminded her. "That this was all about giving something freely to Ren?"

"Right," she said, rubbing her damp palms against the legs of her jeans. "It's not to oblige him to anything. We're just...reaching out. Making a statement."

Cami slanted her a glance. "Some of our statements are a little more forceful than others."

"You think I'm nuts."

"I think you might be the bravest Lemon kid of them all."

Cilla smiled at that. "Wait until Beck finally returns home and regales us with tales of wrestling alligators and riding on the backs of panthers."

"You know what you're doing is way scarier than either of those."

Cilla squeezed shut her eyes. "Not owning up to it won't make it any less true," she said.

"Exactly why I'm hoping I never fall in love," Cami replied. "I'll just settle for singing about heartbreak."

"That doesn't sound like a vote of confidence."

"Oh, Cilla..." Cami started.

She held up her hand. "I know, I know. This was my idea, I'm aware of that. And I'm aware I said I was willing to do this no matter the outcome."

But she wanted it to go...well.

So there was nothing left to do but get out of the car and walk into the compound. She bent to talk to Cami through the open passenger window. "See you later."

"Count on it, sister," the other woman said.

Sister, Cilla thought. *Wouldn't that be nice?*

Then she made her way into Gwen's house. It was

filled with late afternoon sunshine and the scent of coffee. She noted the pot on the coffee maker's element looked fresh, but she didn't need to pour caffeine into her nervous stomach, especially as she'd had two shots of tequila—one before, one after—her final stop.

On slow feet, she sought out Ren, knowing he must be there because of the coffee and because of his car she'd seen in the drive. At the entry to the bedroom they'd been sharing, she halted, her heart slamming into her ribs so hard she had to grip the doorjamb to steady herself.

He was packing.

Of course, he was packing.

The sharp breath she inhaled must have alerted him to her presence. He looked up, his hands around a stack of T-shirts. "There you are," he said.

She couldn't immediately find her voice. Though she'd known he was planning on leaving that night, to see him collecting his belongings, actually preparing to walk away from everything they'd had...it stole her very breath.

"You've been gone nearly all day," he said, his brows drawing together as if he disapproved.

"I—" She coughed to force out the words. "I left you a note."

"It's my last day."

"Yes." That it was, made her miserable. That he said it in a disgruntled tone—as if he thought she should have been nearby during the remaining hours—gave her hope.

She wasn't supposed to have hope, though. She was supposed to be giving, not expecting. But she was a member of rock royalty too, the youngest princess, the one abandoned by all the others, and it was hard to blast through her own guarded nature.

"Ren—"

"Hand me that sweatshirt, will you?" He gestured to

the bureau just inside the door.

Automatically, she picked up the folded garment. She squeezed the soft, thick cotton and paced toward him. He stepped forward to retrieve it from her, then cocked his head, his hand falling to his side. "I smell tequila."

"Um..." She'd been shaking when she'd taken the last shot and spilled a little on her shirt.

"What have you been doing?" he asked, pinning her with his gaze.

"Uh...I was with Cami." She was the one who'd suggested the booze.

Ren's expression turned dark. "She took you out to get drunk?" Rubbing his hand over his forehead, he looked away. "Cilla, I'm sor—"

"No! It's not what you think." Embarrassment joined all the other emotions pooling in her belly. He thought she'd resorted to drinking to get through his last day? Stepping closer, she pushed the folded sweatshirt against his chest. "Here."

His gaze shifted down. "What's that?" he asked, his focus on the large bandage covering the lower half her forearm. "Did you hurt yourself?"

It had hurt, all right. But the pain had been toward a higher purpose and she'd born it pretty stoically, if she did say so herself.

"Cilla." Ren grabbed the sweatshirt from her hand, tossed it down to the bed, and took a firm grasp of her fingers. "How'd you get hurt?"

"Um..." She hadn't thought this part through well enough, she realized. Her gaze darted to the tattoo on the wrist of the arm that was holding hers. His tattoo. Then she glanced back up.

Ren had frozen, his gaze riveted to the bandage. A long moment passed. "What have you done?" he asked, his tone...

She couldn't decide what word described it best. Icy? Angry? Forbidding?

"*Cilla*?"

Oh, God. The moment was here. It was really here and it should have a soundtrack of strings and woodwinds, but instead the only accompaniment was his harsh breaths as he lost patience with her and he began picking at the edge of the adhesive. She thought about jerking out of his hold, but the whole point was for Ren to see the statement she'd decided to make.

The permanent declaration.

His expression stony, he peeled the dressing partly away, exposing the new tattoo. It was surrounded by a faint cloud of pink that she'd been assured would diminish as the skin healed. His grip on her tightened. "Fuck," he muttered, staring at her marked flesh.

The inked design was a stark black point that started at her wrist then rose to curve along her forearm, the image the reverse of the one he'd gotten so long ago.

She cleared her throat. "I got a—"

"I know what it is," he said, his voice rough. "Just tell me it's temporary."

Her stomach twisted, but she soldiered on. "You know it's not. This morning I...I took a photo of your design with my cell phone when you were sleeping. Then Cami drove me to this artist she knows."

Squeezing his eyes shut, he groaned. "Cilla..."

She sucked in a breath. It was scarier to think of saying these words than facing a hundred needles wielded by a dozen shaven-headed, multiply pierced tattoo men. But it had to be done. *Not owning up to it won't make it any less true.* "I love you, Ren," she said, her voice quivering just the slightest. "I'm in love with you and I wanted you to know...I wanted to show you I'll feel this way forever."

"God damn it." He dropped her hand, then spun to stare out the window. "You little fool."

"I'm not—"

"You can go back. Get the artist to turn it into a Winnie-the-Pooh or something."

Now there was insult added to injury! "I'm not a child, Ren," she said, her voice sharp. Then softening, she placed her fingertips on the small of his back, ignoring his flinch. "Please listen. Please know."

"Know what?" He practically barked the question.

He was being deliberately obtuse, but she didn't let that stop her. "It's right here, written in black-and-flesh. You're...you're the other half of my heart."

"God! You have no idea—"

"I know I'm right."

He spun back, glaring at her. "I'm the wrong man, don't you understand?"

"You think that, but—"

"Solitary is what I do best. Detachment is what I'm good at." One finger rose to point at her. "I'm no good at being with you."

Tears pricked the corners of Cilla's eyes. What had she expected? That one look at her new tattoo (her only tattoo) and his resistance would melt? That he'd fall into her arms with his own profession of undying love?

Yes, she admitted to herself. And yes.

Brisk knocking on the front door had them both jolting. "What the hell?" Ren said.

Cilla glanced at the alarm clock on the bedside table. Was it that late already? "I'll get it." She started toward the sound.

Ren caught her elbow before she'd taken a full step.

"What's going on?"

"I don't—"

"*Cilla.*"

"Fine," she said, frowning up at him, his gorgeous face set in furious lines. Her whole plan was crumbling around her. "The rock royalty is coming over for another party."

"Christ, Cilla." He let go of her to run his hands through his hair. "Why?"

Her eyes were stinging again. "Even if you don't want me, you're still part of the Lemon kids. You could be part of our tribe."

He shook his head.

She decided to give him the rest of the bad news. "Your other siblings are coming over too. Nell and Clark."

"Damn it," he said, his voice hot. "You haven't heard a word I've said, have you? You haven't learned a single thing about me."

Now her own temper kindled. A breaking heart was good fuel for a fire, she found. "I suppose you're right, because I didn't realize how stupid and stubborn you can be. I told you I'm in love with you, but you didn't even consider it for a second."

"Consider what?" he ground out.

"Us. You didn't for a second consider there could be an us."

"Us?" His eyes narrowed and he said the word as if it tasted bad. "I suppose that means I don't get you either, Cilla. What the hell is up with that tattoo? With talk about an 'us'? After the way we were raised, I never imagined you could somehow tangle up emotions and sex. The fucking Lemons should have been good for teaching how little one relies upon the other."

His snide tone clawed at her insides and his dismissal

of her grand gesture made her feel like a fool.

Pounding renewed at the front door. "Tell them all to go away," Ren ordered.

She whirled to exit the room, her throat clogging with a choking combination of misery and disappointment and deep, unfulfilled yearning. Still, she hung onto her mad, because that was what would keep her upright until he was gone. "You're going to have to reject them yourself," she said over her shoulder. "Don't worry though—you're very good at it."

His parting shot was more deadly than hers. "Damn you, Cilla. I'm never going to forgive you for what you've done."

In Gwen's kitchen, Ren gripped his beer, held tight a plate of the food that had been brought by Cami, and told himself he just had to endure a couple hours of rock royalty togetherness before it would all be over. Forever.

I'm in love with you and I wanted you to know...I wanted to show you I'll feel this way forever.

Remembering Cilla's words, the dread that had hung over him like a dark cloud the last several days dropped like a net and tightened viciously, making it nearly impossible to breathe. He coughed, trying to force open a pathway for air.

Payne looked over, his fork, laden with Mexican rice, halfway to his mouth. "You okay?"

Hell, no. By succumbing to temptation and having sex with Cilla, Ren had screwed up everything. He'd told her that he'd never thought she'd tangle sex with sentiment, but he'd known she'd fancied herself in love with him.

Still, he'd counted on that infatuation popping like a flimsy soap bubble once he took off. Instead, she'd be left with a permanent mark in the shape of an incomplete heart.

He didn't want that for her. He didn't want her to view it as a grim reminder, the way he viewed his.

He *wanted* her to fall in love.

Just not with him.

"Ren?"

Stalling, he took another sip of beer and ran his gaze about. This time they'd congregated at Gwen's cottage. Cami had provided trays of street tacos and other Mexican food and the rock royalty princes had lugged in beers and sodas—enough food and drink for an army.

The only good news was that his mother's other kids, Nell and Clark, hadn't made it to the gathering. Homework, maybe. Second thoughts about hanging with a half-brother they'd never know. Whatever.

Anyway, the cottage felt overcrowded as it was. He didn't see Cilla, but the rest were draped over every available surface. Walsh, Brody, and Reed were gathered around the kitchen table playing some intricate dice game.

Playing.

Ren set his untouched plate on the counter and turned to his half-brother. "What do you remember about growing up here?"

Payne's gaze slid to him and he frowned. "What do you mean? Are you talking about the Lemons and their wild parties?"

Trying to ignore the new throbbing at the base of his skull, Ren shook his head. "I'm not talking about the band. I'm talking about us."

His brother shrugged. "I don't know what you're getting at."

"I just think we should have been a closer unit. You, me, and Cami. And the three of us with the other Lemon kids. Why didn't that happen?"

"I don't know." Payne shrugged again. "Because dysfunction makes a shitty glue? Maybe that's why we're anti-social."

"I'm the anti-social one," Ren pointed out. "You have a relationship with our sister. You run a successful business. You don't break laws or lie."

"I do fib about my marital status," Payne said, grinning. "I've got this completely fake ex-wife who I claim has shut down my ability to commit—though I must admit about half the women I meet take that as a challenge when I tell them about her."

Ren stared at the other man. "You've actually made someone up?"

He shrugged again. "I call her Lily."

Huh. Lily was the name of Payne's high school girlfriend. There was some story to why they'd broken up, one that Ren had never bothered to uncover. *Because dysfunction makes shitty glue.*

Shaking off the distracting thought, he returned to the original subject. "What's your first childhood memory?"

"I feel like I'm at a shrink's," Payne complained, digging into his food again.

"Just answer."

"I don't know. Six? Seven? Turning somersaults on the grass by the tennis court."

"Nothing earlier? Christmases? Halloween?"

"Holidays? Bean never was big on those, right? Gwen brought us a cake on our birthdays, though."

Ren ran his hand through his hair. It seemed as if Payne was as hazy about their early years as he. "What about your dreams?" At times his were strange. Full of frantic whispers and wild weeping. "Anything weird there?"

"I sleep like a baby," Payne said quickly. "Just like all

the other sinners in the world." Then he moved off, joining the dice-players a few feet away.

Ren rubbed at his neck, trying to erase the tension gathered there. Shifting his gaze to the clock, he began calculating how much longer before he found peace.

Bing entered the room, brushing past Ren on his way to the refrigerator. Seeing Cilla's brother only brought his guilt to the forefront, and to escape both, he started edging backward.

Before he'd made it four steps, he was pinned by a pair of Maddox-blue eyes. "Don't go anywhere," the other man said. "I need to have words with you."

Damn.

They found a semi-private spot on Gwen's front porch. Though small, it offered a sweeping view of the compound. Ren's gaze snagged on the windows of the Castle's tower, where he thought he detected movement.

"What the hell's going on with my sister?" Bing demanded. "She's in a mood."

"Uh..." Ren mulled how to answer. She'd pulled on a sweatshirt to cover the bandage—he needed to let her know both should come off soon, the new tattoo needed air—and had busied herself helping Cami set out the food then dishing it out for everyone. A while back he'd lost sight of her. "You'll have to ask her."

What else could he say? He wasn't about to share their last conversation. Ren didn't want to *think* about their last conversation. His head hurt, his chest ached, and he wished like hell he'd never returned to Laurel Canyon.

"Women," Bing muttered now.

Ren glanced over, then followed the other man's gaze. Across the compound, Alexa Alessio was walking alone through the citrus orchard, her sleek hair a dark flag against the back of her red sweater. "What's going on with her?" Ren asked.

"Huh?" Bing switched his attention to Ren. "Who?"

Christ, as if an idiot couldn't see his fascination with the woman strolling between the lemon and orange trees. "Alexa. I see she came with you two again."

Bing grunted, then refocused across the compound. "She's having some issues. It's good for her to get out."

"Nice for her to have both you and your twin concerned for her."

Bing let out a short, dry laugh. "She and Brody are BFFs. She doesn't give me the time of day."

Interesting. There was something deeper going on there, Ren could tell, but he tamped down his curiosity. It's not as if he'd be around to see how the situation played itself out.

Cilla's brother seemed to have lost interest in grilling him, anyway, distracted by the lovely Alexa, so Ren used the moment to slide his phone from his pocket and check the time. Maybe he could announce the airline had notified him by text that the plane was leaving early...like when did that ever happen? Okay, how about a traffic tie-up? That would work. He could tell them all if he didn't leave immediately, he'd miss his flight. Everybody knew the 405 freeway was a bitch around the LAX exit 24/7.

He decided on a test run with Bing. "Well," he said, noting the other man didn't even glance his way. "It looks like I have to get going earlier than I thought."

"Yeah?" Bing didn't seem bothered by the announcement. As a matter of fact, he began descending the porch steps, his attention still on Alexa. "Have a good trip."

Ren saluted his receding back and had a hope that all the impending goodbyes would be so easy. Even Cilla shouldn't be difficult, as long as he avoided looking at that bandage, her body, her expressive eyes, her valentine mouth...

Oh, shit. Rubbing his chest, he sucked in a breath and ordered himself to get on with it. Turning toward the front door, its knob rotated before he could touch it. When the wood panel swung open, two figures stood framed by the jamb. Ned and Clark, his teenage half-siblings stared at him, shy smiles on their faces. "We came through the back door," the boy said.

His sister combed the ends of her hair with her fingers, a nervous gesture. "We wanted to say goodbye."

Ridiculous how he felt so...so touched that they'd made the effort. Suddenly he couldn't see himself hustling immediately out of the house. A few more minutes couldn't hurt, could they? "Did you see the food?" he asked. "Did someone direct you to the sodas?"

He glanced around as if expecting Cilla to appear out of thin air. She'd help make the youngsters more comfortable—she'd done it before. "We'll get you something to eat and drink and then we'll find a place to sit down and talk."

Yes, ridiculous, how he wanted just a bit more time with them. Still, there it was. "I need to give you my email address," he heard himself say. "We'll exchange cell phone numbers."

Wasn't that odd as hell? Because he was leaving for London in a few hours with every intention of never making contact with any of his relatives—or the rest of the rock royalty—ever again. Hadn't he been fine all those years alone? But maybe this last exchange would be how he made peace with it...and with them all.

"Um..." Nell slid a glance toward her brother. "There's something else."

Ren shook his head. "You won't find me on social

media."

"There's *someone* else," Clark amended, "here to see you."

"What?" Ren's brows drew together. "Who?"

The teenagers shifted so that a person standing behind could step onto the porch. Ren froze, as his pipe dream of imminent peace evaporated.

His mother gave him a stiff half-smile. "Hello, Renford," she said.

Chapter 15

"You," Ren said to the woman who'd birthed him. *What the hell could she want?*

"It's been a long time," she said, as Nell and Clark retreated into the house, the door shutting behind them. Her fingers toyed with the top button of the navy blue cardigan she wore over a matching sweater. "You look...good."

"Thanks."

Another half-smile curved her mouth. "Grown up."

He continued staring, as in his memory he heard his half-sister's throaty voice singing, her tone both sweet and sad.

Motherless children have a hard time
When their mother is gone

Shaking the words from his head, he shoved his hands in his pockets. His fingers closed around his phone, and he thought of that excuse he'd been concocting. Traffic on the freeway. A plane to catch.

Time to go.

It would be a way out of this conversation Alison Renford Holzman appeared to want to force on him.

The coward's way out.

Fuck it. Ren was no coward.

Withdrawing his hands from his pockets, he crossed his arms over his chest. "What brings you here?"

Her gaze moved off his face for a moment to scan the view. The sun was going down, and its dwindling light got caught in the long branches of the eucalyptus. "The compound hasn't changed much. The trees are bigger. You boys are bigger." Another of those strained, almost-smiles. "When I left, you and Beck were toddlers, Bing, Brody, and Walsh babies. Reed was just a tadpole in his mother's belly, Payne too. The girls had yet to be born."

Ren realized he'd never known exactly when she'd left him with Bean. And it surprised him that she'd mention the names of all the rest. "You know about the other Lemon kids?"

One of her thin shoulders lifted. "Gwen and I kept up a correspondence of sorts."

"Of sorts? What does that mean?"

"About five years ago I began writing to her. We exchanged letters regularly since then."

Ren frowned. "It's a thirty-minute drive."

Alison shrugged again. "We preferred keeping in touch that way." She paused. "Though she never shared she was sick, so I missed my chance to say goodbye."

He could hardly rebuke her for her ignorance, considering he *had* known and still not visited before Gwen's death. "She was a special woman," he said.

"Yes. And speaking of special..." She glanced down at her feet, shod in sensible-looking flats with understated gold buckles on the toes. "Thank you for your kindness to

Nell and Clark. They enjoyed the chance to meet you...to know you."

And didn't that just give him a guilty pinch? It was his intention to never see them again, or even keep in long-distance contact, despite the noises he'd made about sharing email addresses and cell phone numbers. "I like them," he heard himself say.

It was true.

Alison looked up, her gaze meeting his. "They told me you met my father. That you visited him frequently."

"And I was told at the home where he lived that you never visited." See? He'd come by his talent for detachment naturally. "Not once."

The shot must have hit its mark, because the woman who'd given birth to him winced. "I had a...difficult relationship with my father."

Another thing they had in common.

"My father—your grandfather—was a professor at USC before retiring and returning to London. My mother was younger, American, but she died when I was entering my teens. Whether it was losing her, or whether it was just me...well, there came a time I was game for anything."

"And along came Bean," Ren said.

She smoothed a hand over her conservative bob of hair, not one of its locks out of place. "I was seventeen and went backstage at a concert at the Hollywood Bowl. A friend's older brother worked security—" She broke off and a wry little laugh escaped. "Like you, I suppose."

"My company doesn't let underage girls anywhere near the bands."

"Fake I.D.," she said.

"We're pretty good at spotting those," Ren replied.

"Anyway," Alison continued. "The rest...the rest was sex, drugs, and rock 'n' roll."

"You don't have to tell me about that."

"No." She looked away again. "And I probably shouldn't."

"But you want to tell me something. Why you left me behind?" Ren guessed.

Color crept up her neck to her cheeks. "I thought it was a better situation for you, here at the compound. Your father was rich. You had a family of sorts in the other boys. When I left, I had no idea how I was going to support myself, let alone a child."

"And you knew Bean was going to be the kind of paternal figure any boy could want or need," Ren said drily.

She closed her eyes, clearly in more pain. "I was a twenty-year-old who hadn't finished high school. I didn't have any maternal skills myself."

"Nell and Clark prove differently."

Her shoulders relaxed at the mention of her two younger children. "I'd like to think some of who they are is testament to my parenting skills. It took me a long time to go from that young woman who abandoned her child to the person I am today. Their father—between undergrad and med school he worked at a tutoring center for people working toward passing the GED—believed in me even when I didn't. He loved me, even when I thought myself unlovable and undeserving. He didn't accept for a minute that I was unable to form a long-lasting bond."

A chill rolled down Ren's spine. *Unlovable. Undeserving. Unable to form a long-lasting bond.* Now it was his turn to look away. He stared out over the compound, seeing none of it. The descending dusk might as well be full dark.

He believed in me when I didn't. He loved me.

"But now I'm not so sure about the scope of my

maternal influence," Alison said.

Ren glanced over. "Yeah? Why's that?"

"Because of who you are, Ren. I remember that twenty-year-old—the same age I was when I left behind a baby—who showed up on my doorstep."

He'd been bristling with attitude but still unprepared for rejection. "You gave me a box—the mementoes of my babyhood you'd kept. You gave them away."

Her flush deepened and she looked down at those gold buckles. "I thought...so much time had passed. I didn't know the correct thing to say, to do, and I didn't feel I had a right to hold onto anything that had to do with you."

"But you think you know the correct thing now?" He couldn't disguise the edge to his voice.

"No." She shook her head. "But even if you don't care about my opinion—and I can understand why you wouldn't—I'm going to say how happy I am you became the man my children met last week."

"I don't know what you're talking about."

"You're not that twenty-year-old I met in Pasadena any longer."

He had to laugh. That kid had been big trouble and heading for more. Somehow he'd pulled himself back from the brink. "You're right."

"So, like me, you learned. You grew up. You didn't need a mother or a better father to become who you are."

"I—"

"To become someone who reaches out to others, like you did to your grandfather, like you did to Nell and Clark, like you're doing here, with the kids of the Velvet Lemons."

The ones he'd been about to leave behind forever. Suddenly agitated, Ren ran his hand through his hair. "Listen, I...I need to take a walk."

The woman who'd given birth to him put her hand on his arm. "You made it, Ren. That's what I came to tell you. I don't expect you ever to forgive me, but I couldn't forgive myself unless I said those words. It takes courage to create your own identity, to stop believing old stories about who you are or that limit who you can be."

Courage. Fuck it. Courage.

"Gwen said you and the other Lemon kids weren't very close as adults...but it looks like that's changing. She'd be so thrilled you were bringing them together. That you'd learned to treasure them."

That was it. Ren was done. He pulled free of the woman's hold and hurried down the porch steps, away from her, Gwen's house, everything that had happened.

Separating himself.

Darkness was descending. The sky was the pale purple of an old bruise. He felt like that all over. Aching.

His mind teeming with thoughts he didn't try to catch and his chest filled with jagged emotions that he tried over and over to dodge, he paced mindlessly about the compound, taking none of it in. Not any of the Lemon houses, not the tennis court, the pool, the pool house. When the automatic landscape lights flipped on, illuminating hibiscus bushes and wrapping the trees and the tennis court fencing in what looked to be fireflies, Ren squeezed his eyes shut against the new brightness.

Why the hell hadn't he left hours ago?

Why wasn't he leaving now?

With that in mind, he spun back. It didn't matter what was going on at Gwen's or who was still there. He'd slip in, slip out with his bag, run from them, run from all of it like a thief in the night.

As he strode in the direction of the cottage, a light came on in the tower of the Castle. Ren glanced up at the open window, a reflex, but the quick look became a stare. His feet stuttered to a halt.

A yellow glow behind her, Cilla was framed by more fairy lights. They lit up her face as she looked outward, her elbows braced on the sill. She couldn't see him where he stood in the shadows of a towering eucalyptus, but he was close enough to make out that new mark on her wrist— apparently she'd been given good advice about bandage removal—and the pensive expression on her face.

The matching tattoo on his skin began throbbing like it was just inked hours ago and that look on her face hurt too, as it mirrored the wretched state of his soul.

Because of what he'd done to her.

Ren remembered thinking she was too well-armored to let any man in. That she'd leave the man who fell in love with her dismayed and frustrated because he'd only get a shallow taste of Cilla's sweet and sexy essence.

But he'd been all wrong.

She'd let in Ren. For a short time, she'd opened herself and her heart to him.

Then he'd turned his back on her.

Like his mother, he'd considered himself undeserving, unlovable, unable to form a long-lasting bond. Despite what Cilla professed to feel for him, he'd rebuffed her.

Alison Renford Holzman's voice echoed in his head.

He believed in me when I didn't. He loved me.

Cilla had given him that same belief, that same love.

And he'd thrown them back in her face.

Curling his hands into fists, he cursed his emotional clumsiness. His ineptitude with what that beautiful woman had offered to him. What he'd predicted had come true. Thanks to him, thanks to his rejection of her love, he'd wrought his worst fear.

Thanks to him, Cilla Maddox, was made as

inaccessible to love as if she were truly locked up in her Rapunzel tower for the rest of her life.

His eyes closed, trying to reject the renewed pain on his skin, in his chest, somewhere deep in his soul. He'd done this to himself, to Cilla, because he couldn't love her back.

Except...

Fuck.

Except he did.

He pressed his fist to his chest, trying to calm his hammering heart. Shit.

Love.

It swamped him, drowning his breath and making him sway on his feet.

Shit. Could he do something with the feeling? Actually ask to become a permanent part of her life?

Could he ask her to trust him after his rejection? Could he imagine he'd be given a second chance to breach her castle walls?

Did he even have what it took to make that play?

It takes courage to create your own identity, to stop believing old stories about who you are or that limit who you can be.

Could he do it?

And another voice sounded in his head, one that came from some place deep within. *Go for it, Ren.* It sounded, oddly, a little like Gwen.

I dare you.

"What's up, bro?" a voice asked from the darkness.

Ren jolted, then recognized his half-brother in the shadows. "Shit, Payne. You're quiet as a ghost."

"I've always thought at least one is lurking about here," he said.

Pushing away the unsettling idea, Ren gave his

brother a speculative glance. He'd perform a favor without questions asked, wouldn't he? Ren could send him for his bag and meet the other man at his car, avoiding awkward goodbyes and further emotional turmoil. Then, in hours, stretched out on his airline seat-turned-bed, with the low roar of the jet engine in his ears, he could turn back time and restart his old, solitary life once he hit the ground in London.

"Payne—"

"So what's up with our Rapunzel?" he said, lifting his chin to indicate Cilla who could still be seen at the window, her facial expression and body language telegraphing her unhappiness.

"I'm in love with her," Ren blurted. *Fuck me.*

Even in the darkness, he could see Payne's eyes widen. "Uh...yeah?"

Ren inhaled a long breath. "Yeah."

"What are you going to do about it?"

"Nothing, right?" He forked his fingers through his hair. "It was you who pointed out I don't know anything about a normal relationship."

"That might work in your favor in this case," Payne said. "As another Lemon kid, Cilla doesn't know anything about one either, so you can probably get away with fucking it up a little at first."

"I don't want to fuck it up at all," Ren ground out. "I want to..."

"What?"

Do it right. Make her happy. Let her make me *happy.* But what would convince her to give him that chance?

"I should forget all about this," Ren muttered. "About her."

"Or you could give it your best effort," Payne said, and then his mouth curved and his teeth glowed white in the darkness. "I dare you."

The second iteration of that phrase seemed to hang in the air. *I dare you.* He'd never been able to resist it, and he wouldn't do it this time, because at the words a plan instantly formed.

He might not have a whole hell of a lot of hope it would win Cilla over...but he'd always been a cocky badass and so he had to give it a try.

And just like that, he went from the idea of an attempt to a commitment to winning.

To winning what he'd always lacked and what he'd always, he realized now, needed.

Cilla had gone through the motions. She'd had to, as the party had been her idea. But once the guests were digging into the food and drinks, she'd escaped to her childhood refuge. The tower room wasn't spacious and now was barely furnished (if you could call a single free-standing mirror barely furnished) but it gave her distance from what was going on at the other end of the compound.

Ren making his goodbyes and then making his way out of Laurel Canyon.

She'd whispered to Cami to come get her when he was gone and the other woman had given her a sympathetic glance, then nodded.

You little fool.

Staring out over the compound, more of Ren's words replayed in her mind.

After the way we were raised, I never imagined you could somehow tangle up emotions and sex. The fucking Lemons should have been good for teaching how little one relies upon the other.

She wanted to be angry with him over that. Instead, she just felt tired and sad and in her chest she was aware of a new presence. Her heart had been returned to her.

Broken.

Her spirit felt that way too. She'd thought Tad Kersley's actions had stomped on her confidence, but Ren's rejection of her love had done something different. He hadn't messed with her sense of self (funny, falling in love, reciprocated or not, had demonstrated being rock royalty did not mean she was emotionally stunted as she'd always thought, which was a good thing), but realizing she'd lost her other half made her more lonely than ever.

She glanced down at the new tattoo, as tender as she felt inside.

Maybe she'd love again, she thought, trying to cheer herself up. Now that she knew she could, it was something to strive toward.

A strange scraping sound caused her to frown. Narrowing her gaze, she stared out the window again, trying to determine the source of the noise. When it wasn't immediately apparent, she pressed her hips against the window sill and leaned out the opening.

Nothing.

Then movement below caught her eye. Not below on the ground, but below on the *wall*.

Her breath caught in her throat and she bent farther at the waist. "Ren! What are you doing?"

Not that she couldn't tell. Not that she couldn't see, in the wash of light directed against the outside of the Castle, that Renford Colson was climbing the rough-hewn bricks. He glanced up at her, his toes wedged in a deep crevice, his fingers gripping another. "Climbing up to you, Rapunzel."

She gaped at him, her heart beating like mad. "You're crazy. Get down. Get down at once!"

He was panting a little. "Safer moving up, baby.

Though I'm sure you wouldn't be too unhappy if I land on my head."

"Stop being ridiculous. You broke your arm doing this once."

"Cheated this time," he said, on the move again. "Payne and I dragged out an extension ladder. Got me up a good twenty feet."

Cilla rolled her eyes, even as her heart continued its accelerated rhythm. "Oh, well, then."

It took hours (in real time, possibly minutes) before he was at the window. Cilla moved back as the top of his head reached the sill. Then he was staring at her, his fingers grasping the bottom of the window, his feet presumably braced on something stable.

The fairy lights didn't soften the angles of his cheekbones and jaw, but there was a gentleness in his gaze that made her belly tighten.

She licked her lips. "What are you doing?"

"Coming for my Rapunzel," he said.

Her fingers gripped each other at her waist. "I don't understand."

"I remember Gwen reading you the story."

"A fairy tale."

"Yeah." He studied her face as if looking for something important there.

"The prince falls, you know." She took another step back. "In some versions, the witch pushes him to the thorns below."

His brows rose. "Is that what you want to do to me? I wouldn't blame you."

She shook her head, because she couldn't trust her voice. All she wanted was for this to be over. But he continued staring at her so she had to say something, anything, to get him on his way before the tears that were hot behind her eyes spilled onto her cheeks.

"It's okay, Ren. I get maybe you're feeling bad for what happened between us, but it's okay. *I'm* okay." Or she would be, she told herself. Some day when she found a way to forget about him.

"He goes blind," Ren said.

Cilla blinked. "What?"

"The prince. Rapunzel's prince. I remember the story too. After he falls or is pushed, he's blinded by the thorns and only regains his sight when he rediscovers the beautiful woman he loves."

"Okay." What was this all about? "Now that you've proven your grasp of—"

"But that's not the way it went for us."

Cilla didn't know how much longer she could hold back the tears. "Ren, you should go. Climb over the window sill, go down the stairs, go back to London."

He did part of that, hoisting himself up with his arms (she cursed herself for noticing the power of those muscles) so one long leg and then the other could step onto the floor. She took a few more paces back, until her shoulder blades met one corner of the small room.

Ren stalked closer, then stopped a few feet from her. His long hair was disheveled, there was tension in his jaw, and a strange light in his gaze.

Her belly clenched again and she felt that inexorable, sexual pull. His charisma calling to something inside of her. Trying to ignore it, she closed her eyes.

"I was blind before I fell in love with you," Ren said, his voice low. "Not after."

Her eyes popped open. He'd come another step closer and now his hand reached out and his palm cupped her cheek. She flinched at the delicious goodness of it and he frowned.

"Have I hurt you that much?" he asked.

"I don't know what's going on," Cilla whispered.

His thumb stroked her face, spreading dampness so she knew a tear had escaped after all. "I couldn't see myself loving anyone. Being with anyone. Having a future that was filled with love and family."

"Ren—"

"Then you showed me how it could be. You showed me how sweet are the ties that I thought would never be for me. You made me want them. Fiercely."

This was a dream. She'd fallen asleep in the tower room and this was wish fulfillment. Still, Cilla couldn't help herself from placing her palm over the hand on her face. "You feel real," she told him.

His smile curved his wonderful lips. "I am real, baby. This is real. What I feel for you is real."

No. "You told me you'd never forgive me."

"Because I'm an ass. Because at that moment you'd made me want something I was afraid I could never have."

"See? You don't want my love."

His free hand tucked her hair behind her ear. "You're the first person to offer it to me in a long time...maybe ever. I didn't know what to do with it."

She rolled her eyes. "Plenty of women have been willing to offer you love, Ren. I'm pretty sure of that."

"Maybe." He leaned down, touching his forehead to hers. "But there has been only one woman who made me want to offer it back. My love, my heart, my life. Everything."

The words weren't making sense. "Everything?"

"All I've got, baby."

Fear suddenly cooled her blood and slowed her heartbeat to a funeral knell. Once they'd gone, nobody had ever come back for her and she didn't think she could trust any of this. Trust Ren. "No," she said, shaking her head and trying to slide away from his touch. "This will hurt too much if it doesn't go right. You should leave. I should leave."

Ren's hands moved to cup her shoulders. "Neither of us is going anywhere. At least not without each other."

"It won't work." She looked up at him, desperate. "How could it possibly work?"

"Because I'll make it work," Ren said, his gaze confident, his touch gentle. "That's what I do. I fix things. I make them come out right."

Another tear rolled down her cheek. "Are you trying to tell me you can create happy endings?"

He smiled down at her. "For you and me, guaranteed."

Her years of loneliness still resisted the promise. "Ren..."

Looking about the room, one of his hands slid down to grasp hers. Then he pulled her toward the opposite corner, in front of the freestanding mirror. Their images were reflected in the glass. Ren, dark-haired, and muscled. Cilla, looking wide-eyed and unsure of herself.

"What do you see?" he whispered, his mouth against her temple, stirring her hair.

The most beautiful man she'd ever imagined. "I don't know."

"Look lower, baby." His fingers squeezed hers.

Her gaze traveled down and snagged on their tattoos. With their hands entwined, the dark designs kissed at the bottom and then again, forming a perfect heart. "They match up," she whispered.

"Like we do," Ren said. "Two halves of a whole."

Cilla's resistance melted. Her walls fell. The last of her self-protection conquered by the certainty in her lover's voice.

She turned to him. "You love me," she said.

"God, so much."

"You love me," she said again, thrilling at the words.

"Forever," he promised.

Then he sealed the vow by drawing her close for a heated, claiming kiss.

As they pressed together, heart-to-heart, guitar notes floated through the compound. Ren's head lifted and Cilla stared into his eyes that were filled with passion and tenderness. The song Cami was playing (it had to be Cami) seemed to twine around them. Cilla knew it instantly. It was steeped in Laurel Canyon lore, about a house not far from them.

It had been written in the early years of the Canyon's musical history, before the Velvet Lemons had arrived and long before their nine collected children had come on the scene to live their odd and often solitary childhoods.

Maybe that was changing, Cilla thought.

She believed, finally, that her life had.

Her palm cupped Ren's beloved face, so long in her dreams and now the star of her future.

"You see how it's going to be for us?" he asked, his voice husky, his gaze searching her face. "How it's going to be beautiful?"

"Yes," she whispered. In the distance, Cami played the chorus of the song and Cilla whispered to Ren, paraphrasing the lyrics. "Everything will be easy 'cause of you."

The End

Made in the USA
Middletown, DE
18 March 2015